Dear Reader,

The reissue of *Fallen Angel*, my first book, is finally here. Over the years, I have received many requests for this book from readers and bookstores. I was unable to help because it was out of print for several years. Now, thanks to Monique Patterson, my wonderful editor at St. Martin's Press, *Fallen Angel* has a new life with a beautiful new cover and added length.

I'm writing this letter to thank you for waiting, and also to assure you that the title change, *Someone to Love Me*, is not meant to confuse you. We all value you too much for that. The change just updates the book and better captures its essence.

If I may, I'd also like to thank Leticia Peoples, the dynamic publisher of Odyssey Books, Inc. In the early 1990s Ms. Peoples saw the need for romance books with strong African-American men and independent women who share dreams and a lifetime of happiness, and made it happen with grit and determination. *Fallen Angel* would not have been published without her vision.

I can't close without thanking you for your unending patience and support for the continuation of "The Graysons of New Mexico" series. You made it happen. Morgan Grayson's story, *You and No Other*, is scheduled for 2004. You'll find an excerpt in the back. Until next time.

Wishing you love and happiness,
Francis Ray
www.francisray.com
P.O. Box 764423
Dallas, TX 75376

D0775709

ALSO BY FRANCIS RAY

Like the First Time

Somebody's Knocking at My Door

I Know Who Holds Tomorrow

Trouble Don't Last Always (formerly The Turning Point)

Rockin' Around That Christmas Tree (with Donna Hill)

You and No Other

ANTHOLOGIES

Rosie's Curl and Weave

Della's House of Style

Going to the Chapel

Welcome to Leo's

Gettin' Merry

Someone
to Love Me

FRANCIS RAY

St. Martin's Paperbacks

ISBN: 0-312-98677-7
EAN: 80312-98677-3

Printed in the United States of America

St. Martin's Paperbacks edition / December 2003

St. Martin's Paperbacks are published by St. Martin's Press, 175 Fifth Avenue, New York, NY 10010.

10 9 8 7 6 5 4

DEDICATION

My parents, McClinton and Venora Radford,
who were always being there for me

and

My husband, William, and our daughter, Michelle, who
continue the tradition with love and understanding.

CHAPTER ONE

"What time shall I pick you up?" asked the uniformed chauffeur as he brought the white Rolls-Royce to a smooth stop in front of the brightly lit Colonial mansion in North Dallas.

"Miss Grant?" the driver prompted, turning his good ear toward the backseat when no answer came from the dim interior.

"Um. I heard you, Jacob. I was just trying to think of an excuse for missing this little gathering," Michelle Grant answered.

Jacob chuckled. "I knew you were up to something when it took you over an hour to get ready. But Mr. Forbes told me when he sent me to pick you up at the airport that no matter how long it took, I was not to come back without you."

"That's what I thought," Michelle murmured, her shadowy outline finally moving into the pool of light spilling from the house to reveal the slender curves of a young woman, her arms

stretched over her head with a weary, uncon-
scious grace.

"I would have preferred staying home, but
Alex has his mind set on my meeting Brad Jamison tonight." She groaned, uncoiling her body
from the plush seat.

Jacob caught her reflection in the rearview
mirror as she patted back a yawn, the strap of
her high-heeled black sandal dangling from her
fingers. His craggy face softened into a smile. "I
think you might like this one, Miss Grant. Very
few of the men I've picked up for Mr. Forbes
have shaken my hand and looked me straight in
the eye the way Mr. Jamison did."

A smile touched the sensual fullness of
Michelle's lips. "Oh, Jacob, if Alex liked the
man, you'd never say anything against him.
However, our dear boss may be in for a surprise
when he sees me tonight. It's very difficult to be
witty and charming when you have had only
eight hours of sleep in the last seventy-two. I
may scare your Mr. Jamison to death if I look as
tired as I feel." Sighing softly, Michelle opened
her beaded clutch and took out her lit compact
to check her lipstick.

Still looking in his mirror, Jacob studied the
almost imperceptible droop of Michelle's bare
shoulders. He knew she was overworked, but
he, like Alex Forbes, also knew two important
things: even exhausted, she possessed one of the

sharpest minds in commercial real estate in Dallas, and nothing could distract from her exquisite beauty.

Long black lashes cast crescent shadows on her almond skin, momentarily hiding her volatile light brown eyes. Her cheekbones were high and delicately carved, her nose dainty. From the natural arc of her satiny brows to the minute thrust of her determined chin, she was stunning. Her long black hair, swept atop her head in a loose coronet, resembled coiled silk. No, Jacob mused, a man might look at Miss Grant and be scared, but not for the reason she was thinking.

Maybe that was why the rumors had started. Momentarily, a frown hardened Jacob's features before he got out of the car and opened Michelle's door. His gnarled hand extended to help her onto the pavement. "Will midnight be all right, Miss Grant?"

"I guess so. Two hours should be enough time to meet Mr. Jamison." Whirling in her four-inch heels, Michelle walked up the stone steps and rang the doorbell.

Her summons was answered before the musical chime ended. Dressed in his usual black tails, the butler peered down at her with studied indifference. Gerald was a dying breed in Dallas, a proper English butler.

"Good evening, Gerald."

"Good evening, Miss Grant. Mr. Forbes and

his other guests are in the main ballroom. Please follow me."

Knowing it was useless to point out she knew the way, Michelle followed the stiff-backed servant down the elegant hallway. Opening an ornately carved door that dated back to the eighteenth century, Gerald bowed slightly from the waist, and raised his white-gloved hand in an invitation for her to enter.

Stepping into the magnificently appointed room, Michelle was immediately surrounded by the fast tempo of music from a live band and the hum of conversation. The French-inspired room—with its gilded mirrors, damask-covered chairs, and nymphs frolicking on the ceiling—was ageless in its beauty. Overhead two large Waterford crystal chandeliers bathed the jovial crowd in sparkling light as they had for the past three generations of Forbeses. Alex had something she would never know—a sense of heritage.

"Good evening, Ms. Grant. Champagne?"

Michelle turned to see a white-coated waiter standing with a tray of long-stemmed glasses, and smiled when she recognized him. "No thank you, Greg. Worn out as I am, I might fall asleep after one sip."

Greg's youthful brown face knitted into a frown. "You're still coming to speak to my class tomorrow night, aren't you?"

"Cedar Valley College, room 410 at seven thirty. 'The Real Estate Boom in Dallas,'" Michelle replied. Greg had asked her to speak two months earlier.

"Thank you, Ms. Grant. I know how busy you—"

"I'm not that busy," she interrupted gently. "Besides, someone helped me. By the way, have you seen our boss and host of this get-together?"

Greg hooked a thumb over his thin left shoulder. "Mr. Forbes was near the bar a few minutes ago."

"In that case, I'd better head in that direction. See you tomorrow night, Greg."

From experience Michelle moved easily through the throng of people who were dancing, laughing, and having a good time in general. Besides Greg, there were three other waiters to make sure the guests had enough to nibble on and to drink. Of course, somewhere unseen was Gerald, making sure everything went smoothly.

Not locating Alex in the group of people clustered around the bar, Michelle decided to work her way to the raised platform on which the band was performing and use it for visual leverage. Surely if she didn't see him, he'd spot her.

Halfway there, someone gripped her bare arm. Her initial spurt of irritation quickly turned to anger when she looked into the smug face of Stan Gabriel. Stan was the most persistent of the men who chose to believe her success was achieved by measures other than hard work.

"If you don't mind, I would like my arm back," she said evenly.

Bold eyes swept over her svelte body hungrily. "My offer still stands, Michelle. As head of commercial loans for the bank, I could do a great deal for you."

"I make it on my own or not at all. But if I do decide to take the plunge, I won't waste my time in the shallow end of the pool," she said, letting her gaze drift down his thin frame with open disdain.

The corners of his mouth twisted into a cruel imitation of a smile. "Always ready with the smart answers, aren't you? Always cool under pressure. I wonder what it will take to shatter that composure?"

"That's something you'll never know." Her voice hardened. "Now turn my arm loose or I'll call your father-in-law over and see how he feels about you using your position to harass his bank clients."

He released her arm. "One of these days," he threatened and strode away.

"Never," Michelle whispered, massaging her arm. If Stan touched her again, her threat might become a reality. There was more than one bank in town. What concerned her was how many people actually believed those vicious lies that had begun circulating recently, that she had slept her way to the top. Who hated her enough to start them?

If anyone with half a brain would just stop and think for a moment they'd know better. Sex wouldn't sway a savvy businessman. Besides, with her hectic schedule and her ever-growing client list, when would she find the time? Her mouth tightened into a narrow line. Gossipers seldom worried about the truth or who their lies hurt.

"There's my favorite person," floated a deep male voice over her shoulders. On hearing Alex Forbes' familiar drawl, Michelle turned and thrust Stan and the rumors from her mind. She smothered a laugh as Alex lifted her off the floor to accommodate his six feet. As he set her down, his white teeth flashed in a devilish grin. Alex, dark, bearded, and muscular, had never reminded Michelle more of a black Viking warrior than now. To those unfortunate enough to cross him, he could be as fierce as one, but she had only known his gentler side.

"I wasn't always your favorite person if memory serves me correctly. You almost had me arrested," she teased, recalling the bedlam after she had been found hiding on the floorboard of his Silver Cloud. After graduating from high school, she'd decided on a career in real estate because she could take the required courses at night after work, and the profession had the potential for a big income. After meeting the qualifications, she was issued an "inactive" license and needed to obtain the sponsorship of a broker to begin practice. Hiding in Alex's car had been her last desperate effort to see him for a job interview. Her numerous calls had not been returned.

He'd taken her to his office and grilled her on real estate law, then thrown problematic scenarios at her. Ninety tense minutes later he had hired her.

"You aren't going to let me forget that, are you?" Alex asked, his eyes twinkling.

"No, I'm—" The words abruptly died in her throat. Stan, standing in a circle of men, nodded in her direction and said something; they all laughed. Michelle stiffened.

"What's the matter, Michelle?"

Lifting her gaze, she saw Alex frowning and forced herself to smile. "Nothing, Alex. I'm just a little tired. Trying to close those double deals in Houston was more than I expected."

A smooth thumb and forefinger lifted her chin. "Never try to fool a fooler, Michelle."

"Am I that obvious?"

"Only because I know you're hurting and there's not a damn thing I can do about it. I'd hoped you hadn't heard those lies," he said bitterly.

"Stan made me aware of them when I went to the bank last Monday to pick up some papers. It seems he wanted to know why I was rebuffing him while having a fling with all of my male clients. He pointed out his usefulness."

"Stan is a fool! Son-in-law or not, I don't see why Marvin, as president of the bank, keeps Stan as loan officer. He has the intelligence of a turkey and the morals of an alley cat. Come to think of it, he does look like a skinny, plucked turkey." Michelle's face lost some of its tenseness at the picture Alex painted. He slid a comforting arm around her small waist before continuing.

"You're twenty-six years old and one of the most successful Realtors in the state. Last month at the National Association of Realtors' conference you walked away with an armful of awards. Anywhere there's competition, there are going to be rumors. Your meteoric rise in commercial real estate was perfect for the tongues to wag," he said, his fingers tightening.

Michelle's eyes narrowed. "It might seem meteoric to some, but you know as well I as do that I worked fourteen to sixteen hours a day, made cold calls, followed up on the slightest referral, and did without lunch to be able to send cards and gifts to clients as thank-yous and on their special occasions."

He touched her cheek in a gesture of friendship and comfort. "You worked your behind off. And when it gets out you closed two more deals with one of the largest investments firms in

Canada this weekend, the tongues will wag even more. But you got where you are on your own. You're the best."

She relaxed under his warm regard, then smiled impishly up at him. "Does that mean you're going to give me a raise?"

"Ouch." He chuckled, a rich deep sound. "That's my girl. For a moment I thought I was going to have to call Nick."

"You can't. He's in Austin trying to raise funds for the Winslow Rehabilitation Center," Michelle answered, but deep in her heart she knew there was nothing her brother could do to fill the growing emptiness she felt.

Astonishment arched Alex's brow. "He's out of town without you?"

Michelle nodded. "His friendship with Jodie Daniels touched something within him that nothing else has accomplished. I think finally he's accepting he'll always be paralyzed from the waist down and in a wheelchair. After her death six weeks ago, I was afraid he might become withdrawn again, but he hasn't. In fact he's doing so well he's being considered for the public relations director position when the rehab center opens."

"How near are you to finalizing all the plans?"

"In three months we'll have the groundbreaking ceremony. A year ahead of schedule because of Jodie's father." She shook her head. "Without Clint Daniels selling his ranch to us below market value I'd still be looking for a site."

"When is Nick coming home?" Alex abruptly asked.

Her brows furrowed. "Tomorrow afternoon. Why?"

Alex gave an exaggerated leer and tweaked the jet-black bearded growth on his chin. "Maybe I could come over and keep you company in that big house you love while he's away?"

The smile started at the corner of her lips, then burst into full bloom. "When would you have time to fit me into your schedule? I bet somewhere in this room a woman or two is planning my quick demise."

"Say the word," he countered, amusement shining in his dark eyes.

A lacquered red nail playfully flipped up the lapel of his expertly tailored black evening jacket. There had never been anything between them but friendship, and they both knew that special spark would never be there.

"One day I might take you up on that offer you keep throwing at me. However, not tonight. Now, where is the reason you had me put on my working clothes and rush over?" Michelle asked, glancing down at the clinging white jersey knit gown caressing the supple curves of her slim body. Open-backed to the waist and cut to a dramatic V in front, it had been known to raise the blood pressure of more than one male and the envy of several females.

All her eveningwear, was designed to be provocative and daring. Her daywear was the same. Even before the current style of baring belly buttons and as much skin as possible, she had raised eyebrows and pulses. Dallas might have a cosmopolitan image, but the city was deeply rooted in Southern morality, and conservative. She went against the grain.

Hearing the self-derision in her voice, Alex frowned. "You still hate using the flamboyant image, don't you?"

"I'd hate not eating even more," Michelle said tightly, her face set in determination. It galled her even more that the way she dressed gave further credence to the rumors. But for the moment she was helpless to change either. Altering her image wouldn't stop the rumors, but it might adversely affect her client base. Financially, she couldn't stand a big drop in commissions, and a pretty face and flash of skin never failed to reel them in. But it was her prowess in the market that sealed the deal and kept them coming back for more. "Let's get down to business."

Noting the slight tilt of her chin, Alex linked his arm through hers as they began to edge their way to the other side of the room through the amicable crowd of people. When a full minute had passed without an interruption by anyone, Alex began to give Michelle the information she wanted.

"You know by now that your potential client is Brad Jamison. We were at Columbia University together and even then he was a shrewd businessman. He may be your biggest challenge yet."

Michelle was unimpressed. "What does he want?"

"What he doesn't want is easier answered. His family owns Computron, a computer manufacturing firm, and they may be in the market to move their operations from California. Brad has been CEO since his father died eight years ago. It's your job to see that Computron comes to Dallas, and of course, that they use us exclusively."

"That's a tall order."

Alex nodded. "If anyone can pull it off, you can. You're the best I have to offer and only the best will get results with Brad. He wants choice sites in North Dallas, east of Grapevine near Dallas/Fort Worth International Airport, and by Cedar Creek Lake. He knows what he wants and won't settle for anything less."

"I'm surprised he has time for business if all the stories I've heard about his romantic escapades are true," Michelle said dryly.

"It's true Brad is a man who enjoys female company, but Computron has shown a profit each quarter since he took over." Alex glanced at Michelle. "Don't worry. He doesn't pounce unless you know he's coming. Now where did that sister of mine run off to with Brad?"

Michelle tensed. "I thought Cassie was in Europe."

"She was, but she came home the day you left for Houston. It was her idea to give this party to introduce Brad to some of our friends and associates. I thought I mentioned her coming home when I talked with you on the phone this morning. Anyone else would have jet lag, but not Cassie," Alex said proudly.

"Yes," Michelle said. How could any man as astute as Alex be so blind to his snobbish, troublemaking little sister? Cassie had made it plain from the first time Alex had told her how he had met Michelle that she was beneath her. Alex's concern for and mentoring of Michelle made Cassie's dislike take on a more subtle flair, but it was still there.

To Cassie, wealth and your name on the social register meant more than people. Michelle couldn't claim either. She came from a long line of poor but honest laborers. Her father had died when she was a baby, her mother when she was five. She'd lived in foster care until Nick had signed a contract to play professional football, but three years later his accident ended his career. When Michelle met Cassie, she and Nick hadn't known where their next meal was coming from or how they'd pay the rent.

All that had changed. Yet, no matter how

much success Michelle had achieved since then, Cassie would always feel smugly superior. Grimacing, Michelle thought the evening couldn't get any worse.

"Brad, are you listening to me?" Cassie Collins asked, the underlying sensuality of her voice designed to gain any man's attention and keep it.

Brad Jamison glanced down at Cassie's pretty heart-shaped face surrounded by dark auburn curls, and patted her hand. "Of course I am."

Cassie smiled and leaned closer. Brad patted her hand again. Absently he heard her tell him about a wealthy financier who had begged her to stay in Paris. Brad silently wished them both well if the man was to be husband number three for Cassie, then went back to searching the crowd.

Where was the stunning woman in white? Or had he just imagined her? No, he hadn't lost that much sleep in the past hectic weeks. But when he had first seen her, it had taken a couple of moments to believe that she was real.

It wasn't just her strikingly beautiful face; it was the seductive innocence she wore like a cloak, almost daring a man to take it off and discover the sensual woman beneath and make her his. The way her dress flowed over the curves of her body like a lover's caress, he was seriously considering accepting her unspoken challenge.

Brad's face dimpled into a pure male smile. His self-imposed celibacy was making him poetic. He continued to scan the crowd, this time searching for Alex as well. Before Brad could carry out his plans to meet the mystery woman, he'd have to meet Michelle Grant. His mouth flattened into a thin line.

If he got any indication on meeting her that the rumors were true, he'd find another Realtor. He didn't conduct business that way and steered clear of people who did. His mother had taught him early that some career women sacrificed anything and anyone in their quest to reach the top.

His free hand clenched at the unwanted memory of his mother dressed in glitter and diamonds hurrying out of the house with his father for a dinner party, him standing in the foyer with a book for her to read to him, and what she'd said:

"I don't have time. The nanny can read it to you."

Brad's jaw clenched, but not before he saw again the tears streaming down the little boy's bewildered and hurt face. He couldn't have been more than five years old. At that age he'd been young enough to keep trying to win her affection. But she always had someplace to go or someone to see. She'd never attended any school functions unless he was being given an award . . . then she'd show up and play the role of the proud, devoted mother.

Although they now lived in the same city, he steered clear of his mother. Not even for Alex would he associate with another self-centered woman.

"There they are," Alex said enthusiastically.

Michelle's gaze followed the direction of his gesturing hand to several people standing in a small alcove about fifteen feet away. One of the men stood out.

He was tall and magnificently male—lean and ruggedly built. His body, exquisitely detailed in a black tuxedo, commanded attention, as did the sharp angles and rugged planes of his handsome chocolate-colored face. His well-trimmed mustache was jet black. Although his head was tilted downward toward Cassie, his narrowed gaze was aimed at Michelle.

The sudden tingling sensation in the pit of Michelle's stomach acknowledging his male magnetism surprised, then annoyed her. Only one man had ever made her body react that way. Their gazes clashed. In the space of a heartbeat she knew the eyes moving over her in a bold appraisal were black and electrifying.

She knew this man. She had met him a lifetime ago.

Dazed, she returned the bold stare. She recalled the way his black hair glinted in the
moonlight, its springy softness beneath her fingers. Her long wait was over. He'd come back
into her life as unexpectedly as he'd entered it
nine years ago. Not a day had gone by that she
hadn't thought of him, thanked him. Her trembling fingers gripped Alex's arm as a mixture of
fear and excitement raced through her.

Cassie, standing by the man's side, noticed
his attention was elsewhere and followed the direction of his gaze. Standing on tiptoe, she whispered something in his ear. The sensual warmth
left his eyes, leaving them as cold as icicles.

Michelle found it impossible to look away as
his gaze traveled with a chilling thoroughness
back over the exposed length of her thigh before
lifting briefly to the plunging V of her gown,
then coming to rest on her face. Never before had
she felt so exposed in a dress, and never would
she have expected such coldness from *him*.

"Michelle, what is it?" Alex questioned, feeling her nails dig through his coat into his arm.

"My angel."

Only two whispered words, but they were
enough. Alex's head whipped around, his eyes
locking with those of Brad Jamison.

"The man who rescued you? Are you sure?"

Michelle nodded numbly.

"Alex, please stop staring and come over
here." Cassie's voice rang clearly over the live

band, the chatter, and the thumping of Michelle's heart. "Brad is waiting to meet Michelle."

"Hang on, Michelle. Brad has that reckless look in his eyes."

Michelle dismissed Alex's words with only momentary hesitation. Brad hadn't recognized her. Her face was more defined, her body certainly had more curves. Then, there was the dress. Once she explained to B.J. he'd understand. She'd waited years for this opportunity, and not even the potential cutting words from Cassie would spoil the moment. Michelle's smile dazzled.

"Brad," Cassie cooed sweetly, clinging to his arm with unmistakable possessiveness. "This is the employee I was telling you about. Michelle Grant, Alex's little protégé. Michelle, Brad Jamison."

Michelle watched with narrowed eyes as Cassie swayed closer. Was B.J. another of Cassie's conquests? *No.* Fate wouldn't be that cruel, to see him again only to lose him. "Mr. Jamison. Cassie."

"Ms. Grant." Hard eyes flicked over Michelle, noting Alex's hand riding on the curve of her waist. "I can see why you're so sought after. It's a wonder a man can remember to sign his name to a contract. You'll find I'm not so easily distracted."

Stunned, Michelle barely managed to stop her gasp at Brad's innuendo. A hushed silence fell around them. Michelle barely noticed. The coaxing velvet drawl she remembered that had calmed her fears was now encased in steel. The man from her past was gone and in his place was a man who looked at her with distaste. Once she might have crumpled from such contempt. Oddly, *he* had taught her to face her adversaries head on.

Alex pulled her closer to him and Brad's mouth tightened at the protective gesture. Once he had given her his strength, his warmth, but now. . . .

Her chin lifted. She stared at him with cool, flat eyes. "Mr. Jamison, I'll endeavor to make sure we never have a chance to test your theory. Excuse us, please. Alex and I were about to get some air."

With Alex's support, Michelle made her feet move across the polished hardwood floor. She had learned in foster care. And later in boarding school, to ignore pain when it was threatening to rip her apart. Never let them know you care. Never cry.

The soft click of the terrace door behind her let Michelle release the rigid control on her emotions. She sagged against Alex.

"I'm sorry, Michelle. I've never seen Brad that way," Alex said tightly. "But friend or not, he's going to apologize to you."

"Please call me a cab. I'm going home." Her ragged voice was hoarse and thick with the effort of suppressed tears. She'd foolishly hoped and prayed to see B.J. again and he'd crucified her without a moment's hesitation.

"Sorry, but this is one time I have to say no. You know some of the people inside are having a field day thinking the flamboyant Michelle Grant has finally gotten hers. You have to go back inside," he said.

"I don't care," she said, finally able to move out of his arms, her endurance at its limits. Her lack of sleep, the rumors, and seeing B.J.—it was too much.

"Yes, you do. You care too much. That's your trouble. I can't let you run away. You never have before," Alex pointed out, sympathy in his voice.

Fighting back tears, Michelle wrapped her bare arms around her slim body, trying to stop shaking. Her mind was reliving another spring night, when an angel had healed her heart and touched her soul.

"Michelle," Alex said softly. "I'm not going back without you."

Shutting her eyes tightly, Michelle fought the need to run and hide, to nurse her wounds in private. Alex was right. Some of the people inside thought her an unscrupulous bitch who would stop at nothing to get ahead. Yet, how many of them had ever had to beg for food or a place to stay? Hunger was a harsh and merciless teacher.

Her back straightened. "All right, Alex. Go back inside. I'll join you in a minute."

"Mi—"

"Please."

After a brief moment, she felt the reassuring touch of his hand on her shoulder, then seconds later heard the sound of music as the door opened, then silence. She was alone.

Taking a deep breath, Michelle stared out over the well-manicured lawn and instead saw the sandy shoreline of San Francisco. Every detail was vivid in her mind. She'd been terrified and powerless to save herself from her own foolishness. Then her angel had appeared.

B.J. had saved her when she didn't think she was worth saving; Brad Jamison wouldn't spit on her if she were on fire. She had to forget and go on with her life. But some dreams died hard.

She had been like a miser, hoarding each precious detail, of her memories, taking them out only in the hushed stillness of the night to examine and savor, replaying each moment in her mind. Now she was trapped by her own mind, with no escape from the harsh reality of a dream turned nightmare.

The soft tread of footsteps on the brick patio brought her head up. "Alex, I told you I don't think I can go back inside right now."

"It's not Alex." Tall and imposing, Brad stepped out of the shadows.

CHAPTER TWO

Michelle stiffened, then began to hurry toward the stone steps leading away from the terrace. A lean brown hand on her forearm stopped her. Wrenching her arm away, she whirled around to face him.

"Don't touch me!"

A black brow arched upward. "Why not? Does it bother you?" His deep drawl slid across the night, evoking so many memories she wanted to cry out.

"Are you conducting a survey on the subject?" she asked.

He smiled, revealing a flash of perfect white teeth. "There may be hope for you yet, Michelle Grant. Now, why don't we go back inside? Alex is waiting."

Michelle drew her head back, her eyes searching the chiseled features in the moonlight for some hidden innuendo and finding none. Looking at him only served to remind her how com-

pellingly handsome and how utterly unobtain-
able he was. "I can find my way alone." She
tried to go around him only to have her path
suddenly blocked.

"Would you like to start over?"

"No." The man she remembered was gone.

He smiled without warmth, sliding his hands
into the pockets of his tailored slacks. "Not even
if it meant I decided to relocate in Dallas and
work exclusively with you?"

"Not even if I were a big enough fool to believe such a proposal."

Black eyes narrowed. "You're not what I expected."

"That makes us even. Now, if you don't mind,
get out of my way."

"But I do mind, Ms. Grant," he said quietly. A
tapered finger reached out to quickly glide over
the delicate curve of her cheek in a light caress.

Michelle stepped back instantly, but the damage was already done. "Why don't you leave
me alone?" She forced the words through trembling lips.

"Because your eyes give you away. They are
as deep and as mysterious as the sea, but if one
looks closely enough, like the sea, its secrets will
be revealed. Only this time I see pain, pain I
caused. I'm sorry," he said softly.

Wordlessly, Michelle stared at Brad, stunned
by his apology as well as by his analogy to the
sea where they had first met. She sensed com-

passion when earlier she had only been subjected to his scorn.

Annoyed at the softening his words caused, she said, "I'm too tired to play whatever little game you have going. I'm sure Forbes Realtors can find someone else to assist you."

The corners of his mouth lifted. "If you think I'm here trying to entice a Realtor, you're not as smart as I've been led to believe."

Disconcerted, she looked away. "Just get out of my way and I'll make sure we never see each other again."

"And if I don't?"

Michelle heard the challenge in his voice, no longer subdued by moonlight and velvet, and whipped her head around to meet his steady black gaze. All traces of tenderness were gone. His face was expressionless. She could feel his coiled alertness, power leashed and waiting. The casual stance was gone. Obviously he wasn't going to let her leave until he was finished, and to force the issue would be sheer stupidity.

When Michelle made no move to leave, Brad braced a hip against the stone balustrade and folded his arms across his wide chest. "I thought not. Your beautiful skin would bruise easily if I had to detain you and we both know Alex would be angry, deal or not. Therefore you'll stay because you'd rather fight your own battles."

"Another analysis of my character, Mr. Jamison? It's a wonder you can find the time for your company with all the free counseling you do."

Brad appeared undisturbed. "Do you realize some of your business associates had me believing you would do anything to close a deal? I was almost convinced when Cassie introduced us and I saw you wearing that dress. I stopped believing when I saw the light go out of your eyes and your bottom lip start to tremble," he finished softly, unfolding his arms and coming to stand in front of her.

The question of "why" was unmistakable in his voice. Her anger drained away as his gaze traveled over her face and searched her eyes. She answered, needing him to understand. "Competition in real estate is fierce. I had exactly one sale in my first six months. The commission barely paid one month's rent."

She took a deep, steadying breath, recalling Nick's suggestion that she dress a little more daringly to get the attention of potential clients. He reasoned that people in Hollywood did it all the time and people noticed. She had argued that she wasn't comfortable with the idea, and besides, Dallas was more conservative than New York or LA. She'd stopped arguing when they were served with an eviction notice. Within the week after wearing a figure-hugging rented gown to a charity function with Alex, she had two new listings and a sale.

Her steady gaze met Brad's. "Now they call me."

"If you're as good as Alex claims, you could have made it without all this," he said, gesturing toward her dress.

Her composure snapped. "And perhaps I couldn't. I was tired of living off people's charity. I needed to succeed and if it took acquiring a certain allure for people to look at me long enough to know I had a brain in my head, so what? It sells." Her bitterness against him and her own image spilled over into her voice.

His mouth twisted. "So you prostituted your—"

A sharp crack shattered the stillness of the night. Before Michelle could land another blow to his cheek, her hand was completely enclosed within Brad's. Blazing black eyes narrowed to slits. Michelle met his glare without flinching.

"*Principles* was the word I was going to say." He bit out each word distinctly, easily pulling her twisting body against his.

Michelle's breath hissed from between clenched teeth as her breasts flattened against his chest. Needles of desire raced through her veins like wildfire . . . fierce and consuming. Instinctively her hands pushed against his chest, but the seeping warmth beneath her fingertips undid her. She had waited too long to touch him. Her knees trembled as his breath stroked her face.

"I guess I had that one coming, but never try it again. I don't like hysterical women and I suggest you remember that if we're going to be working together."

His hand loosened and slid down to hold her wrist in a gentle vise, making her skin tingle. His faint, spicy aftershave lotion stirred her senses. There was no way for her to work with him and remain emotionally detached. "I . . . I don't think—"

"It's obvious your thinking is not up to its usual high level of intelligence." Ignoring Michelle's outraged expression, Brad placed her hand over the lean hardness of his arm and started back inside.

Bright lights and curious stares greeted them as they stepped onto the polished sheen of the ballroom's floor. Michelle saw Alex, but before she could move in that direction, Brad slid his arm around her waist and swung her onto the dance floor. Other couples and the haunting melody of a song about unrequited love immediately surrounded them.

Michelle's protest lodged in her throat as Brad boldly fitted her body snugly against his, breast to thigh. Not a wisp of air stood between them.

"Why are you doing this?" she asked unsteadily.

"Since I'm the one who caused the problem, it's only right that I should repair the damage," he explained, his thumb making circular motions in the small of her bare back, his other thumb doing the same thing on her wrist. "One turn around the dance floor should convince people you haven't lost your touch."

He smiled into her angry face. "Loosen up, Ms. Grant, or some people might begin to think you've finally met your match."

She stumbled. Brad easily covered the mis-step by whirling with her, his arm tightening around her waist, jutting her hip against his un-mistakable male hardness. Her heart lurched. She tilted her head back to give him a stinging retort, but the words were stopped by the barely leashed passion in his face.

A thousand thoughts raced through her mind, but the one pushing everything else aside was that Brad Jamison was a dangerous complication, one she couldn't handle at twenty-six any better than she had at seventeen.

The song ended and Michelle moved out of Brad's arms. "Thank you, Mr. Jamison, but I won't need your assistance any longer. Please excuse me." Michelle walked off the floor. The hairs prickling on the nape of her neck told her Brad was right behind her.

Brad knew where she was heading. This time, being right gave him little satisfaction. His mouth thinned, his mustache becoming a black slash above his mouth as he joined Alex and Michelle.

"Alex, I think you have some property I

might want." Brad's gaze touched Michelle briefly before meeting Alex's.

"I'm not in direct sales, Brad," Alex answered stiffly.

"In that case, I'll see you in your office in the morning at nine, Ms. Grant." His eyes glinting under the bright lights, Brad turned in one smooth motion and walked away. Lithe strength and raw masculinity radiated from every line of his body.

"Are you going to be all right, Michelle?" Alex asked, his eyes searching her drawn face.

"Of course I am. I always bounce back," Michelle assured him brightly, but her voice lacked conviction.

Michelle's conviction had deteriorated even more when, an hour later, she crawled beneath the peach-colored sheets on her bed. With each restless turn, she recalled the rush of the waves and the silken caress of a man best forgotten.

Rising up on her elbow, she pounded the down pillow with a tightly clenched fist. Why hadn't she thought there might be a connection between B.J. and Brad Jamison? The reason came to her almost at once. She had always thought of him as her angel, her savior, the man who had rescued her from her own stupidity. At seventeen she thought she could take care of herself. Richard Ewing had proven her wrong about that and a great deal more.

As she turned over in bed, the sheets rustled and once again she was a lonely seventeen-year-old who was so hungry for love that she had left Nick—his career over, his future uncertain—and run after a man who said he loved her.

Ignoring her brother's warning that if she left she was not to come back, she had boarded a plane for San Francisco. All she could think of was seeing Richard and finding out why he had left her a note saying he didn't want to see her again.

The seven weeks they had been dating were the happiest of her life. Finally, after all the years of feeling unwanted, someone really wanted her, not because of the state check or because her brother was a professional football star, but for herself.

At San Francisco International Airport, she had hired a taxi to take her to Richard's cousin's beach house. In her heart she never doubted that once she talked to him everything would be all right.

Five seconds after knocking on the door, she realized she had been wrong. Richard had stood in the doorway and laughed in her face. Nick was no longer a salable commodity in professional football, and that meant her usefulness had come to an end. He sneeringly pointed out that Nick had been stupid to go riding in the rain on his motorcycle during contract negotiations. Skidding into the back of a car not only ended his career, but also Michelle's ability to keep Richard in the style to which he had grown accustomed. It was a well-known fact that Nick spent lavishly. With all the medical bills he was bound to incur, in a matter of weeks there would be nothing left.

"I walked out on my brother and made a fool of myself in the process because of you," Michelle cried in agonized disbelief.

Richard shrugged. "It was your choice, sweetie. Now leave. My girlfriend and her parents will be here soon."

Michelle didn't move. This time she studied Richard unhurriedly, feature by feature. This time she saw beyond the handsome nut-brown face. His brown eyes were no longer warm and loving, but hard and cold. Richard had used her and she had let him. She felt the screams of betrayal building at the back of her throat and forced them down. An outburst would only humiliate her further. "I hope you get everything you deserve," she said finally.

Richard threw back his head and laughed. "Oh, don't worry. I will. Marilyn's parents are loaded and she's even crazier about me than you were. What's more important is that she has poise, breeding, and class. Things you'll never have. I don't want you now and I only tolerated you then."

Her composure had snapped. She slapped Richard with all the force of her five-foot-three frame, totally disregarding that he was a scant inch from six feet.

Fury stole across his face. He grabbed for her. Whirling, she ran down the wooden steps and along the beach. It was futile. He caught her less than thirty feet away. They fell into the fast-rushing waters of the incoming tide. Begging Richard to stop proved useless, so she began to pray.

A man, tall, dark, and imposing, appeared out of nowhere. He lifted Richard like a twig and tossed him several feet away. Richard hit the ground heavily and started to rise, but checked his movement with one look from her rescuer. Richard lay in the sand, panting and scowling. The stranger's mention of calling the police brought a quick babble of words. Michelle's relief turned to shame as Richard told how she had come looking for him.

"It's all her fault, she was the one asking for it."

"Please, don't call the police. My brother . . ." Her voice trailed off, her head lowered. She was ashamed enough without Nick finding out and the story getting in the papers.

"You get off this time, but I'm on this beach a lot. Touch another woman without her permission and you'll answer to me."

Turning his back on Richard, the stranger

gently took Michelle by the arm and led her to a
house farther down the beach. Leaving the
wooden front door ajar, he ushered her inside.

"Friends call me B.J. I know you may have a
low opinion of men right now, but I won't hurt
you," he said gently, his voice deep and soothing.

Her arms wrapped tightly around her waist,
Michelle's gaze traveled up six feet plus of con-
ditioned muscles clad in snug-fitting jeans, over
a powerful chest bared by his unzipped black
sweat jacket, past the dimpled thrust of his chin,
the sensual curve of his lower lip, the full black
mustache, the straight nose, then stopped at the
black eyes staring calmly back at her.

The eyes convinced her. There was something reassuring and gentle in them. Despite
his obvious strength, he hadn't used it indis-
criminately. More important, she needed to believe him. She needed someone to lean on just
for a little while, and B.J. looked as if he had
enough strength for both of them. She closed
the door.

He nodded his head to the left. "Bedroom and
clean clothes through there. After you're cleaned
up, I'll take you home."

She burst into tears. Through her sobs she
told him about Nick's ultimatum. There was no
home to go to. B.J. didn't comment until she had
showered and eaten half a sandwich. Then he
began to talk, not only about how she might feel,
but also about Nick and what he must be going

through if he could no longer care for her or himself.

The night was well-aged by the time he made her see that life wasn't over because of one mistake, and to lie down in self-pity would give Richard a kind of power over her. B.J.'s nonjudgmental attitude, his understanding and patience, gave her the courage to call Nick.

B.J. had also given her the first tempting taste of real attraction—something entirely different from the foolish schoolgirl infatuation she'd felt for Richard. Standing with him near the iron steps leading up to the waiting taxi, she realized again how horrible the night might have ended if not for her angel. He was the only person in her memory who wanted to give without wanting anything in return. Nick wanted total obedience. Richard wanted her brother's money. B.J. just wanted her safe and happy. On impulse she stood on tiptoe to kiss him good-bye on the cheek. His head turned, his lips accidentally finding hers.

At her startled gasp he'd caught her arms with his hands, then stepped away to stare down at her. "Please don't be frightened. I won't hurt you."

She hadn't known how to tell him it wasn't fear that caused her body to shiver, but an unexpected need to press her lips back against his, to feel his arms around her. It was as if she had been waiting all her life for this moment, this man.

"It's ... it's not that ... I. ..." She couldn't put into words all the emotions swirling through her. She'd thought she loved Richard, but now she knew better. Gathering her courage, she stepped out of his arms. "Good-bye. I just wanted to know how it felt to kiss an angel."

"Please change your mind and let me take you to the airport," he said, a frown marring his handsome face.

She smiled sadly and shook her head. She still thought it best to say good-bye here. She had hurt her brother enough. Nick could never find out she wasn't safe in a hotel room as she had told him. The only regret she had was in not being able to tell B.J. her name. There had been a great deal of media attention focused on Nick's injury and many of the stories had included her name. "I won't ever forget you."

B.J. stood there, moonbeams dancing around his broad shoulders, his face silhouetted. "Remember what I said. Spit in the devil's eye if he tries to stop you from getting what you want out of life."

"I'll remember." She glanced down at the pink jogging suit she was wearing. "Where shall I send the clothes?"

"Don't bother. Alice has more than enough. At least that's what her husband is always telling me."

The horn blared.

"I guess the taxi driver is getting impatient."

She swallowed the sudden lump in her throat. "Thanks for being there and for giving me the courage to try my wings." Turning away from the face she would carry in her heart always, she ran to the waiting taxi, determined to make something of herself and to one day find her angel again.

She hadn't found him; he had found her. Except he didn't remember her. Had she really expected him to? *Yes!* her mind screamed, just as she had remembered him.

But their reunion wasn't the fantasy she had envisioned. He wasn't attracted to her; he was attracted to the image Nick had persuaded her to create. Why was it so difficult for people to care about the woman behind the image? Somehow she had to accept that it was and go on as before. At least it had allowed her to do something she had always dreamed: buy a home, thirty-two-hundred square feet of comfort and luxury on a wooded lot in the middle of Dallas.

It was the first real home for both of them. She'd lived in boarding school while Nick played football. His near-empty apartment certainly hadn't been a home. After his accident his medical expenses had taken what little money he had left and they had been forced to live in a one-bedroom efficiency. Because of her success they didn't ever have to worry about being evicted again. Smoothing out her pillow,

Michelle lay down and sought the forgetfulness of sleep.

Precisely at eight forty-five the next morning, Michelle pushed open the glass front door of Forbes Realtors. The smile and greeting she gave the receptionist, Dana, was friendly, but the dangerous glint in her eyes sent an entirely different message. Michelle didn't slacken her pace until she reached her office, located near the end of the atrium complex.

The large sunny room resembled a comfortable den more than an office. A sofa and loveseat covered in supple white leather sat in one corner of the room. A combination bar and entertainment center was within arm's reach. On the glass cocktail table sat a fresh-cut arrangement of flowers in a crystal vase. The walls and the carpet were soft blue.

Sitting behind her cherry desk, Michelle opened her briefcase and took out the contract for the two hundred acres she had sold the day before. The usual sense of accomplishment and pride she experienced after a sale wasn't there. Her mind was on one thing—rather, one man. But Brad Jamison would be out of her life in fifteen minutes.

The strident buzz of the intercom came exactly at nine.

"Ms. Grant, Mr. Jamison is here to see you,"

came the breathless sound of the receptionist's heavily accented Southern drawl. Brad had made another conquest.

The smile forming on Michelle's face shifted into a frown. "Please tell Mr. Jamison I'm sorry, but I have a prior appointment, and refer him to Mr. Sims or Ms. Rogers."

Now all she had to do was wait five seconds. A gentleman would reschedule or see another Realtor, but a renegade like Brad . . .

He came charging through her door in four seconds instead of the expected five. Bold and devastatingly handsome in a dark gray suit, Brad strode angrily across the plush carpet until he stood in front of her. Firmly planting both hands on top of her desk, he glared across the short distance separating them. "We had an appointment."

Michelle slowly leaned back in her swivel chair, away from the assault of his lethal maleness. He had no right to make her body react as if it were still going through adolescence. Her palms were actually damp.

"*We* is an incorrect statement. You threw an appointment time at me and walked off. I'm already booked for the day and I have no intention of breaking a single appointment," she said. "Would you expect any less if the situation were reversed?"

The harsh lines faded from his face. Straightening to his full height, he brushed aside his jacket and slid four fingers into his pants pocket, revealing a trim waist and a flat stomach. "Who is the appointment with?"

Michelle shook her head. If nothing else he was persistent. "I hardly see how that has anything to do with the situation. Besides, there is such a thing as client confidentiality."

Long slender fingers raked impatiently over short curly hair. "I need to leave Dallas this afternoon and I wanted to get some idea of the potential sites before I left."

"I understand." Ignoring her sudden feeling of loss, Michelle picked up the phone, pushed the intercom button, then dialed.

"Yes?"

"Dana, please ask Mr. Sims and Ms. Rogers to step into my office." Placing the receiver back in its cradle, she sent Brad her best professional smile. "Please have a seat, Mr. Jamison. I'm sure one of them can assist us."

Black eyes studied her for a long moment, then he turned and sat down in a slate blue leather chair near her desk. Hitching up his trousers, he rested one long leg over his other knee. Sunlight filtered through the window over his black hair and Michelle had to grip her pen to fight the urge to walk over and touch him. She forced herself to meet his disconcerting gaze. If he could remain unaffected, so could she.

Brad let his gaze touch every visible inch of

Michelle's body. He didn't see how, but she was even more beautiful in the revealing light of day. The apricot linen suit she wore gave a warm glow to her almond complexion. He only wished she'd take her hair out of that darn knot. He visualized it flowing over his pillow, her eyes glazed with desire just before he—

"Mr. Jamison, how long have you been in Dallas?"

Brad saw the anger glinting in Michelle's eyes and smiled lazily. She knew what he was thinking, and from her agitated breathing, she had been thinking the same thing. "Apparently not long enough," he answered, raking her with another heated look.

Her mouth tightened, and she could have kicked herself when his mouth curved into a smile. The scoundrel knew he was making her uncomfortable. Well, he was about to get his.

Her office door opened, and Michelle moved to greet the man and woman entering. Out of the corner of her eye she saw Brad stand.

"Good morning, Lucy, John. Mr. Jamison, I'd like to introduce you to Ms. Lucy Rogers and Mr. John Sims. You probably saw each other last night at Alex's house."

Michelle waited until the handshakes were over, then sprang her trap. "Mr. Jamison, I took the liberty of calling them this morning because of my full schedule. Either one is very capable of helping you. Since I have an appointment with Alex in two minutes, you're welcome to stay and use my office."

Michelle watched Brad's face contort with fury and felt a prickle of unease. Hating herself for doing so, she made a hasty retreat from the office.

She was still shaking when she knocked on Alex's door and heard him say, "Come in."

Looking up from his cluttered desk, he frowned at her pale complexion as she closed the door and walked unsteadily across the room. "Michelle, what is it?"

The abrupt opening of the door and the reverberating sound as it slammed shut interrupted her reply. She whirled. In two long-legged strides Brad reached Michelle, his jaw tight.

"I don't know what you're trying to prove, and frankly I don't care. You're the one chosen to show me properties. Now if you're too emotional or too insecure, I'll find another Realtor or another city. It's your choice. You have five seconds to give me an answer!"

CHAPTER THREE

Wide-eyed, Michelle glanced toward Alex for help. The only indication that he might be upset was the way he gripped a gold pen in his fist. He'd back her in whatever decision she made, but he wouldn't fight her battles for her.

Steeling herself against Brad's anger, she said, "I'm sorry, Mr. Jamison, if the two agents are unsatisfactory, but naturally I assumed you wished—"

The sharp slice of his hand through the air stopped her explanation. "You were stuffed down my throat as the Realtor to see. I admit that I was out of line last night, but we both know you paid me back. Now, are you going to act like a professional or some child who can't handle criticism? You have four seconds."

Her hand clenched by her side. "An important man like—"

"Three seconds."

Michelle studied Brad's chiseled features.

They were inflexible. He wasn't bluffing. He'd walk out and not look back. She'd be rid of him, but Forbes Realtors would lose one of its biggest potential sales of the year. It wasn't fair to Alex to let her personal feelings interfere with her job. She wasn't that unsure of herself. A smile touched the curve of her lips. She was about to spit into the devil's eye.

"Is one o' clock satisfactory?" Michelle asked and heard the mingled sounds of Alex's sigh of relief and the creak of his chair. At least someone in the room was happy.

Brad gave a negative shake of his head. "I have an appointment for lunch at half past one. An hour later would be better."

"I have a closure at three."

"Perhaps if I saw your appointment book, we could figure something out."

Michelle opened her mouth to remind him of confidentiality, then snapped it shut. The sooner he saw no time was available, the sooner he'd leave. "Certainly, I'll get my book."

"I'll go with you."

Her smile was chilly. "As you wish." Brushing past Brad, she left the room. Behind her she heard Brad apologize for his "rude entry" and Alex's "forget it." Gritting her teeth, Michelle continued down the hall and into her office, with Brad close behind.

A scarlet-tipped nail flipped through the crisp white pages of her appointment book until she stopped at May 2. Gripping the book firmly, Michelle turned to Brad.

He took the leather-bound book without hesitation. To her surprise, he began to thumb back through. Outraged, she pulled the book from his hand.

Apparently undisturbed by his action, Brad crossed his arms and met her angry gaze impassively. "You can tell a great deal about a person from looking through their appointment book. Do you want to know what I learned about you?"

"Another free analysis, Mr. Jamison?"

"You're well organized, you're neat, and you don't try to cram clients together. You have very few cancellations, and an impressive number of SOLDS written in bold red letters. You work hard, don't you?" he asked, a note of surprise in his voice.

"Doing my job, or doing whatever it takes to make a sale?" she asked tightly.

His eyes glinted. "I told you I was sorry for that remark. I'm not proud of the way I acted, but I will not keep apologizing or let you continue to throw it in my face."

Brad's blunt reprisal left her no comeback. Michelle noted the proud carriage of his head and realized she had pushed him far enough. Brad Jamison pushed back. He was right, she was overreacting.

In all of her seven years as a Realtor, she had

never treated a client so callously. And there had been many who deserved worse. Brad had no way of knowing she had woven a tapestry of dreams around him. She had to get her emotions under control.

"I'm sorry, Mr. Jamison. I didn't get much sleep last night and I'm a little testy," she admitted, not realizing what her admission implied until Brad's gaze narrowed speculatively on her face, then dropped to her lips.

"That makes two of us," he said, somehow managing to look hopeful and outraged at the same time.

A blush intensified the color of her cheeks. "I ... er ... meant that I'm keyed up from the closure of two important deals in Houston." Nervously, she fingered the long strand of pearls around her neck.

His answering smile was as wicked as it was heart-stopping. "If you say so, Ms. Grant." His warm gaze roaming slowly, seductively, over Michelle's suddenly heated flesh definitely said he didn't believe a word she said.

His eyes touched her in all the places he wanted his hands to delight in touching. From the curve of her slightly parted lips, past the tantalizing thrust of her breasts, over her small waist, and down the soft lines of her hips and shapely legs, which were shown to perfection in her slim skirt. When his gaze lifted abruptly to hers, there was an open challenge glittering in his eyes.

"Do you think I can fit?" he asked softly.

"What?" Her heart knocked against her ribs.

"Do you think I can fit into your schedule?"

Michelle struggled to bring her wayward thoughts back to the situation at hand. "There is simply no time, Mr. Jamison, and I have no intention of altering my schedule to meet your needs." Walking around her desk, she sat down. The man was impossible—and dangerous to her peace of mind.

"You haven't looked yet," he said, gesturing toward the appointment book.

"I don't have to," Michelle replied, placing the disputed object on the far corner of her desk. "Please leave your number and I'll have the receptionist call as soon as something is available."

Brad was completely still except for the muscles clenching in his jaw. If anyone else had treated him this way, he would have walked. But Michelle Grant fascinated him almost as much as she made him want to shake some sense into her beautiful head. It had been a long time since a woman aroused his interest as well as his body.

From beneath the safety of her long lashes, Michelle noted Brad hadn't left. She picked up a client's folder and tried to study the speculations for a piece of frontal property on Elm

Street, but her mind refused to relinquish Brad Jamison. She kept remembering how well his suit fit, how magnificently male he was.

The annoying buzz of the intercom jerked her mind from its traitorous thoughts. Irritated with herself, she punched the blinking red button and snapped, "Yes." Instantly she regretted the harshness of her tone. Dana's hesitant answer only made her feel worse.

"I-I'm sorry to disturb you, Ms. Grant, but there's a long-distance call for Mr. Jamison from California on line two."

Lifting the receiver from its base, Michelle handed Brad the phone. It was only seven-thirty there, so it was safe to assume the call wasn't business. The lines gathering between his brows only increased her vexation. He was probably trying to figure out which of his lady friends it was.

As he took the phone, their fingers accidentally brushed. An undeniable current of warmth passed between them. Their startled gazes locked for a long moment. Brad recovered first. Jabbing the flashing red button, he barked, "Jamison here."

Totally out of character, Michelle leaned back in her chair to listen. However, in a few minutes a scowl deepening the lines between Brad's eyes and around his mouth made her wish she had left. His voice was like a blast of frigid air.

"Dammit, I told them to watch her closely! When?" he ripped out, shoving his hand into his pocket. "I want a complete breakdown from Kent when I get back."

He shook his head once. "No. Don't call anyone. I'll take care of this myself," he ground out between clenched teeth. His tone brooked no argument. "I'll be there in three hours. Have a car waiting for me at the airport. You just make sure Edith is all right."

Brad slammed the phone into the cradle. He turned cold black eyes upon her. She resisted the urge to shrink back into her chair. His body was taut with barely controlled rage. Michelle realized she had yet to feel the full force of his wrath, yet somehow sensed it could easily be unleashed if he were pushed too far.

"You have a reprieve, Ms. Grant. I have to leave immediately. Today is Wednesday; you have until Monday to set up an appointment with me. Think long and hard. I won't ask again." His face unyielding, he spun on his heel and strode from the room without giving Michelle a chance to reply.

Watching his rugged frame disappear, Michelle felt an unexpected sadness wash over her. The relief she had expected to feel when she saw the last of Brad Jamison wasn't there. Instead she felt an acute sense of loss—and, if she were honest, pique. He certainly hadn't wasted

any time rushing back to California to rescue another woman in distress. Her unfair thoughts
caused her to wince.

Brad had been there when she needed him
the most. He had lit the dark places in her soul
and banished the shadows. He revealed to her a
world that could be. If some other woman
needed his help, she couldn't think of anyone
better equipped to assist her.

Rising from her desk, Michelle stood looking
out the large plate glass window behind her
desk. She saw none of the towering gold buildings surrounding the Galleria or the busy traffic
on LBJ Freeway. Why couldn't she forget him?

Every man she had ever dated, she had measured up against her dark angel. Each one always lost. A psychiatrist could probably tell her
the reason behind her feelings, but it still would
not help her banish them. B.J.'s memory had
seen her through hunger, pain, fear, and disillusionment; prodding her, making her believe it
was possible to succeed. Now her dream lover
had taken on human form again, and there was
no defense within her to withstand him.

The hard rap on her door brought her head
around. "Come in, Alex," she answered, recognizing his knock before she saw him advancing
through the door. The corners of her mouth
lifted in a poor imitation of a smile.

"I'm sorry, Alex. My objectivity along with

my professionalism stayed home this morning," she said, sitting down.

Perching his hip on the edge of her desk, Alex took her cold hands in his. "You avoided talking last night, but I think it's time we did," he said softly, his gaze skimming over her pinched features.

She shrugged one slim shoulder. "There is nothing to say that you don't already know. Brad Jamison is the man who helped me when I ran after Richard Ewing and he didn't want me," she stated, the disillusionment evident in her voice. Alex was the only person she had ever told about that night, and even he didn't know the entire story.

Alex seemed to choose his next words carefully. "You expected him to remember, didn't you?"

Closing her eyes briefly, Michelle tried to pull her skittering emotions together. "Stupid, wasn't it?"

"No, it wasn't. Brad touched something within you that night that made you want to go on. He helped you to see beyond the misery you were feeling to the promise of a better tomorrow. Anyone would have remembered him. But are you sure the man was Brad?"

"It's him. He told me his name was B.J. I never told you because I foolishly wanted to have something of him that only I knew. At the time I thought they were the initials for his first and middle name." She sighed. "Yet, even if he hadn't told me his name, I would still remember his piercing black eyes, the warmth of his touch," she admitted, unaware of the wistfulness in her voice.

Alex's breath expelled on a ragged sigh. "I guess that settles it. We called him B.J. in college." Michelle's nails bit into the palm of his hand. "I'm sorry, Michelle."

"For what?" she asked, trying to keep her voice light.

He reached out to touch her face. "Because things didn't work out the way you wanted. Because you ask so little for yourself and always give so much. Because somehow it doesn't seem fair."

"Don't worry about it, Alex. I learned a long time ago that life is seldom fair. I guess for a little while I forgot and tried to beat the odds," she informed him blithely, withdrawing her hands and forcing a smile to her face.

Alex wasn't fooled. "What are you going to do now?"

Michelle shifted uneasily in her seat. She knew he was referring to both the professional and personal relationship. "Brad scares me."

Alex gave her a half-smile. "He has that effect on most people. On the other hand, there aren't many things that intimidate him. What he wants, he goes after and usually gets. It probably comes from being Kyle Jamison's only child and heir."

Michelle's mouth dropped open. "*The* Kyle Jamison? The man who parlayed his oil fields in East Texas into a multi-million-dollar conglomerate?"

"The same. Brad's mother was just as much of an achiever in the publishing industry. She made *Mystique the* fashion magazine for the fashion-conscious women of America. Growing up with parents like that, 'I can't' was definitely frowned upon."

To Michelle, who had never known her father and barely remembered her mother, it gave her a little more insight into Brad. "No wonder he is so impatient and intense."

"Remember that when he's being a little over-bearing, not to mention arrogant." Alex stood. " 'No' is not a word he likes to hear. He actually thrives on competition."

Michelle glanced at Alex sharply. "I get the feeling you're trying to tell me something about Brad other than his business acumen."

The look Alex sent her was shrewd, level. "Don't go dumb on me, Michelle. I'd have to be blind not to see the sparks flying between you two. They could set green kindling on fire." Michelle's indignant gasp failed to stop his flow of words.

"I must admit I was surprised by the attraction. In the past Brad has taken a wide berth around women who devote long, hard hours to their career the way you do. He wants to come first in any relationship." Alex looked thoughtful. "Probably because he had such a hard time getting affection from his parents, especially his mother."

As if aware of what he had admitted, Alex gritted out an expletive. "I had no right to tell you that."

"How could his parents not love him?" she blurted, stunned by what she had heard.

"He wouldn't want your or anyone else's pity. Women have been chasing him since his voice changed. That is, until you. But as I said, he goes after what he wants, and I think we both know it's you."

"If that's so, why did he go rushing off to see some other woman?" she questioned sharply, then gasped at her slip of the tongue.

Alex's booming laughter heightened the color in her cheeks. "I don't know. Why don't you ask him when he gets back? He's not a man to give up easily and you'll see him because you're no coward." He flicked his forefinger across her nose.

Michelle slapped the air where his hand had been.

Chuckling, Alex walked to the door. "If you want my advice, go after him. Next to me, he's probably the best man for you. But you better learn to cook something besides grilled cheese sandwiches."

Michelle watched the door close and smiled. The crack about her cooking had done it. Cooking was an art she had never cultivated, and frankly had no desire to. In the foster homes there were always other chores she'd opted to do, and at the boarding school the recipes she learned were impractical; then after Nick's football career ended, there was no money or time with her working two jobs. Brad would just have to eat her cooking the same as Nick did.

Her smile froze. For the first time since their disastrous reunion, she was thinking of them in the future tense. Absently gnawing on her bottom lip, she admitted what she had been trying to deny. She wanted Brad to be a permanent part of her life. The first thing she was going to do was stop acting like a prickly pear. This time she was going to give him memories two lifetimes couldn't dim. Light, tinkling laughter bubbled from her at her temerity.

CHAPTER FOUR

The grandfather clock in the far corner of Michelle's office struck the quarter hour, drawing her firmly back to the present. There was a client to pick up at ten and she prided herself on her punctuality. Daydreams about Brad would have to wait. In the back of her mind a small voice tried to whisper about the woman he had gone to see. Her heart refused to listen.

For the second time in her life she was going to follow her heart. She could only hope this time things would end differently. Grabbing her attaché case, she stood.

Passing the receptionist, her steps slowed, "I'm sorry that I snapped at you, Dana."

The petite woman's head came up, her face wreathed in its usual smile. "That's all right, Ms. Grant. I know how hectic it's been for you. I make your appointments."

"Speaking of appointments. If I have a cancellation, please give it to Mr. Jamison. Otherwise, give him my next available opening. Mr. Forbes has his phone number," Michelle said matter-of-factly, but the knowing look on Dana's pretty face said she was not fooled.

"You can count on me, Ms. Grant," Dana said in a conspiratorial tone.

Michelle's brow knitted at the implication, but before she could decide whether to say something, the phone rang, and Dana turned her attention to the call. Chafing at the situation, Michelle mumbled good-bye and turned away.

Still wondering if she should try to straighten Dana out, Michelle lifted her hand to push against the brass bar plate to open the door. The sound of her name caught her attention just as her hand settled against the cold metal. Sighing at the delay, she retraced her steps.

"Yes?"

Dana, who knew how Michelle felt about being punctual, quickly explained, "That was your brother. He said his reservations were changed. You're to pick him up at the American Eagle terminal at six thirty-five." Ripping off the crisp white sheet of paper with the information on it, Dana handed it to Michelle.

"I can't." Michelle frowned, looking at the message. "Did he leave a number?"

Springy curls brushed against her cinnamon-colored cheeks as Dana shook her head. "No, I asked him to wait, but he said he had to go."

Mumbling her thanks, Michelle turned away

from Dana's sympathetic look. They had gone through this before. If Nick wanted to make sure she did as he asked, he left no way for her to return his call. Sometimes, he acted as if he were thirteen instead of thirty-three.

Pushing open the door, she stepped into the bright sunshine. Jacob, as expected, waited beside the Rolls. Nodding absently, she got inside, Nick still occupying her thoughts. With all her problems she didn't need him constantly testing her love. For a split second she thought of not showing up.

Almost instantly she regretted the idea. Before his accident, Nick was always there for her. Why shouldn't he expect the same from her? It wasn't his fault their roles had been reversed that rainy night. He had lost his career and his dreams. But that would all change once the rehab center opened.

Leaning back against the plush leather seat, she knew she'd be at the airport as requested. Somehow she'd make the usual hour drive to Cedar Valley College in time for her lecture at seven thirty.

At six thirty, Jacob pulled up to the curb in Love Field Airport. Opening the door, Michelle stepped out as soon as the car came to a full halt. The brisk, hot wind whipped black strands of hair from her chignon, giving a soft delicate beauty to her face.

Entering the cool terminal, Michelle absently brushed her hair behind her ear, causing her cropped jacket to open and reveal high, firm breasts pushing against the sheer white material of her blouse. More than one head turned to follow her progress to the security checkpoint.

The first sight of Nick, as it had for the past nine years, made her heart constrict in pain. Her husky brother, who was once the star running back for one of the best professional football teams in the country, would never run or walk again. He would be locked in the mechanical chair that was now his legs forever.

He had gone from touchdown to touchdown, breaking and setting records with only minor injuries, only to pay a devastating price for riding his motorcycle far too recklessly. There was nothing the doctors could do to bring life back to the powerful legs that had carried his team to a winning Super Bowl.

Smiling through her sadness, she said, "Welcome home, Nick."

A boyish smile lit his weary face. "It's great being back, Shelly."

She breathed a little easier. She could tell Nick's moods by the way he greeted her. "Shelly" meant he was all right. "Michelle" meant duck for cover.

Greeting the skycap carrying Nick's luggage, she leaned down to brush her lips against her brother's cheek and winced. "Ouch. I'll be glad when that thing is fully grown," she teased, referring to his week-old beard. Falling into step beside the motorized wheelchair, she followed Nick down the concourse.

Instead of the smile she expected, he frowned and rubbed the short, stubby growth on his face. "Sorry. It's been a long time since I had to worry about a woman's tender skin."

Her steps faltered, but her smile remained. Once again she had stumbled into a painful area. After his accident, Jodie was the only woman Nick allowed to get remotely close to him. Michelle guessed he'd done so because Jodie had posed no threat to his fragile ego or his manhood.

"Are you saying that I'm not a woman?" she asked, deliberately misunderstanding his statement. He opened his mouth, but she cut him off, saying, "Never mind or you might talk yourself into eating my cooking for a week."

"Please, anything but that," Nick begged, and they both laughed.

Outside the terminal a swift glance at her thin gold watch told Michelle she was going to be late. Tipping the skycap, she got inside the car and waited for Nick to hoist himself in beside her. She and Jacob had learned not to give or offer any help unless Nick asked for it.

"I have a speaking engagement at Cedar Valley and Jacob is going to drop me off," she explained, glancing through the rear window to see the wheelchair being stored. "I'm sorry you'll have to spend your first night back alone."

Straightening his legs, Nick gave her a small smile. "You mean I can send out for pizza, and not have you pester me about the fund-raising trip."

"That's right. So tell me now or I'll be forced to wake you up tonight." She leaned back. "I'm all ears."

"You're all heart too," he said quietly, reaching over to squeeze her hand. "Don't give up on me."

Knowing he was referring to his quip in the airport, she closed her fingers around his. "You didn't give up on me. Now talk."

He did. "The three-day trip was a success. Thanks to you and your contacts, the businessmen and -women were more than ready to help out." He made a face. "I drank enough tea to last a lifetime at a couple of the luncheons in the women's homes, but seeing the checks pile up on the table afterward was more than worth it."

He patted the inside pocket of his tan raw silk blazer. "I have another twenty thousand dollars to add."

"That's wonderful. Mr. Nash will be thrilled," she said, referring to the chairman of the board of the Winslow Foundation.

Nick grinned. "I called him from Austin. He couldn't stop praising me."

"And well he should," Michelle said, then listened as Nick continued to relate what had happened in Austin. Not one time did he tell her of anything but happy experiences.

Never had she been prouder of him. Working first with Jodie, and now with the Winslow Foundation was helping him to realize that his life wasn't over because he was in a wheelchair. Her earlier thoughts of not picking him up caused her to feel ashamed.

"It sounds as if everything went fine," Michelle said.

"Things would be finer if we had about eighty thousand dollars more for the physical therapy equipment. Got any new clients you might be able to get a donation from?" he queried.

Brad immediately sprang into her mind. "I do have one. Brad's family owns a computer firm and they might relocate here."

His hand tightened briefly on hers. "I never heard you call any of your clients by their first name before. Is he someone special to you?"

In spite of the disapproval in Nick's voice, she answered honestly. "He could be."

"Be careful," he cautioned. "You haven't dated much so you don't know how devious men can be."

"All right, Nick," she said, hating the warning

almost as much as the thought that he might be right.

Nick's mouth tightened at her crestfallen expression. "Honey, I'm sorry. I still look at you as my little sister and I worry. I don't want you getting hurt by some fast-talking jerk."

Her irritation vanished. "I know, but this is one time I have to work things out for myself."

He squeezed her hand. "I guess you do, but right now get your things together. We just turned onto the campus."

He was right. The glistening white buildings sitting amid oak trees on the hilly countryside loomed before her. "So that's what Jacob whispered to you when I was talking to the skycap. You were to keep me busy so I wouldn't notice how fast he was driving."

"No comment." He glanced at his stainless-steel watch. "You have five minutes to spare."

Shaking her head, Michelle picked up her briefcase just as the door opened. Jacob's craggy face smiled down at her. She couldn't do anything but smile in return.

"I still say you should have been a race car driver." Once she was on the sidewalk, her gaze touched both men. "Greg, one of the students, is bringing me home, so you two stay out of trouble. 'Bye."

Turning away, she followed the curved, tree-lined walk leading to the main building of the college. Less than fifteen feet away she saw Greg hurrying toward her. Trying to forget how little sleep she had obtained in the last four days, she lifted her hand in greeting.

Michelle inserted her key in the front door lock, then turned to the four young students hanging out of the windows of Greg's battered Ford. "Good night and thanks for seeing me home." Pushing the door open, a shaft of white light greeted her. The hall light had a timer that switched it on at eight P.M.

"Good night, Ms. Grant. Sorry we kept you out so late," Greg shouted, unconcerned about disturbing the neighbors since the house was situated in the middle of a densely wooded acre lot.

The car ground into gear, jerked, then lurched like a bucking horse in the circular driveway. To a chorus of "good night" and "thanks," the vehicle backfired and disappeared down the winding road.

A weary sigh escaped Michelle as she closed the door and leaned back against the stained glass framing the portal. She should have been in bed hours ago, but the hopeful, almost hungry eyes of the students kept her from leaving, even when the security guard ran them off campus and they had to retreat to an all-night café.

She remembered too much of herself in them to walk away. With pen and paper in hand, they had tried to jot down every word she uttered. They saw the trappings of success she possessed, and they were eager for some of the same. However, she also wanted them to know about the bad times, the no's, the doors shut in your face, the sales that fell through.

Then, if you were lucky and persistent, and the sales started coming regularly, then came the fourteen-hour days, and very little time for yourself or your family. Success was not without its price tag. What was? Her thoughts went to Brad, but she firmly pulled them back.

Pushing herself upright, she went to her bedroom in the back of the rambling, one-story ranch house. Shell lights led the way. For some reason, neither she nor Nick liked total darkness.

The press of a button threw a soft yellow light across the spacious bedroom. Here was her sanctuary, her retreat. From the first moment she'd stepped into the room three years ago, she knew it was what she had always dreamed of: a home where she belonged and no one could take from her. An enclosed patio with a small rock waterfall to lull her to sleep and remind her of the ocean made the house perfect. The house had been a real bargain. While it had still taken a sizable chunk of her savings to make the down payment, she'd never regretted her decision.

In her memory there was never a time until she was twenty that she had not shared a room or a bed. First the foster homes, then after Nick's success there were the dorms of her private school, and after his financial problems there was the lumpy sofa bed in their one-bedroom efficiency. The brass, king-sized four-poster draped in white voile on a raised platform was a far cry away from that.

Plopping down on a peach silk–covered chaise longue, Michelle slipped off her shoes and rubbed the bottoms of her aching feet. Knowing that resting there longer meant not getting up until morning, she picked up her shoes and went to the closet. Uncharacteristically, she let the shoes fall from her fingers, then pulled a lacy aqua nightgown and robe from a padded hanger and went to the bathroom.

Draping the sleepwear over a vanity chair, she turned on the tap of the tub, liberally sprinkling Gold Leaf bath salts under the running water. After undressing, she stepped in and let the scented water close around her.

Ten minutes later, Michelle emerged, feeling as if she could sleep for a month. Drawing the pins from her hair, she brushed through the long silky strands once, twice, then put the silver-handled brush on the dresser. To heck with it, she was going to bed.

Unwanted, a pair of black eyes flashed before her and she realized falling asleep was not going to be easy.

Her fingers had just touched the white satin comforter when the phone rang. Her gaze darted to the digital clock on her nightstand. Who would call at two in the morning? All she needed was a heavy breather.

"Hello."

"Where the hell have you been? I've been trying to reach you all evening."

It was no heavy breather. It was Brad Jamison.

CHAPTER FIVE

The swiftness of the verbal attack surprised her almost as much as the identity of the caller. Her hackles rose. The initial spurt of joy faded at the uncalled-for reprimand.

"It might surprise you, Mr. Jamison, but I've been able to tell time since I was five years old. If all you wanted to do was chime the time, I'll say good night," she said crisply.

"Please don't hang up." A long sigh heaved through the phone.

She could almost see him run his fingers over his hair. "Give me one reason why I shouldn't."

"I didn't mean to yell at you."

"I'm sure you didn't," she said, her voice heavy with sarcasm.

"You don't sound as if you believe me, Michelle, but I'm telling the truth. I guess the problems here have me edgy. When I spoke with Alex earlier he said you were usually home by twelve. After I tried repeatedly to reach you and couldn't, I became worried."

The tiredness in his voice and his concern for her touched her almost as much as the sound of her name on his lips. Besides, she didn't think Brad let many people know he had any weaknesses.

"What kind of problems?" Very much aware she had not accepted his apology, Michelle stepped out of her slippers, then lay across the handmade comforter that had taken her six months to obtain on special order. A little humility would do him good.

"There was a break-in at one of the research labs."

She came upright. "Is everything all right?"

"Things are fine," he quickly reassured her. "It just made me mad. They couldn't get any information without the access code and only one other person besides myself knows it."

"Isn't that dangerous?" Her annoyance forgotten, her hand tightened a fraction on the receiver.

"Torture and kidnap is only in the movies," he said, amusement in his voice.

Michelle relaxed, then recalled his time limit. "I asked the receptionist to give you an appointment as soon as one is available." Silence stretched on until she became uneasy. "Brad, did you hear what I said?"

"Yes," he answered, his voice hesitant; then

he continued. "That's why I tried to call you earlier. I shouldn't have given you an ultimatum. If anyone had said the same thing to me, they'd be looking for another firm to represent them."

Michelle smiled and stretched out on her back on the bed. "I think I hear another apology somewhere in there."

Brad chuckled. "I guess you do. Are you going to accept any of them?"

"I suppose so," she said. She'd never been able to stay upset with those she cared about for long. Which was exactly the reason Nick got away with trying to run her life all the time.

"Thank you. I really did have good intentions when I called."

"You probably haven't had any good intentions since you started wearing long pants," Michelle bantered lightly, then sobered when she remembered the woman he had rushed to California to rescue. Before she realized it she was asking, "How is Edith?"

"What did you say?"

The harshness of the question caught her off guard, but Michelle realized it was deserved. His personal life was none of her concern. Trying to make her voice light, she explained, "This morning, or rather yesterday morning, when you took your call in my office you seemed upset that Edith was in trouble. I . . . er . . . just wondered how she was."

"How much do you know about computers, Michelle?"

"Just enough to know that they scare me," she admitted, annoyed and thankful that he had changed the subject.

"E.D.I.T.H. stands for Electronic Data Internal Transmission Hardware. It's a system I designed to interface computers," he explained, his voice sounding inordinately pleased and smug.

"Oh," Michelle said. *Now he knew she had eavesdropped* and *that she was jealous!*

"If you're going to be my Realtor, you'll have to understand a little about what I do and what my company requires. I'll have my secretary FedEx some specifications and requirements to you. Or you can fly out here?"

"You want me to come to San Francisco?" That had her sitting up again.

"We'll talk more about it after you receive the information," he said casually. "You have visited clients before, haven't you?"

She had, but the possibility of them being together in San Francisco made her nerve endings zing. "Yes, of course."

"Good. I'll see you next Friday at one thirty. Someone called my office while I was tied up and assured my secretary that that was the earliest possible date unless there was a cancellation," he told her. "Now go to sleep. I shouldn't have called you so late, but I wanted to tell you

about the appointment. Good night, Michelle.
Pleasant dreams."

"Good night, Brad," she said softly and hung
up the phone. Her hand still on the receiver, she
stared out the French doors leading to the waterfall surrounded by lights. It was going to be all
right. Her dream might come true after all.

Brad couldn't believe what was happening to
him. He was acting like a kid, pacing the floor in
the reception area of Alex's firm and staring out
of a window anxiously awaiting Michelle's return. An impatient hand thrust itself over his
curly coal-black hair. What was there about
Michelle Grant that rebuffed and invited at the
same time? Undeniably she was one of the most
beautiful women he had ever seen, but early in
life he had learned that the old adage "Beauty is
only skin deep" held a wealth of meaning.

His mother was beautiful and charming, but
she was vindictive when she didn't get her way.
She'd proven that to him when she sold the old
south-of-Dallas homestead his maternal grandparents wanted him to have just to spite him. The
ranch meant home and love to him. To his mother
it was a way of making him bend to her wishes.
She'd miscalculated. He'd bow for no one.

But if it was the last thing he did, he planned
to buy back that ranch. Perhaps after he'd gotten
his company's relocation site settled, he'd let

Michelle see if she could talk the present owner, Clint Daniels, into selling. Brad's people certainly weren't having any success.

Thinking of Michelle caused the hard lines of his mouth to soften. She intrigued him. Perhaps it was because she was a puzzle he had yet to solve. One moment she was vulnerable, the next spitting like a wildcat. Past girlfriends might have been angry with him, but they never showed him that anger until after the relationship was over. Michelle didn't take guff from anyone for any reason. He liked that independent spirit about her.

Looking out of the huge plate glass framing the flowering pink crape myrtle–lined parking lot, Brad's attention was caught by a shiny white Rolls turning in. The car cruised to the front of the building and stopped. Recognizing the gray-haired driver as Alex's chauffeur, Brad continued watching, expecting Alex to emerge from the door Jacob opened.

Brad's eyes widened in surprise, then narrowed in speculation when he saw one, then another shapely leg appear. He didn't need the sudden tightening in the pit of his stomach to know to whom the legs belonged. Unknowingly, he took a step closer to the window. The appreciative look on his face shifted into a frown as a giant of a man got out of the car, swept Michelle into his arms, then pressed a hard kiss to her cheek.

Anger surged through Brad. He was reaching for the door when he saw Michelle lean her head back, exposing the graceful curve of her neck. A smile shaped the softness of her lips as she stood easily in the man's arms, like a friend or a lover. The word "lover" pounded in Brad's brain like a relentless drum; his fingers curled into a fist.

Unable to turn away, he watched as strands of Michelle's silky black unbound hair were lifted by the wind and draped caressingly over broad shoulders encased in a brown sports jacket. Laughing, Michelle reached up to pull the errant strands behind her ear. The man's hand followed and enclosed hers within its massive grip.

Another gust of wind molded Michelle's vivid red-and-green floral print dress to her shapely figure and around the man's denim-clad legs. With a muttered curse, Brad spun and walked to the far side of the waiting room and took a seat.

Large hands gripped the smoothness of the arms of the beige leather side chair. She had played her little innocent act and he had fallen for it. He didn't stand in line. From now on it was going to be strictly business. Ignoring the knot in his gut, he prepared to wait for Michelle.

"Thank you again, Michelle," Mason Jones said, his arms enclosing Michelle's tiny waist. "You did it again."

"I should be the one thanking you, Mason," Michelle answered, smiling up at the man who had given her her first listing and whose multi-faceted development company continued to deal exclusively with her. "Without you, I don't know how far I might have gotten in this business."

He shook his dark head. "You would have made it, Michelle. You have too much talent and drive not to succeed," he countered, finally releasing her. "And remember, without your help on this deal I don't think I would have been able to talk Mrs. Radford into selling her property so we could finalize the plans for building the shopping mall."

"We were lucky. If I hadn't been able to find that vacant lot so her house could be moved, we both might still be talking. It helped that one of her old neighbors lived only a block away," Michelle said. "You may not realize it, but it's hard to move away from what you've known for forty years. But I knew you'd build around her and she'd be landlocked or surrounded by things utterly confusing and alien to her. I've seen it happen."

Mason nodded. "I knew you were on her side as much as you were on mine. That's what makes you so valuable; you always have both the buyer's and the seller's best interests at heart."

"Thank you, Mason," Michelle said, and

glanced at her watch. "Now if you'll excuse me, I have another appointment in five minutes."

Mason leaned his head to one side and studied her sparkling brown eyes. "This client must be mighty important. You've been checking your watch every five minutes for the past hour," he teased, crossing his arms across his wide chest. He smiled at the flush in Michelle's cheeks. "I was only funning, Michelle. It's about time you took some time out for yourself. You better go inside. In case you didn't know it, men don't like to be kept waiting to see a beautiful lady." Flashing another grin, he turned on booted heels and strode to a red Mercedes sports car.

Threading her fingers through her tousled hair, Michelle started toward the office building, her bottom lip tucked between her teeth. Was she so easily read? If so, she'd have to get herself under control. In the past she had always prided herself on giving each client her undivided attention. Brad made that impossible.

Gripping the leather handle of her Louis Vuitton attaché case, she vowed not to let her personal life infringe on her business life. She had worked too hard to succeed. With the rumors going around, she needed to work harder, not daydream about a man whose presence in her life was fleeting at best.

She had no illusions about her ability to keep Brad's attention. Women in his past lasted only a few weeks. If he was the same man she had met nine years ago she might risk it, but he wasn't. Letting herself become emotionally involved would be a disaster. Being made a fool of over a man once was more than enough to last her a lifetime. The happiness she had felt earlier about seeing Brad was now tempered with restraint.

Pushing open the glass door, Michelle walked inside the cool waiting room. Immediately her eyes were drawn to Brad lounging in one of the leather chairs.

Despite her vow, her heart lurched. He looked more handsome than ever in a tan silk sports coat and a beige shirt open at the collar. Drawing in a steadying breath, she continued toward him. His long legs unfolded, and he stood, shoving his hands into his wheat-colored slacks in a now-familiar gesture of impatience.

Trying to control her own emotions, it took Michelle a few seconds to realize that there was almost a ruthlessness in the gaze traveling over her face and searching her eyes. Self-consciously, her hand fluttered over her windswept hair. Her decision to wear her hair down for him no longer seemed a good one. Confused by his silence and his rigid stance, she retreated behind a wall of professionalism.

"Welcome back to Dallas, Mr. Jamison. I trust you haven't waited too long."

"Long enough, Ms. Grant."

Her finely arched brow lifted at the briskness of his tone. "I don't understand."

"You will."

His stare drilled into her. She refused to cower or regret that the laughter they'd shared on the phone was gone. She'd learned long ago that at times, life sucked. "If you will follow me to my office we can discuss some of the sites I plan for us to see today."

Inside her office, she waved him to a chair and placed her case on her desk. "If you'll excuse me for a few minutes, I need to freshen up." Not waiting for an answer, Michelle went into the bathroom. Pulling open a drawer, she took out a brush and pulled her hair into a sleek chignon.

Looking at the picture of the sophisticated woman staring back at her, Michelle felt more capable of handling Brad in his strange mood. Taking a deep breath, she left. She was not surprised to see him leaning against the leather chair facing her desk. Sitting, she took out a folder marked "Computron."

Brad had watched Michelle march back into the room, her hair scraped back into the tight knot he hated, and gritted his teeth to keep from snatching the pins out. With a talent he had learned long ago, he listened to her go over the four sites she planned to show him and the reasons she chose them, while he studied the almost imperceptible squirming of her rounded bottom in her chair.

For the first time since he saw her being kissed, the knot in his stomach eased. It appeared he made her nervous. Good, because she made him act like a jealous fool and he didn't like it one bit.

Michelle looked up, wondering if her suggestions were acceptable, and saw Brad studying her. "Any questions, Mr. Jamison?"

"No. Why don't we go look them over?"

"Certainly, Mr. Jamison," she agreed, shoving the folder into her leather case. She was going to get through this no matter how difficult.

Brad straightened. "I don't think you want to go out looking like you do."

Her satiny brow arched. "Is there something wrong with the way I look?"

"Your lipstick is smudged at the corner," Brad explained.

Michelle's tongue flicked out and she lifted her finger to correct the problem. He watched her lips open wider, then close over her retreating tongue. Never in his life had he wanted anything more than to follow her tongue with his own.

Clamping a tight rein on his desire, he finally said, "I didn't want you to damage your image." Cool, impersonal fingers lightly touched her elbow and led her from the room.

The warm day did nothing to ease the tension

building within her. Nothing was going as she had envisioned. She kept her gaze on Jacob as he opened the door for them. "Thank you, Jacob." Michelle slid across the glove-soft white interior to the far side.

"Good afternoon, Jacob," Brad greeted him with a cheerfulness that had been lacking when he spoke with Michelle.

"Good afternoon, Mr. Jamison," the chauffeur said, smiling broadly.

"Field and Main," Michelle instructed, then casually placed her attaché case on the seat beside her. She wanted as much distance between them as possible.

"Yes, Ms. Grant," Jacob acknowledged.

The car was speeding on the toll road before Brad spoke, his voice tight. "Isn't this Alex's car?"

"Yes, it is," Michelle answered. "However, the top producer in the firm gets the exclusive use of it for the following year."

"How long has Alex done this?"

She glanced at his rigid body, already knowing where the conversation was heading. "Two years."

"How long have you been top producer?"

Michelle's hesitation answered her question before she did. "Two years."

"I see." Brad glanced out the window. "Where is the first property?"

Michelle ignored the censure in Brad's voice.

He was a client and nothing more. "Downtown at Field and Main. I know you want to build, but I thought in view of the problems you're having, you might want to think about moving your more delicate operations into a lease property," she explained.

He barely glanced at her before he turned back to the tinted window. "I haven't decided to move anything to Dallas," he said, a biting edge of steel in his voice. "I don't remember your mentioning a lease property in your office."

Michelle took the reprimand stoically. "I'm sorry. I did fail to tell you. If you'd rather not see the building, I can tell Jacob to go to the next site."

Brad gritted his teeth at the coolness in her voice. She hadn't been that way with her last client. But snapping at her would only make it more difficult for them to work together. It wasn't her fault he still wanted her no matter what he thought of her business tactics.

Thoughts of how she had persuaded Alex to let her have his prized car, and how private the backseat was with the tinted partition separating the passengers from Jacob, was making Brad crazy and clouding his objectivity. Computron had to come first. Her idea was a good one.

"We'll see the building," he finally said, seeing none of the traffic.

"As you wish," came the brisk reply.

Brad clenched his teeth to keep his colorful response locked behind his teeth.

For the next two hours Brad not only got a chance to see the possible sites for his firm, but to learn why Michelle was so good at her job. There was no detail she left to chance. From future expansion to employee parking and day care, she covered it all. And everyone greeted her with respect. Not a single man got out of line. Admiring glances followed her every move, but she appeared not to notice.

The only time she became agitated, Brad realized, was when he accidentally touched her. She'd jump, flash those big light brown eyes at him, then move away. Finally, when they were standing on the shoreline of Cedar Creek Lake, he could take no more.

"Michelle, if you skitter away from me one more time, I swear I won't be responsible for my actions," he told her.

She gazed at him with wide, uncertain eyes. "I'm sorry. You . . . you make me nervous."

"You do the same thing to me."

From his tone and expression, Michelle knew the admission was given grudgingly and he was not happy about it. "We don't seem to be able to keep from rubbing each other the wrong way." She glanced around for Jacob; his attention was on a fisherman who was casting from the bank into the placid waters of the lake.

Brad stepped closer until his cologne blotted out the smell of honeysuckle and filled her senses. "Rubbing you the right way is something I wouldn't mind doing."

"No," she choked, and stepped back.

His eyes took in the weary look in hers, and he checked the motion to pull her into his arms. Which was the real Michelle Grant? The shy, breathless woman standing before him or. . . . His mind refused to form the word. Looking at her trembling red lips, her manicured fingers desperately clutching her notebook, he could almost believe she was innocent. He wanted to believe.

"I think it's about time we had lunch. If I remember, Las Colinas is the last stop and there is an excellent restaurant in the Omni Mandalay Hotel." Brad smiled. "Are you hungry?"

"I am, a little," she admitted, relieved he was no longer scowling at her. "I didn't eat breakfast."

"Come on, then. Lunch is on me," he said, leading her back to the car. Once inside, he asked, "Why didn't you have breakfast?"

Not wanting to tell him she was too nervous about seeing him to eat, she instead made Mason the reason. "The appointment prior to yours was to see the last holdout in a multi-million-dollar shopping center. Luckily we were able to figure out the reason for her six-month refusal."

A muscle twitched in Brad's lean jaw. "He must have been grateful."

Michelle looked at Brad and realized their brief camaraderie was over. She continued, but her voice lacked its earlier enthusiasm. "I suppose, but he's the type of person who enjoys life to its fullest. I made my first sale to him when I started. It was not a tenth as important as today's, and I think my ribs will be just as sore. He's a good friend."

Brad's anger at himself was swift. How could he keep on misjudging her? Until he met Michelle, he had prided himself on his ability to read people correctly, or at least let them prove themselves. He shamefully admitted he had never given her the chance. Never again. "He's a very lucky man. Someday I hope you'll call me a friend."

Lean fingers closed over her slender ones. She studied his face a long time, then withdrew her hand. "How is E.D.I.T.H.?"

Brad accepted that she wasn't quite ready to overlook his poor behavior and set out to prove he could be trusted. "E.D.I.T.H. is fine."

"Are you sure there is no danger?"

He cocked his head to one side to study the frown touching the smoothness of her brows. "I'm sure, Michelle. There is no danger. Computer thieves are usually nonviolent, sneaky cowards. Besides, only three people other than you know that I'm one of the two people who have the entry code," he said with quiet emphasis.

Intense astonishment touched her face. She was shaken to the core. "But you don't even like me. Why trust me with a secret like that?"

Now it was Brad's forehead that furrowed in thought. "It's not that I don't like you, Michelle, it's that sometimes I don't understand you. As strange as it may seem, I trust your integrity to keep our discussion confidential."

"Thank you, Brad," she whispered, taking the initiative to touch him for the first time. Their eyes met and she felt a warm current rush through her. "I will never betray that trust."

"I know, Michelle," he answered, his voice deep and sensual. His intense gaze wandered over her face. How he wanted to taste her, to savor her. Without thought, he moved closer to her on the seat, his fingers following the curve of her face. Her head tilted backward against the soft white leather.

Brad Jamison was not a man who asked permission, and he did not do so now. But he was also a man who knew the value of things and took Michelle's offering with consummate skill and gentleness. With a featherlike brush of his mouth across her parted lips, he showed her tenderness, and also the pleasures he could give her.

Michelle moaned at the delicious shivers the kiss sent flowing through her, and slid her hands around his neck. She wanted more, much more. Brad's hand curved around her waist, bringing her closer, damning the fact he couldn't take into his hand the soft breast pressing against his chest. However, he could taste all the sweetness of her mouth.

Hesitant at first, Michelle soon was caught up in the kiss. Sharp teeth nipped her bottom lip, then suckled away the sweet pain. Intense passion heated her blood. She arched closer.

"Brad, it's been so long. Love me."

CHAPTER SIX

"No," he whispered raggedly, lifting his head. "We can't."

Michelle opened her eyes in the instant of his rejection, the sensuous fog lifting. Humiliation swept through her. She was lying on top of Brad, pressing him back against the seat wantonly, her fingers clutching his head.

With a muffled cry, she snatched her hands back and began to move away. Strong arms stopped her progress.

"Please," she managed, her voice shaky and foreign to her ears.

"I wish it were that easy." His arms tightened as he pressed his chin against the top of her head. His body trembled almost as much as hers did.

Michelle frowned her confusion. "I thought you didn't want . . . want . . ." Her voice trailed off.

Brad laughed, a sound like silk tearing. "I

want you. But I'll be damned if I'll give any credence to the talk about you and your clients."
Michelle stiffened, and Brad cursed under his
breath.

"Listen, Michelle. What I am trying to say,
and doing a bad job of it, is that I mean during
business hours. I want you to be able to continue
your policy of not having a personal relationship with a client while you are working. I'd be a
fool and a liar if I said I didn't want to see more
of you after hours. I think you want the same
thing," Brad finished softly, his hand gently caressing the curve of her back.

He waited for her to say she felt the same way.
One moment stretched into the next and the
next. She remained stiff in his arms, her head
bowed, her hands clasped in her lap. He took
matters into his own hands.

Sitting up with her in his lap, his hands
moved to the front of her dress. Deft, experienced fingers opened the top button on her
dress. Frantically pushing out of his arms,
Michelle scooted to the other side of the car.

"What do you think you're doing?"

He stared calmly back at her. "Would you
have stopped me five, even two minutes ago?"

Michelle opened her mouth to tell him *yes*, felt
the yearning still shimmering within her, and
couldn't utter the lie. Instead she clutched the
front of her dress.

"If I hadn't stopped when I did, neither one

of us would have cared if we were in the middle of Main Street during a parade or if only a tinted partition separated us from Jacob," Brad said.

He was right. "Thank you."

"I did it for both of us, Michelle," he said softly. "You want me as much as I want you, whether you are willing to admit it now or not. We're going to make love, but when we do, you and I will have all the time we need to enjoy and savor our passions." His hands moved hers aside and redid the button.

Her head lifted to meet black eyes filled with banked desire. A shiver ran down her spine at the possessive look he sent her. The question of their making love was no longer *if* but *when*. Tingling sensations raced over her body and she didn't know if they were caused by fear or by anticipation.

Brad leaned against the seat and folded his arms. "Why don't you tell me which property you think is best for Computron?"

Moistening her lips, she nodded. That, she could handle. Slowly at first, then more confidently as she gathered her frayed emotions together, Michelle told Brad the merits of the rapidly developing area around Las Colinas.

When Jacob pulled up in front of the Mandalay, Michelle was back in control. In a matter of minutes they were inside and settled at a secluded table in an alcove of the Enjolie. To

Michelle's questioning look at the swiftness of their being seated and the excellent table in the popular French restaurant, Brad smiled.

"I asked Dana if we had time for lunch and she said yes, so I made reservations. I hope you don't mind?" he said with boyish charm.

"I'm flattered."

"Good. Then maybe you'll accept this as my appreciation for your overlooking my bad manners in the past." Leaning over, he reached under the table, picked up a long narrow flower box, and handed it to her across the table. "I hope the occasion never arises again when I'll make you unhappy."

Her hands shook as she slid the lid off the box. A soft sigh of wonder escaped her lips. Nestled among a bed of heather and fern was a single, perfect blood-red rose. Reverently she picked up the flower and lifted it to inhale the intoxicating fragrance. Dewdrops clung to its half-open petals. No gift could have meant more.

"Thank you, Brad."

The appearance of the waiter to take their orders forestalled any further talk, and Michelle was somehow glad. She needed more time to examine her feelings. Things were changing and moving too rapidly for her. Brad ordered for both of them and then they were alone.

"What if I don't like grilled salmon?" she asked lightly.

"I checked with Dana," he answered, lifting his wineglass.

"What else did you ask Dana?"

"You'll find out . . . in time. Now why don't you try one of these puff-pastry appetizers?" he suggested, picking up one of the light pastries and popping it into his mouth.

Knowing she was not going to get any further information, Michelle picked up her glass and sipped the dry red wine. Her eyes widened. Chinon Les Varennes. Her favorite. Dana was definitely going to hear some words from her when she returned to her office.

"You're very pleased with yourself, aren't you?" she asked, setting the glass down and running a finger over the velvet smoothness of the rose.

"Why don't you ask me that question in a couple of months?" he bantered, covering her hand with his. Picking up her hand, he kissed her palm, his hot tongue stroking her skin.

Michelle jumped as if she had sustained an electrical shock. Currents of desire rushed through her body. Her heart hammered in her chest. "Brad, please. Remember what you said."

He didn't move. His gaze caressed the curve of her face, then swept to the rapid rise and fall of her breasts, then shot up to pin her with a heated look.

"My mind remembers, but my body has a

way of reacting all by itself. Do you have any idea how soft you feel? How it drives me crazy to hear that little purring sound in your throat? To know that beneath that silky dress your breasts are—"

"Brad," she said, trembling. "If you don't behave, I'll leave."

"I will for now. But one of these days you're going to admit to the same feelings," he told her, then sat back in his seat and picked up his napkin. "Here comes the waiter. I'm starved."

Once they were served Brad took pity on Michelle and settled down to become a charming luncheon companion. She was surprised to learn he had a keen sense of humor to match his sharp wit. They had just been served cheesecake for dessert when Brad's cell phone rang.

"Excuse me. I need to take this call." He stood up to leave.

"Brad?" Michelle said. He shook his head to her unspoken question about E.D.I.T.H. The hard glitter was back in his eyes. Wanting the Brad of moments ago, she said, "Hurry back or they'll think you skipped out on me."

She was rewarded with a heart-stopping smile. "That is something I'll never do."

Then he was gone, his last words bringing a secretive smile to her lips. She watched his lean, rugged body weave its way around the tables amid admiring stares from the women and envious ones from the men, and felt a perverse sense of pleasure that he was with her.

"So all of that talk about you making it on your own was nothing but lies," snarled a male voice.

Michelle glanced up, but she already knew she'd see Stan Gabriel. "Why don't you speak louder, Stan? I don't think the people in the lobby heard you."

His thin face hardened. "Still the smart—"

"Don't start throwing names. You'd lose," Michelle warned, tracing the rim of her wineglass with a steady forefinger.

Stan's thin face leaned closer. "I've got a few names the Greater Dallas Board of Realtors might like to hear."

"Anytime, Stan ol' boy," Michelle agreed, leaning back in her chair, the coldness of her gaze unsettling. "Why don't we invite your wife and father-in-law to the meeting? I'm sure after hearing what I have to say, they'd both have names of their own they'd like to call you."

His jaw slackened. He tried to smile, but the muscles in his face refused to cooperate, and instead created a cruel caricature. He gulped and straightened. "I was only kidding, Michelle. Let me buy you and Jamison a drink."

"I wasn't, and if you ever bother me again, I can assure you that your father-in-law and I will have that talk," she promised, her voice like chips of ice. Numbly he moved away. It was then she saw Brad, his body taut.

"Does that happen often?" he asked tersely as he jerked out his chair to sit. His gaze never wavered from Michelle.

Of all the people to overhear Stan, Brad was the worst. Drawing upon all her inner strength, she shrugged a slim shoulder, and answered his question. "Not very."

She reached for her water. Her hand shook so much it took a moment to control it before she could pick up the glass. Taking a sip, she looked at Brad. "Is everything all right?"

Eyes the color of midnight narrowed. He had seen her hand and wondered how long it had taken her to learn to control her emotions—and at what price. The thought made his voice rougher than intended. "Are you going to let that bastard upset you and do nothing?"

"I can't help what nasty little minds like Stan's conjure up. The main thing is to be the best I can be. Please, let's finish our meal."

He picked up his fork, only to pause with it in midair. "That fool only reminds me of how stupid I was. Doesn't it bother you, knowing what people are saying?"

Yes, but that is my own secret. Aloud she said, "I have to take the good with the bad. I could deny the accusations until hell froze over and it wouldn't make any difference. In fact, it probably would only make the rumors worse. My clients have come to expect a certain image, and if some people want to make more of it, then there is nothing I can do."

"Can't or won't?" Brad challenged.

Michelle had had enough. Her gaze met his defiantly. "All right, I won't. I didn't grow up rich like you did. I've worked hard for everything I've accomplished and I have nothing to be ashamed of. If you don't like it, that's your problem, not mine." She reached for her purse.

"If you move another inch, I'll tie you to that chair," Brad warned. "Yes, my parents were rich, and they expected only perfection from me. Whatever I was in, I had to be the leader. If I made ninety-nine, they always wondered why I couldn't have put forth the extra effort for a hundred. The only time they trotted me out or paid any attention to me was to show their friends what a good job they had done."

Michelle's heart turned over. Nothing was worth the pain she saw in his face. "Brad, I—"

As if the words had been held back too long, they spilled forth. "After I graduated from college, I walked. I got a job without my father's help and worked my tail off to make it." He looked at her with haunted memories in his eyes. "A lot of times it was rough, but I never went back. I knew I would succeed. People think I inherited my shares in Computron. I bought them." He sighed, rubbing his neck. "All that I'm trying to say is that you have what it takes to make it without the facade."

"I never had a chance to finish college." She stood, picked up her purse, and left the table.

Brad watched the erect stiffness of her back as she moved across the room, and he wanted nothing more than to ram his fist into someone, preferably Stan Gabriel. Throwing some bills on the table, he noticed the rose he had ordered when he'd made the reservations and muttered an explicit curse.

How could he keep hurting her, when all he wanted to do was take her in his arms and love her? The damn rumors were driving him crazy. Michelle wasn't like that, and having people think she was, was turning him into a self-righteous fool.

When he caught up with Michelle, she was halfway across the parking lot. The hurt look in her eyes made him feel worse. "If I make another stupid remark, you have permission to kick me where your mother taught you."

"My mother wasn't around to teach me much of anything," she said flatly. "My father died when I was nine months old. My mother when I was five. The great State of Texas raised me." Bitterness tinged her words.

Brad realized too late that nothing in his life could compare to the misery and uncertainty Michelle must have faced growing up. It was amazing that she had accomplished so much. He at least had known there was a home to return to. Striking out on his own was his rebellious way of getting back at his parents. There was no way of telling how his life might have gone if his grandfather's letter begging Brad to come home had not caught up with him in South America nine years ago.

He had come home to heal, to get the stench of death from his nostrils, to walk the cool, serene beaches of the San Francisco coastline. He grimaced, remembering the nightmares he had fought through to become whole, and what he had done to be alive to dream at all.

Out of nowhere came the frightened face of a young girl on the beach who was running from her own demons. Somehow her innocent trust of him, her shy kiss, had helped him to believe in his own worth again. Would she have come to him so freely if she had known that he had been a mercenary? No, he had no right to judge Michelle or anyone.

"I'm sorry," Brad said, attempting to draw her into his arms.

Michelle pushed him away. "If you don't mind, I have another appointment at four."

Brad saw her close herself away from him and knew he was losing. Rage consumed him. "Wait in the car. I forgot something." Turning on his heels, he reentered the hotel.

Something about his measured strides bothered her. Acting on instinct, she followed him inside. She was just in time to see him stop in front of Stan, who was dining alone. His pinched face lost all color when he looked up and saw Brad.

Planting his hands palm-down on the table, Brad leaned over and spoke. Whatever he said, Michelle could see that Stan was shaken. Beads of perspiration popped out on his forehead. Unsteady fingers tugged the knot loose in his tie. Patting him none too gently on his thin shoulder, Brad straightened to leave.

Seeing Michelle, his angry expression disappeared. "Save it," he ordered gruffly, taking her by the arm.

As soon as they were near the Rolls, Michelle jerked her arm away and swung around to face him. "How dare you do that!"

Brad was equally incensed. "No one is going to treat you that way as long as I'm around."

"You seem to forget you said the same things to me," she shot back, and saw the remorse in his eyes. But she had to make him understand.

"Besides, how long will you be around? A week? A month?" she questioned, unable to keep the longing from her eyes. "In the meantime I have to live here. Before the day is over, the news will be out that the son-in-law of the president of one of the largest banks in Dallas and one of my clients had a fight over me." Fumbling in her purse, she found her oversized sunglasses and put them on. "I can take care of myself."

"If I were around longer, would that make a difference?" Brad asked, taking a step closer.

Michelle fought the urge to say yes, and tried her original logic on him again. "They're only words, Brad."

She had called him by his name. Brad breathed easier. "That rat should be showed up."

"That rat has a very nice wife and two children. Velma Gabriel is one of the kindest persons I know. It's not her fault that she fell in love with Stan."

"She can find someone else to love," Brad said without missing a beat.

"You can't mean that."

"I can. She'll probably be thankful to get rid of him."

Michelle shook her head at the carelessness of his words. "Yes, she'll be thankful to have people laughing behind her back and her life shattered."

"Come on, Michelle. You make it sound as if it's a life-or-death situation," Brad said, obviously losing his patience with the conversation.

Michelle looked into his black eyes and wondered how to make him understand true love between a man and a woman. He was a man who obviously never had to do anything except crook his finger to gain the adoration of any woman he wanted.

"Didn't you hear me? I said she loves her husband. For some women there is only one man, one love. You'll do anything to try and keep that love alive. Tell yourself lies, make excuses, because to admit the truth would put you through hell." She remembered how stupid she'd been about Richard. "Leave Velma with her dreams."

A lean, dark finger caressed her cheek. "Who stole your dreams?"

"Leave me alone," she gritted out, then whirled and continued to the waiting car, angry with him for making her almost reveal herself; with herself for still wishing Brad could be different. But trying to reach Brad was like trying to scale Mt. Everest with your bare hands: impossible and potentially lethal.

He matched her step for step. "I told you once, leaving you alone is something I can't do. Sooner or later I'm going to figure you out."

"Why bother?" she asked, taking a seat inside the limo.

He climbed in and sat beside her. "Because it matters. *You* matter."

CHAPTER SEVEN

His answer splintered through her, making a mockery of her attempts not to care. Knowing her emotions were clearly written on her face, she turned away. "Please, can we just leave?" she murmured, gazing out the window.

Brad closed the door himself and came to a decision. "Do you mind if Jacob drops me off at the airport? My plane leaves in thirty minutes."

"Of course not."

"Thanks." Folding his arms, Brad sat back as Michelle gave Jacob their new destination.

The silence remained thick and strained during the twenty-five-minute drive to Addison Airport. As soon as the car stopped, Brad spoke. "There are some specifications I'd like you to see if I decide to go with leasing initially. If you will come with me to the plane, I'll get them for you."

Michelle looked at him suspiciously. "Can't you just tell me here?"

"If it was that simple, I wouldn't have suggested we go aboard."

"Of course." She was acting childish.

As soon as she emerged from the car, Brad lightly grasped her elbow, forcing her to admit her own needs and fears. With every step she longed to throw herself into the comfort of his arms, yet at the same time she had to beat down the impulse to run back to the safety of the car. She admitted ruefully that she was out of her depth trying to deal with Brad.

The posh interior of the Gulf Stream was elegant, but understated. Brad waved her to a navy blue lounge chair, then took a seat a few feet away, directly in front of her. Crossing one long leg over the other, he said, "Michelle, I'm usually a very direct and reasonably intelligent person. I say what I mean and I take great pride in keeping my word."

"What has—"

"Please," he interrupted, holding up his hand. "Let me finish. Twice I have told you to trust me, and twice I have abused that trust. Since I am usually not such a fool or such a self-righteous bastard, I assume it's because we haven't had time to get to know each other better. I'm asking for that time."

Michelle shifted in her seat. "I'm not sure that would be a good idea."

His hand slapped against the padded arm of

his chair. "I knew I should have ordered Mack to take off as soon as we were aboard." At her stunned look, he smiled devilishly. "Fortunately for you, I didn't think you'd like that very much."

Michelle surged to her feet, and took a step away from his compelling maleness. "You can't treat people as you please."

Brad stood. "If I treated you as I pleased, you'd be in a lot more difficulty. Now, please sit down." She took another step back, then another. He matched her steps.

"You interest me. Something a woman hasn't done in a long time. We're both adults, and I for one don't like playing games. Now, name a city you'd like to visit, or shall I escort you off the plane?"

"You don't act as if it would bother you if I chose to leave," she said, watching him closely.

In one step he closed the distance between them. Cupping her chin in his hand, he looked deeply into her eyes. "It would bother me a great deal."

Slowly his lips descended to meet hers, giving her time to move away if she wanted. But Michelle couldn't move. She wanted this. Finally his mouth, feather-light and tantalizingly persuasive, met hers. He pressed the slimness of her body against the solidness of his. With whimpering need, she sought to deepen the kiss.

She became fully aware of his thighs against hers, his hardness pressed against her, and moaned softly.

Stretched to his limits, Brad lifted his head and gently pulled away from Michelle and temptation. Yet, his hand continued a relentless sweep of her back as if he couldn't make himself let go of her completely.

The glazed look of passion in her brown eyes almost made him drag her back against his body and damn the consequences. Taking a deep breath, he said, "I'll always have that to remember you by."

Trembling and weak-kneed, Michelle swayed back into his arms. It would be so easy to accept his strength, his warmth, but for how long? Having Brad, then losing him, was something she wasn't sure she could endure. Totally shaken, she closed her eyes and let the gentleness of his embrace shield her from her doubts.

Brad held Michelle in his arms, very aware of the possessiveness of his hold. His body ached with the pain of unfilled desire, but he wanted something more. He felt protective and carnal. Michelle was a woman a man could tussle with in bed, and hold in the bright light of day. He was not going to lose her by pushing too fast.

"I have to stay in San Francisco for a couple of weeks. Will you have dinner with me when I return?" he asked, kissing the top of her head and inhaling the tantalizing fragrance of her perfume.

Michelle wanted with all her heart to say yes, and for the first time in nine years, she didn't try to figure out the consequences of her actions. "Yes."

"Thank you," he whispered, brushing his lips across hers. "Now, I better take you back while my intentions are still good."

"What did I tell you once about your good intentions?" Michelle bantered.

"As odd as it might seem, you're the only one who can make me forget them," Brad replied, then led her down the ramp and onto the pavement.

Not knowing how to answer, Michelle said nothing. Getting inside the car, she waited for Brad to close the door.

"Think of me sometimes," he said and pressed a brief, hard kiss to her lips. Then he turned and walked quickly away.

"I have no choice," she whispered, her fingers touching her lips.

For the rest of the afternoon, Michelle's busy schedule kept her traveling from one site to the other. Her last appointment was two energetic ladies who were looking for the perfect spot to open their clothing boutique.

It was after six when she finally closed her office door. Every muscle in her body ached. She wanted nothing more than to sleep for two days.

"Michelle, I want to talk with you."

Michelle stopped, tensing as she always did when she was around Alex's sister. "Good evening, Cassie," she greeted, wondering if there was a time when the other woman was not perfectly groomed and beautiful. Not a hair was out of place. Her lemon yellow knit dress clung enticingly to every shapely curve of her petite body.

"Alex just told me that you had an appointment with Brad today," Cassie said, her disapproval obvious.

"Yes."

Cassie's chin jutted forward. "We have never liked each other, so there is no sense in prolonging this conversation. Brad is mine."

"Does Brad know this?" The uncertainty in the older woman's face was Michelle's answer. "Brad impressed me as a man who can speak for himself. Now, if you'll excuse me, I was just on my way home." Stepping around the bristling woman, Michelle continued toward the front door.

Cassie was running true to form. For some odd reason, she was jealous of anything Michelle had. But Michelle was used to that. Her main concern was the rumors about her. Because no matter how much Brad tried to convince himself otherwise, they bothered him.

Unless he could come to terms with the gossip, their relationship was doomed. Sighing, she left the building to find Jacob waiting for her.

A short while later Michelle opened the front door of her house. If she didn't lie down soon she'd fall down. Jacob stood patiently by her side. "My first appointment isn't until mid-morning, so you sleep in. I'll take a cab into the office."

He shook his graying head. "No, ma'am. I'll pick you up at the usual time. Good night." He returned to the idling car and drove away.

Michelle smiled. Jacob believed in a full day's work for a full day's pay. He was a wonderful, hard-working man.

"Are you going to stand there all night?"

Michelle glanced over her shoulder and smiled at Nick. "I hadn't planned on it, but the sky does look magnificent."

"All right." He laughed. "You got me."

Leaning down, she kissed his cheek. This time she said nothing about the stubby growth. "What did Mrs. Lane leave for dinner?" she asked, laying her attaché case on the navy-and-white sofa and heading for the kitchen. Michelle wasn't hungry, but Nick probably was, and he hated eating alone.

"Stuffed pork chops, I think, and apple pie." He expertly maneuvered his wheelchair around the glass-topped dining table.

Opening the stove, Michelle peered inside,

then lifted the casserole top. "Pork chops it is. Grab the flatware and I'll get everything else." The phone rang as she set the dishes on the table. "Get that please, Nick, and tell them to hold on."

Wheeling over, he picked up the phone from the blue-tiled counter. "Hello." After a short pause he said, "Sure, no problem," and hung up the phone.

She straightened. "Who was it?"

"Some guy. Said he must have the wrong number, but he didn't ask for anyone," he explained, laying out the utensils.

What if it had been Brad? The phone rang again. She jumped to answer it first. "Hello," she said breathlessly, turning away from Nick's inquiring eyes.

Brad's voice was loud and clear. "Hello. You haven't forgotten about our date, have you?"

"No, I haven't." She smiled. "How was your trip?"

"Lonely."

"Oh," she gulped.

"I enjoyed most of today."

Her smile returned. "So did I."

"Well, good night. I'll see you in two weeks."

"Good night, Brad." Still smiling, she hung up the phone.

"Was that Jamison?" Nick asked.

"Yes," she admitted and waited for the disapproval he always showed when men displayed a personal interest in her. No matter her age, to her brother she'd always be the little sister in need of his protection.

She didn't have to wait long. "He seems to have made quite an impression on you," Nick commented, watching her closely.

"Yes, he did," she freely admitted, returning his stare. It was past time for him to see her as an adult and realize she made her own decisions.

"Let's have dinner and you can tell me about him."

"All right," she said, knowing she was going to leave out a great many details about Brad. Her life was her own.

The next several days were hectic for Michelle. Her clients and Winslow Rehabilitation Center took up most of her time. If she wasn't rushing to see a client, she was off to a meeting about the final plans for the center. Nick and Jodie's dream was about to become a reality.

Paraplegics would have a place where they could come and learn that their disability didn't diminish their worth. Living with Nick, she knew how powerless and angry they often felt.

These days she was feeling a little angry herself because almost a week had passed since she had heard from Brad. She rushed home every evening, and refused any business engagements that might keep her out past ten at night. Once, in the shower, she thought she heard the phone, but when she picked it up there was only the mocking dial tone. Deciding she was acting like an adolescent, Michelle sought to put Brad out of her mind. Sometimes she was successful; most of the time she was not.

On one of her most successful days, it took the fourth buzz of the intercom to catch her attention. "Ms. Grant speaking," she said into the phone, her attention still on the papers before her.

Silence greeted her. A frown darted across her face. "May I help you?" There must have been someone there, or Dana would not have put the call through. "Hello?"

"Michelle, it's Clint."

"Clint, how are you doing? I was—"

"I've changed my mind," came the soft interruption.

The smile curving the corners of her mouth froze. "Changed your mind about what, Clint?"

"I can't sell the ranch to the rehab center."

She went cold all over. "What? You can't! You promised," she said. Her voice rose in anxiety, her body tensed. "You can't back out now."

"I know I did, but things have changed," Clint said, regret mingled with determination in his gravelly voice.

A sense of doom swept through her. Her stomach knotted. When she spoke, she tried to keep the panic and accusation from her voice.

"On the strength of your word, I assured Winslow Foundation that everything was going as planned. The workers are scheduled to begin renovation in less than three months. Every decision from employees to delivery contracts was made with your ranch in mind."

"I know you're in a tight spot because of me, and don't think it doesn't eat at my gut, but I've got no choice. If the Foundation can come up with two hundred and fifty thousand dollars more in three weeks, the land is theirs."

Shutting her eyes tightly, Michelle fought the need to scream out loud that it had been his idea to use his ranch. But as a Realtor, she should have waited until the final papers were signed before any plans were made. The Foundation was depending on her to make sure things went smoothly, both as a Realtor and as the financial chairperson of the project. Now, she would be unable to do either.

"Clint, I gave my word. I promised."

"Well, we all know that everything we promise doesn't always work out the way we plan," he said harshly.

The anger drained from her. How many times had she heard Clint promise Jodie that she would walk again, that everything would be all right? Jodie had been a wild free spirit at nineteen. It was hard to believe that she was gone. "Are you changing your mind because of Jodie?

If that's the reason and you need more time, I'll put everything on hold until you give the word."

"Not directly," he hedged.

"Then what is it? Think of all the young people like Jodie who'll be helped," she reasoned, shamelessly hoping to sway him.

"Dammit, Michelle! It's not like you to hit below the belt. Do you honestly think I could forget them for an instant? But for once I've got to think about me and what *I* want and need. You, of all people, know what it takes to care for a handicapped person. This is one time I can't let sentiment stand in the way of good business sense," he argued.

"Clint, I—"

"No, you listen," he interrupted harshly. "You still have Nick, but all I have is a memory of what was and the torment of what might have been. Everyone else might think I sold out, but I expected better from you." The phone crashed in her ear.

Hanging up the phone, Michelle rubbed the pads of her fingertips against her throbbing temples. She didn't need this. There was no way she could raise that amount of money in three weeks.

Sitting up, she flipped open her appointment book. Her last appointment was at three. She wasn't going to give up without a fight. She was going to see Clint and find out why he'd raised the price. Without the center, Nick would stop trying and withdraw into the bitter and angry man he was a year ago. If humanly possible, she wasn't going to let that happen. Nick *needed* this center. So did many other paraplegics.

Later that day, Michelle drove her candy apple–red BMW across the cattle guard of the Lazy R, Clint's ranch. Gravel crunched beneath her tires as she braked in front of a rambling brick house. Getting out, she started up the walkway.

Halfway there, she paused to look out across the meadow and saw the Dallas skyline, rising imposingly under a cloudless blue sky. Off to the left was a man-made pond. In its placid water, Michelle knew from personal experience, trout swam in the coolness beneath the swaying branches of a huge weeping willow. Jodie's rowboat, *The Valiant*, was nowhere in sight.

Biting her lower lip, Michelle turned and started toward the house. The neighing of a horse caught her attention. She glanced around to see Clint, his once straight shoulders slumped, leading Jodie's favorite horse, Excalibur, from the stables.

Clint glanced up, his brown eyes haunted, looking ten years older than the fifty she knew him to be. Not by a word or a sign did he acknowledge her, but merely continued to the house, where he looped the Thoroughbred's reins through an iron hitching post. The sound of his boots was loud on the stone steps, then across the white wooden porch that curved around the front and the left side of the huge old house.

He disappeared inside only to return moments later with a large brown grocery bag clutched in one hand. A foot from her, he reached his other hand inside the sack and drew out a fistful of letters.

"Bills! Bills I can't pay." His voice and his body trembled. "But I'm going to pay every last one of them because they helped Jodie." He rammed them back in the sack. "Think what you like."

Michelle touched his arm, felt the rigid stiffness of his body, and realized the tight control he was holding on his emotions. "Why didn't you say something earlier?"

"I thought I could pay them." Blinking, he looked out toward the pond. "I had it all figured out. How once I sold the ranch to the rehab center, Jodie and I would travel around the country to horse shows, rodeos, or anyplace else she wanted in the camper I had customized for her." He glanced down at Michelle, sadness in his eyes. "Even thought of finally asking Molly to marry me after keeping her waiting for five years. But . . . but I lost heavily in the stock market." He raked his hand across his weary face. "I'm almost flat broke and Jodie's gone."

"I had no idea, Clint." Michelle's hand moved to close over his. "You always spent money so freely on Jodie. Anything she wanted, from another Thoroughbred to a trip to Canada for a horse show."

"And I don't regret one penny I spent." He looked down at Michelle, his large frame towering over her. "Would you have done any less for Nick?"

She drew her hand back. "No." She'd do almost anything to try to make up for his loss. Nick had his first specially equipped Porsche back when she was still driving a ten-year-old Chevrolet. "I'm sorry, Clint. It's just that I want—need—this property so much." Nick had to have his chance and so did other paraplegics.

He nodded. "And you think since Jodie is gone, I don't care? Goodness, Michelle, that's all Jodie talked about was a place for other paralytics to come and shed their fears. But I just can't let it go at the price we discussed. Looking at the bills last night, I remembered an offer I was made a few years back. I contacted the man's lawyer and he said his client is still interested, but the longest I could put him off was three weeks before closing the deal." He stepped back, his jaw clenched. "If I don't sell in three weeks, I may not be able to salvage anything. You'll explain things to Nick, won't you? I don't want him thinking badly of me."

"Yes, I'll tell him," Michelle said, forcing a

smile to her tense features. Yet, how was she going to tell Nick what a mess she had made of things? Or how could she make Clint see that setting a time limit was an old ploy to push a sale through? If the buyer had waited years, he'd certainly wait longer than three weeks to close the deal.

"I'm going away for a few days," Clint said. "Do you still have the key to the gate?"

"Yes." The heavily scrolled, elongated key was in her office. "Are you going to see Molly?"

"No. I have nothing to offer her."

"She won't care that your finances have changed," Michelle reasoned, thinking of the wealthy East Texas woman who drank out of a paper cup or Waterford crystal with equal ease.

"I do," Clint said, his voice flat and final.

Michelle sighed in resignation. "I'll be in touch. Somehow things will work out, Clint," she said, hoping and praying she was right as she started down the walkway to her car.

First Michelle had to get in touch with Mr. Nash, chairman of the board of the Winston Foundation, and tell him that someone had topped their bid for the Lazy R Ranch. She talked; Nash yelled about the terrible position she had placed them in. Since she knew she deserved to be chastised, she took it stoically.

Nick didn't yell or talk when she told him. She

had never felt more helpless, as his face grew taut and somber, as the light went out of his eyes. The only sound after she finished was the wheelchair motor as he left her sitting in the den.

Getting up, she went into her room. One shoulder resting against the sliding glass door, she watched the water spill over the waterfall. She hadn't felt so alone since . . . since nine years ago when an angel had come out of the night to help her believe in herself again. Since then, she had learned to rely on herself. She solved her own problems. She didn't need a fallen angel to rescue her.

Pushing away from the glass, she picked up the mystery book she had been trying to finish for the past two months. She read one sentence, then tossed the hardback onto the chaise longue.

Restless, she prowled the room that had once been her haven, refusing to give in to the overwhelming need to talk with Brad. No matter how much she tried to convince herself how illogical it was for her to remember and need a man from an encounter when she was seventeen, she did. Seeing him again, feeling the warmth of his touch, savoring the taste of him, only made the want more intense. Long ago she had learned that wanting wasn't enough, but tonight, just for tonight, she needed to believe that it was.

Before her courage failed, she dialed Computron, thankful that she memorized numbers easily. It was five-thirty there but perhaps Brad hadn't left his office.

Less than two minutes later Michelle hung up the phone. Brad hadn't left his office, but he was in a conference and the switchboard was holding all his calls. Talking to two other people after telling the operator that it was important did little good. Feeling foolish by that time, she did something she never did: she hung up without leaving her name.

It was going to be a long evening. Getting fresh lingerie from her dresser, she walked into her bathroom and turned on the water in the tub. The phone rang just as she stepped out of her bath ten minutes later. Her heart thumped in her chest, then she remembered that she had not left a message. Chastising herself for the umpteenth time that day—this time for not leaving her name—she hurriedly dried and slipped on her robe.

Her voice was breathless as she rushed to answer the phone. "Hello."

"Michelle, if that wasn't you who called, please lie and say it was," came the deep, masculine voice of her fallen angel.

CHAPTER EIGHT

"Brad." Stunned, she plopped down on the lacy white comforter.

"Was that you who called?"

Michelle twisted the cord around her finger. Was he pleased or displeased about the call? "Yes."

"Then why didn't you leave your name? For the last five days it seemed as though every time I got a moment to call, something came up. Then you call and don't leave your name. It's a good thing Patterson knows accents."

Still unsure of his mood, she asked, "Who's Patterson?"

"Chief of Security," came the succinct reply.

"Oh."

"Is that all you can say?"

Something in his tone struck a raw nerve. "No, that's not all I can say. I called because I had a lousy day and I wanted to talk with someone who I thought would have a little understanding. Apparently, I chose the wrong person. I don't have to call long-distance to find someone to chew on me," Michelle said, her voice rising.

Brad sighed into the phone. "When you tear a strip off a person you do a thorough job."

"You had it coming."

"You're right. I did. I've got a lot on my mind, but I shouldn't have taken it out on you. Care to start over and tell me what happened?" he said softly.

"Everything."

"Is that rat bothering you again?" Brad asked tightly.

"No. It's something else."

"Care to give me a hint?"

"If I told you, you wouldn't think very much of my skills as a Realtor," she said with a weary sigh.

"Don't bet on it. Everyone makes mistakes at one time or another. No matter how much you plan or hope, things don't always work out the way you want them to."

"You'd think I would have learned that lesson nine years ago." Michelle wanted to call the words back, but it was too late. Half of her wanted him to remember, the other half wasn't so sure.

"What happened nine years ago?" Brad asked, a strange note in his voice.

"I grew up," she said trying to keep her voice light and failing miserably.

"Sounds like you didn't have an easy time of it."

She shrugged slim shoulders. "It could have been worse. Now tell me about the board meeting."

"I better not, if you don't want me to lose my temper again."

"Sounds like you didn't have an easy time of it."

He laughed. "Since we both have had a lousy day, let's plan for a great night when we see each other."

"I'd like that."

"Michelle?"

"Yes."

"Whatever it is, I know you'll work things through. You've come too far to quit. You'll accomplish whatever task set before you."

Pleasure filled her. "Thanks, Brad. Bye."

"Bye, honey."

Michelle felt a warm glow at the endearment. But this time her angel might be wrong. She was fighting dollars and cents.

Early the next morning she went straight to Alex's office. Standing in front of his desk, telling him about her blunder was harder than telling Mr. Nash at the Foundation. Alex had always been so proud of her. "So you see, I really did it this time."

"Sit down, Michelle," Alex said, thumping his pen on his cluttered desk. "You're not the first Realtor to make that mistake."

"No, but it . . ." Her voice trailed off.

"It's the combination of Clint shifting the responsibility to you, Nick and the Foundation putting more pressure on you, and all of them looking for you to come through for them. Unfortunately there has to be a winner and a loser."

"I'm in an impossible situation," Michelle replied, then remembered what Brad had said. *You've come too far to quit.* He was right. Now was not the time to give up. Grim determination swept across her face. "I'm going to make some calls. The center is going to open as scheduled."

By the middle of the day, Michelle was no longer so sure of herself. Some people were not willing to donate any more funds. They couldn't understand why more money was needed for a project that was reported to start ground breaking in less than three months. Her answer of "unexpected expenditures" did nothing to change their minds. Donations were the only way to salvage the center and three weeks wasn't enough time to organize a fund-raising drive or a dinner.

Refusing to give in to the doubts nagging her, she placed her address book aside and stood. She was booked solid with appointments until five. Sighing, she picked up her briefcase. It was going to be another long day.

Arriving back at her office after her last appointment, Michelle stopped to pick up her messages. Puzzled by the wide grin on Dana's face, she continued to her office.

Sifting through the slips of paper in her hands, she was three feet on the other side of the door before the sweet smell of flowers lifted her head. Her mouth formed a silent O.

Completely overshadowing her desk was an immense white wicker basket of pink roses and baby's breath. A tingling sensation raced up her spine when she saw the small white box tied with a pink ribbon next to it. Jerky steps carried her forward. A fragile-looking orchid with the faintest tinge of pink lay inside the box. Her hands shaking, she opened the attached envelope and read the card:

To better days and shorter nights. B.

"Beautiful, aren't they?"

Michelle whirled, clutching the card to her breast, and saw Dana standing in the door grinning like a Cheshire cat. "Brad sent them."

"I knew that man had style the first moment I saw him." Dana pointed toward the pink roses. "There are twenty-six in them, one for each year of your life." She sighed dramatically. "If only I could meet such a man. Oops. There's the phone."

The scent of the flowers wafted up and Michelle cupped one perfect bloom, wondering how Brad had found out how old she was.

However, at the moment, it didn't matter. Unable to resist the urge, she pinned the corsage to her jacket, a silly grin on her face.

The smile froze as she looked at the pad on her desk with names for possible donations crossed off. Somehow, it didn't seem right for her to be happy with the opening of the rehab center in jeopardy. Innate honesty made her admit that the opening could be rescheduled if another site could be located. Fortunately contracts were still unsigned and could be renegotiated. Her reputation might suffer, but not irreparably so. The real loser was Nick.

Their only real disagreement had been over Richard. Richard had proven as big a user as Nick had said. Yet, not once since that night had he mentioned her mistake. She could not fail to give him another chance the same way he had given her one. Flicking out the desk light, she picked up her purse to go home.

Nick was waiting for her when she walked through the front door. Seeing the defeated look on her face, he turned away. She reached out to him, then let her hand fall.

"We still have time, Nick."

"Yeah," he said before disappearing into the kitchen.

Silently berating her inability to help, Michelle followed. The plates were already on the table and he was filling the water glasses. "Not talking about it won't make it go away."

His right hand opened and closed, crushing the yellow dinner napkin. He laughed, a brittle, hollow sound. "I've been told that before. Always by people who had no idea what the hell they were talking about. How could they? Their feet were planted firmly on the floor, not on a five-by-seven piece of metal. I know it's not the end of the world. It's just that I was beginning to think I could be useful, could help someone."

"That hasn't changed," Michelle reminded him, gently touching his shoulder. "It may take a little longer, that's all."

He smiled sadly. "Yes, Jodie told me it took eight months to make her first painful step."

"She was quite a fighter."

"That she was," he agreed softly, turning away. Michelle sat down knowing neither of them would eat very much. Tomorrow would be different. It had to be.

The next day proved harder than the one before. Contributors were now afraid that the center was in jeopardy of not opening at all. They were taking a wait-and-see attitude. If the center opened, they'd help, but not until then.

When Brad called that night, she wanted nothing more than to make the distance disappear, crawl into his lap, and tell the world to go away. Somehow the velvet softness of his voice gave her strength to face another day. She was determined to solve the problem she had created by herself. This time her angel couldn't help her.

Brad called the next night, and the next, until the two weeks had passed and he was returning. That morning she couldn't decide what to wear. She had strictly forbidden herself to buy a new dress. But she definitely wasn't going to wear a suit. Her indecision made her keep Jacob waiting for the first time. Mumbling her apology, she stepped into the Rolls.

Michelle strode into the monthly staff meeting and all heads turned. The clinging material of her white jersey dress showed off her figure to perfection. Nodding, she advanced to her seat next to Alex.

"Good morning, Michelle. You look stunning."

Michelle smiled, her large gold earrings brushing against her brown cheeks. "Good morning, Alex, and thanks for the compliment."

His gaze raked the unbound black hair curling around her face. "Is this part of your strategy?" he whispered.

"I don't know what you're talking about."

"Yes, you do. Cassie told me this morning that Brad is coming in from California today."

"I had planned on seeing him," she admitted,

fingering the chunky gold necklace circling her throat.

"Dressed like that, I'd say you're going to knock his socks off." Smiling at her abashed look, he called the meeting to order.

However, Michelle wasn't able to concentrate on anything past Alex's reminder of the yearly retreat at his ranch in less than two weeks. All she could think about were the possible reasons why Brad and Cassie had talked on the phone. Cassie had made it no secret that she wanted Brad. Michelle admitted ruefully that she wasn't in the other woman's league when it came to enticing a man. Instead of listening to Alex, Michelle dwelled on Cassie and her ability to manipulate people and always get what she wanted. Brad was probably at the top of her list.

Two hours later when Alex finally adjourned the meeting, Michelle was tense and irritable. The only thing she was sure of was that she was not going to jump to conclusions. People had done enough of that with her.

"Ms. Grant," Dana called as she passed her desk.

"Yes," Michelle answered, stopping in front of the receptionist.

"Mr. Jamison called to say that he would pick you up for dinner after your last appointment."

Her heart thumped. "When did he call?"

"While you were in the meeting. I told him

your last appointment should be over by seven. By the way, you look fantastic."

"Thank you, Dana," Michelle said and continued to her office, a smile on her face. Everything was going to be all right.

Throughout the day Michelle kept busy, but as the clock clicked closer to seven, she became more and more nervous. Looking at the roses in their graceful decline on her desk, she bit her lip. Nick had been right about her experience with men being limited. What if she was wrong about trusting Brad?

Although belief in Brad had gotten her through some rough times, he was a different man, harsher, less patient, than he'd been nine years ago. Taking a deep breath, she stood and tapped her fingers on the spreadsheet she had been unsuccessfully trying to go over for the past ten minutes. Maybe a talk with Alex would calm her.

She was about to turn the corner to Alex's office when the bubbling laughter of another woman caught her attention. Recognizing Cassie's voice, Michelle glanced around.

Shock lanced through her. Coming through the door, their arms around each other's waists, were Brad and Cassie.

CHAPTER NINE

Intent on each other, the two were oblivious to everything else. Brad gazed down into Cassie's adoring face, and she up into his. Belief in Brad was one thing; being a fool was quite another. Self-preservation came to Michelle's rescue. Her back straightened.

She'd be damned if she'd give either of them the satisfaction of knowing they had hurt her. They were welcome to each other. A man who looked as good as Brad did, whether in a charcoal gray suit as he wore now or in jeans as he had when they first met, would probably keep any woman in tears. She had cried enough.

Michelle strolled to Dana's desk, well aware that she was in their direct path. "If there is nothing else, Dana, I think I'll leave."

"Have fun."

Michelle's smile only slipped for a heartbeat. "I intend to."

"Michelle, how nice to see you. Look who's with me," Cassie said in a cooing voice.

Slowly turning, her face aching with the effort to keep her smile in place, Michelle saw that Cassie was snuggled up against Brad like a well-fed cat. "Hello, Cassie, Brad."

"Good evening, Michelle," Brad said, then casually untangled himself from Cassie's clinging arm and stepped closer to Michelle. "Are you ready to go?"

Her eyes lifted to his, and he wanted to kick himself for the wounded look he saw in her eyes. It wasn't often he offered an explanation, but he did so now. "Cassie and I met outside."

Perhaps it was better if she bailed out while it was still possible to protect her heart. "If you have another engagement, I understand," Michelle said.

"You're more forgiving than I would be if our positions were reversed." He turned to Cassie. "If you have any more problems with investments call me again at the office." Taking Michelle by the arm, Brad led her back to her office.

Once there, she suddenly felt nervous and stepped around her desk. "Thank you for the flowers. They're beautiful."

"So are you. Ready to go?"

"I really would understand if you and Cassie have other plans." Perhaps she had been too hasty in accepting Brad's dinner invitation. She didn't like being this vulnerable.

"The only reason I'm in Dallas is to see you. Not to see Cassie or any other woman. I told you I don't like playing games. It's nice to know that you're jealous, but not if it's going to come between us."

Brad didn't mince words. Neither would she. "That's just it, Brad. I'm not sure this should go any further."

"Then I guess I'll have to convince you." He came around the desk in two seconds and took her in his arms.

Protest stumbled as his lips met hers, parting them deftly, allowing his tongue to probe deeply into her mouth. His hungry tongue glided over hers, rimming the sweetness of her mouth, demanding she respond. She was powerless to resist.

A spark ignited, flickered into a flame, and swept through her. The kiss gentled, no longer demanding, but giving. Her body softened against his. Her arms circled his neck, drawing him closer.

Michelle realized Brad wanted her to feel as much as he did. She had never known a man who gave without thought of taking in return. Pressing her slimness against him, she tilted her head to allow him full access to her mouth, and kissed him with all the passion and need she had held within her for so long. He sensed her change, and settled her between the hollow of his thighs, pressing his hand over the soft curves of her hips, fitting her closer.

Her knees buckled. Trembling fingers clung to his coat lapel for support. She didn't realize the whimpering sounds she heard were coming from her. All she knew was that she was being consumed and she never wanted it to end.

They were both shaking when Brad finally ended the kiss. He held her away from him and waited for her eyes to open before he spoke. "I don't want you to think about anything except that I'm a man and you're a woman."

"Brad—"

"No, don't think," he said, watching the uncertainty return to her eyes. "I've tried to cram a month of work into a week to be here tonight. I haven't eaten all day, I didn't go to bed last night, and *I'm* in no mood for one of *your* moods."

Her brown eyes flashed. Arrogance with a capital A. "You can't tell me what to do. If you—" His lips, gentle and coaxing, fastened on hers, and the fight went out of her.

He raised his head, grazing his lips across her trembling mouth, then settled against her forehead. Defeated, she leaned against his chest.

"It isn't fair," she moaned. "I knew better than to let you come near me."

"Give me your hand, Michelle," he said

huskily. She did and he placed it over his heart.
The erratic pounding pulsed through her fingertips. He watched her eyes widen. "I fight dirty,
but I pay for it."

Seeing the confusion in her face, Brad took the
decision out of her hands. Pressing a quick kiss
to her trembling lips, he said, "We're going to
dinner." His hand riding the small of her back,
he gently prodded her from her office, her purse
in his hand.

Night had just settled over the city as they
stepped outside. Brad gave Michelle her purse,
then opened the door to a Mercedes. Sitting
down, Michelle leaned her head back against
the cool leather.

Brad's long, muscular legs preceded him into
the sports car. Immediately, he turned to
Michelle, framing her face between his unsteady
hands. "It will be all right." Leaning forward, his
lips brushed against her parted ones.

Her lips softened beneath his. The tremor o₁
her body radiated through her hands, which
were clamped tightly around his wrists. Her
nerve endings clamoring, she slumped back into
her seat and tried to stop shaking.

"Tonight you're going to learn to trust me if I
don't explode first."

Placing her palm on his thigh, he switched on
the ignition. The engine roared to life instantly,

taking away the need for Michelle to comment. His right foot lifted, then pushed in on the accelerator, tautening his thigh muscles beneath her fingers. Michelle experienced a responsive tightening deep inside her. Embarrassed, she jerked her hand away and placed it in her lap.

"Either you put your hand back or I'll be forced to put mine on your leg," Brad said, flicking on the turn signal and merging with the traffic on LBJ Freeway.

"Brad!" she yelped when his hand slid from her knee to mid-thigh. The reprimand was unnecessary because his hand was already clamped back around the balled gearshift. The lingering sensation of his hand gliding over her skin, however, refused to go away.

"Sorry, but I can't take my eyes off the road in this crazy traffic. It's almost as bad as San Francisco's. I might upset you more if I placed my hand where I think your leg is," he tossed at her. "Up or down five inches won't bother me, but on the other hand it might bother you."

Since five inches up was precisely where she didn't want his hand, she twisted uncomfortably in her seat. Brad did not make idle threats. Slowly her left hand drifted down to settle on his thigh. "Don't you ever lose an argument?"

Immediately his hand covered hers. "Not when it matters."

Afraid of reading too much into his words, she asked, "Where are we going for dinner?"

He flashed her a quick smile. "Someplace quiet." His hand left hers to shift gears, and Michelle realized he drove like he did everything else, with skill and confidence.

Men and their cars. Nick often told her the only time he felt whole was when he was driving. Then to everyone else he looked like any other man.

"Michelle?" She jumped, and turned to see Brad frowning under the freeway lights.

"I'm sorry. Did you say something?"

"We're almost there."

Michelle discovered the "someplace quiet" was The Warrington Condominium on Turtle Creek Boulevard, very exclusive and very private. After Brad drove into the underground garage and parked, he got out and opened her door.

"I hope you like the menu I selected," he said, leading her to the elevator. "This time I didn't ask Dana."

"I'm sure everything will be fine," she said, her voice stilted. Neither spoke during the elevator ride or the short walk down the hallway.

Unlocking the door, Brad stepped aside and let Michelle enter. Immediately she was immersed in luxury. The huge living room was decorated in white with dramatic splashes of accent pieces in black and a black marble fireplace. Crystal abounded. Her heels sank into the deep white carpeting.

Going down the two steps leading away from the entryway, Michelle tried to think of all the reasons they should be eating here instead of a restaurant. Seduction, albeit an elegant and expensive one, kept repeating itself over and over in her head.

But she had misjudged him once. She wasn't going to do so again. She, of all people, knew how appearances could be misleading.

"I hope you're hungry because I ordered enough to feed four," he said.

She tried to smile and failed. "I'm starved."

Brad watched her closely. "You're also scared I'm going to try and seduce you."

Unable to deny his words, she glanced away.

His thumb and forefinger lifted her chin. Their eyes met. "Thinking that, you'd still stay?"

"I want to believe in you."

"Oh, honey." He pulled her tightly to him. "You don't know how much it means to me to hear you say that. But you have to know that I've wanted you in my bed and under me since the first moment I saw you."

Her mouth went dry. Fighting the images forming in her mind was futile. "Brad, I don't—"

"I said in *my* bed, where even after you're gone I can relive the moment again and again. The scent of your perfume, the feel of your body against me, your hair brushing over my body. I'm a greedy man, Michelle. I want it all. Tonight I only wanted us to get to know each other without all the bother of hovering waiters." He stepped away. "I want you to stay because you want to, not because you think you have to."

Michelle lifted her gaze from his gold tie tack and studied his face. Desire was there; yet there was also tenderness. He didn't have to do this to seduce her or any other woman. His frankness still made her blush, but at least it was there for her to examine. Suddenly she felt very bold.

"I want to stay."

"Let's go eat before the food gets cold." Sliding his arm around her waist, he led her to the terrace. Nestled in a corner near the shrubbery was a candlelit table for two. Twin flames danced in the evening breeze, casting golden reflections on the plates on the snowy white tablecloth. Flanking the serving carts laden with silver-domed trays were two waiters. One quickly lifted a bottle of wine to fill the fluted glasses, then stepped back.

Michelle counted three domes and laughed. "You weren't kidding about the food, were you?"

"When you know me better, you'll find out that I never joke about food. We have lobster, steak, and pheasant," he said, holding out her chair.

"I take it you appreciate good food," she said, looking up at him as she sat.

"It's not hard to appreciate a well-prepared meal after working sixteen hours a day, eating on the run, not eating at all, or eating your own cooking. I can't scramble an egg," he confessed. Taking his seat, he failed to see her bite her lower lip.

Turning to the waiter, he signed the check, then shoved some bills into the man's hand. "We'll serve ourselves. Thank you." Lifting his glass, he proposed a toast. "To a new beginning."

"A new beginning," she repeated, and touched his flute with hers. Brad drank, but his gaze stayed on Michelle.

"Do you know you're staring?"

"It would be difficult for a man not to. You should always have moonlight streaming over your hair, and the flicker of candlelight on your beautiful skin. You're exquisite."

Uncomfortable with his compliment, Michelle blurted out, "You should see me in the morning."

His eyes darkened. "I intend to."

Michelle choked on her wine. When she finally stopped coughing, she gulped down the remaining half and cleared her throat. Through watery eyes she stared across the small table at Brad.

"More wine?" he offered, calmly refilling her glass. "Here, let me serve you a sliver of pheasant breast. There's nothing better than the taste of a plump, tender breast."

Heat rose up from her neck and spread over her face. Her body went hot, then cold. This seductive Brad was something she wasn't sure of any longer.

Brad eyed her untouched plate. "Eat up, Michelle. I have your favorite dessert."

"How can I when you keep talking like that?"

"Like what?"

"Oh, never mind. One day I'm going to come out on top."

"I'm counting on it," Brad said lazily.

Michelle became busy with her silverware. "How was your flight?"

He smiled at her attempt to change the subject. "Bumpy. I hope your day went well."

"It did," she said, then proceeded to tell him about it, pleased by the way he listened and asked her questions.

All through the meal, Brad was the perfect dinner companion and she began to relax. "I always thought you were a man who didn't play fair. After a meal like that and strawberry cheesecake on top of it, how can I be upset with you?"

"That's what I was counting on." Standing, he pulled her to her feet, then led her back inside. Leaving her for a moment, he flipped on the stereo. The haunting voice of Natalie Cole filled the air.

Their gazes touched. Michelle's heart lurched wildly in her chest. Desire curled around her, seeping into her like silent shadows, stealing her will to fight the emotions overwhelming her.

His hand lifted and after the briefest hesitation, Michelle placed hers in his. Gently he brought her to the solid hardness of his body until they formed one continuous line. Caressing fingers moved tantalizingly down the length of her back, creating sensations her dreams had no way of envisioning.

She arched her back, her breasts thrusting forward as a ragged moan tore past her throat. The sound of her need brought reality crashing back. She tucked her head in the hollow of his shoulder.

"There is no shame in being responsive, Michelle. A man wants to know that the woman he's attracted to feels the same way. I can't hide mine any more than you can hide yours," Brad admitted frankly, the proof of his words pressing against her.

Michelle went rigid and tried to move away. A strong arm held her in place. "Relax, Michelle. I'll try to remember to wait until you're ready for the words. For now we'll play by your rules, but know this . . ." A blunt finger lifted her chin and their eyes met.

"Before long the touch of my hand on your body will be as natural and as desired as the warmth of sunshine. The words will come and you won't hide from them." Pulling her back into his arms, he tucked her soft curves into the hard contour of his.

"Brad, I don't know if I can be the way you want. Or if I even want to try," she whispered.

"Just relax and stop thinking." He rubbed the

ball of his thumb over the rapidly beating pulse on her wrist. "Haven't you ever done something because it felt right?"

The memory of kissing B.J. good-bye and the tenderness of his mouth against hers crept into her mind. The memory merged with more recent ones of her body and her mind yearning only for the man in her arms. In a flash of crystal clarity she knew she loved Brad, had loved him since the night they met, would always love him.

Her head tipped back, her lips parted, hunger evident in their trembling softness. She wanted to feel his mouth against hers. She needed it.

On tiptoe, she traced the sensuous curve of his lower lip with her tongue. Shivers of desire raced through her. She felt his arms slide around her back.

His mouth on hers was gentle and demanding, passionate and restrained, and Michelle welcomed each sensation rippling through her. So this was passion. Nagging doubts slipped into oblivion as the intensity of his kiss burned everything else from her mind. The velvet caress of his tongue searched out the dark hollow of her mouth with greedy thoroughness.

His need echoed her own, and she delved her tongue into his mouth. The action only heightened her growing hunger. A moan of frustration erupted from deep within her throat. Pressing closer to Brad, she sought the fulfillment her body craved.

Brad cupped the rounded curve of her hips, fitting her against his arousal. What little breath Michelle had left hissed from her lungs. Her knees shaky, her arms clung around his neck for support.

Swinging her up into his arms, he carried her to the sofa. She never realized when her dress glided off her shoulders because his kisses on her heated flesh replaced it and filled her senses.

Slipping the strap of her lacy bra lower, his hands caressed and his lips nuzzled the satiny skin above her taut breast. He released the rounded globes and took one dark tip into his mouth. Her entire body bucked. His darting tongue paid homage to her, laving and caressing.

Every nerve screaming, she dragged his head up, and their lips fused, hot and urgent. Her fingers trembling, she pushed him away to slip off his coat and shirt. She wanted to touch his skin. Reverently, she ran her hands over his muscled flesh, enjoying the unexpected satiny texture of his chest hair against her palm.

Unable to stop herself, she flicked her tongue over his hard, brown nipple. Brad half-groaned, half-moaned.

Pulling her back into his arms, his mouth fastened greedily on hers, kissing her with a relentless passion, staking his claim. Michelle gloried in the heady embrace.

His hand glided over her bent knee, past her thigh to the top of her panties and paused.

"I want you," he growled.

CHAPTER TEN

I want you, not *I love you.*

Reality came crashing back. Grabbing his seeking hand, she tried to twist from beneath him. "Brad. No."

"Let me love you, Michelle," Brad pleaded, his voice deep, his lips still traveling over her face, his hand unmoved.

"We can't. I didn't mean . . ."

"Michelle—"

"No. Please."

"Damn!"

She flinched. But she knew she deserved worse. Not knowing how to extract herself gracefully from beneath Brad's rigid body, a body she had lovingly undressed only minutes ago, she remained still. No words would make him hate her less. Perhaps it was punishment enough that her nipples ached for his mouth, her body for his.

If there was a chance, even a slim one, that he wanted more than a brief affair, she might take it. She wanted, craved Brad's loving, but she needed a commitment from him. She couldn't give herself to him, then watch him walk away. That was one rejection that might destroy her.

Brad rolled to his feet with the swiftness and the agility of a cat. He raked an unsteady hand over his head. His back to her, he headed for the bar on the other side of the room. "The bathroom is through there." He hooked a thumb toward a hallway.

Pulling her dress together with trembling fingers, she crossed the room on weak legs. Inside the bathroom, she closed the door, but not before she heard a heated expletive. Clamping her eyes shut, she sagged against a mirrored wall. How could she face him again? She had started the whole thing, acted as if she knew what she wanted. She did, but it was for a lifetime, not a night.

Brad's fingers tightened around the whiskey glass in his hand, anger and need shimmering in every part of his body. *Damn! Damn! Damn!* Michelle Grant was driving him crazy. One minute she was climbing all over him as if she wanted him, the next she was grabbing his hand like a virgin. What the hell had she expected him to do? Pat her on the head? She shouldn't have started something that she didn't intend to finish.

Tonight I only wanted us to get to know each other without all the bother of hovering waiters. His words of reassurance to Michelle came rushing back.

Forgetting the drink, he shoved his fingers over his head again. Michelle had a right to say no and expect him to stop. The idea of any man forcing himself on her caused a wave of fury within him. He really had planned a quiet evening until she had set his blood on fire and he had lost control. A first. In the past he'd always been in command of the situation with a woman. The knowledge that he wasn't with Michelle scared him.

He didn't, couldn't need anyone that much. He wouldn't let himself. His grandparents were the only ones who'd ever loved him without conditions and they were both gone. To need no one was the only way not to be hurt. He must not forget the painful lesson his mother taught him.

Looking up, he saw Michelle. Her hair was a tangled mess, her lipstick gone, her mouth swollen from his kisses, her eyes wide and uncertain.

His eyes narrowed. She took a step backward.

His hand fisted; only then did he realize that he had picked up the squat glass again. Banging it on the bar, he started for Michelle. She tensed, but this time stood her ground. The closer he came, the more his anger drained away.

She looked small, fragile, and more beautiful than any woman he had ever seen. The veneer of sophistication was gone. She was vulnerable. He felt a swift, self-directed anger that he was the cause. He wanted to reach out and calm her fears.

Maybe she didn't know how she affected him. Then he remembered her soft body squirming beneath his. His teeth ground together. Another part of him was not so forgiving.

"Why didn't you do something with your hair?"

"I didn't have a comb."

Her simple answer made him mutter another expletive. Whirling, he retrieved her purse and handed it to her. It only took a few moments of her shaky hand rambling in the white leather clutch for Brad to realize there wasn't a comb inside.

"Follow me," he ordered and strode back into the bathroom. He opened a drawer, then another. He didn't want anyone to see her looking as if she had just come from a man's bed. The image made his body harden. He slammed the drawer shut. Opening a third, he finally found a comb.

He handed it to Michelle. It fell from her hand. She stared at him and mutely begged forgiveness. Knowing if he touched her again he might not be able to stop, yet unable to leave her, he picked up the comb, stepped behind Michelle, and gathered her tangled hair at the nape of her neck.

Stroke after stroke, he drew the comb through long black hair that stopped in the middle of her slim back. He continued to let his fingers glide through the silken mass. The sudden urge to bury his face in the black strands and press its fragrant softness against his lips made him throw the comb on the vanity and stalk from the room.

This time he drank the whiskey he had poured earlier. Noticing the slight tremor of his hand, he banged the glass down. How could he let one woman get to him this badly?

In that instant, he looked up and saw Michelle and accepted the answer. As hard as it was for him to admit, she was becoming important to him.

"I'll take you home."

Swallowing the painful lump in her throat, she moved toward the front door. Brad was already there holding it open. Impatience radiated from him. She glanced away. She looked anywhere but at the face of the man she realized she loved. He was probably disgusted at the sight of her.

"If you don't mind, I have an early flight," Brad said.

She looked up. She searched his face for any sign of forgiveness and discovered none. His face was closed, his body rigid. It was as if he had never lit her soul or touched her heart.

When she continued to stare at him, his mouth tightened, his long fingers clenching and unclenching on the brass knob. "If you expect an apology, you'll be standing there a long time."

She recoiled from the hurtfulness of his words.

He made a motion toward her, then stopped. For a brief moment he was unable to hide the remorse in his eyes. In that brief moment Michelle knew that she wasn't the only one suffering, but this time she had to be strong enough to do the healing.

"Before I go, I'd like five minutes of your time."

"Michelle—"

"Please, Brad."

He slammed the door. "Five minutes."

His implacable expression was back and Michelle wanted to shake him almost as much as she wanted to feel his arms around her once again. Her fingers gripped her purse so tightly they ached. Where to begin? He glanced at his watch.

"I take full responsibility for . . . for what happened. I didn't stop to think where my actions might lead." She drew her arms around her waist when he folded his arms and began to study a seascape on the far wall.

"One of the first things you learn in the foster

home is not to get attached to anyone, so you shy away from emotional and physical contact."

"Come on, Michelle," he said, pushing away from the door. "Do you really expect me to believe that you're so starved for affection that you can't help yourself? That you can't think for yourself?"

"The truth is that I wasn't thinking anything when you were kissing me."

He braced both hands on his hips. "Well, you better start thinking. The next guy might not stop."

"The only time I have problems thinking is when you're kissing me." His eyes narrowed and she rushed on. "As for the next guy, there hasn't been anyone in my life for a very long time."

"You must believe that I'm the biggest fool that ever lived."

"I don't know if I should thank you or slap your face for that remark."

"You're beautiful, sensuous, successful. How could that be possible?"

"Because I'm also selective."

Long strides brought him to her. "Men are practically foaming at the mouth when they see you, and you want me to believe that you turned them all away."

"You're coming very close to helping me make a decision, Brad, and it's not in your favor," she said hotly.

He looked at her a long time. His eyes widened. "You're telling the truth! Did you love him or hate him that much?"

How could she explain that both love and hate governed her? Her hate for Richard, her love for him. "Both," she finally said.

"Was he the one who stole your dreams?"

Michelle closed her eyes against the tenderness she heard in his voice, saw in his eyes. When she opened them, he was within arm's reach. Close enough for her to touch and far enough away to give her the strength not to.

"Michelle?"

"I still dream, Brad. I still dream." He took a step toward her, and she retreated. "Thank you for listening. Now if you'll call me a cab, I won't take up any more of your time."

He kept coming. "Not until I have the whole story."

"I told you the whole story."

"I never thought that you were a coward."

"It's not being a coward to not want an affair."

"If you just wanted out, why say anything? I'd bet every penny I have that you haven't told this to any other man."

She backed away from his seeping warmth. "That doesn't prove anything."

His hands settled on her shoulders, effectively stopping her from retreating again. "It does to me."

"The only thing it proves is that I didn't want you to drop Forbes Realtors because of me."

"Do you honestly think I would stop dealing with a company because one of their employees wouldn't sleep with me?"

"No." She tried to pull away. "Can I use the phone?"

"You're going to tell me what I want to know if it takes all night."

"You have an early flight, remember?"

"I've been losing sleep over you ever since we met. I don't know why tonight should be any different," he said softly.

Nothing within her prepared her for the warmth his words brought. "Don't say things like that."

"Tonight seems to be one for total honesty." His finger grazed her chin and she shivered. "Why?"

She squirmed and his hold tightened. "Because I didn't want you looking at me as if I don't exist."

"I should think that would make working with me easier," he probed.

"Because I care about you. Are you satisfied?" she asked, losing patience.

His eyes narrowed. Michelle blushed. "I think I'll pass on answering that one."

"I don't want an affair," she stubbornly insisted.

"If that's all I wanted, we'd already have passed that point in our relationship. Now don't try to pull away."

Her expression turned belligerent. "You make me sound like a pushover."

"I don't court pushovers," he stated, then started for the door. Michelle didn't budge.

"Court?" Her heart boomed in her chest.

"As in date. I'm not clear on the rules, so I'll make this up as we go along." He pulled her resisting body up the two steps to the entryway.

They were in the hall before she found her voice. "Are you sure about this?"

"No, but it beats the alternative," he said as they reached the elevator. At her puzzled look, he continued, "Never tasting your lips again, never holding you in my arms."

"Brad." If he hadn't been holding her arm she would have sagged to the floor.

His warm lips brushed across hers. "Never hearing my name on your lips the way you just said it."

The elevator door slid open. "Going down."

At the sound of the strident voice, Michelle glanced around. The elevator held another couple and an elderly woman who looked as if she had just bitten into an unripe persimmon. It wasn't difficult to decide who had spoken. Flushing, Michelle tucked her head and entered the polished oak and glass enclosure. Brad slowly followed.

Neither spoke on the way to her house. It was as if each was afraid they might say or do the wrong thing.

At her front porch, he took the key from her hand and opened the front door. The ringing phone greeted them. Michelle rushed to pick up the extension in the den. Brad followed her inside, closing the door behind him.

Covering the mouthpiece, she glanced down the hallway to the left, then back at Brad. "Alex needs some figures."

Brad folded his arms across his chest. "Give them to him. I'll wait."

She glanced down the hallway again, then bit her lower lip.

"Michelle, Alex is not a patient man."

She nodded. "The bar is over there. I'll be back in a minute." She left through a hallway in the back of the den.

Brad smiled. She was as nervous as a cat. That was all right, he wasn't too steady himself. Walking farther into the spacious room, he noted the vaulted ceiling, the stylish furniture, the natural stone fireplace, and the wall of windows on the far side of the room. She had accomplished a great deal in a short time and she had done it by herself. She was a unique woman, and somehow, someday, she was going to be his.

Hearing a whirring noise, he frowned. Following the sound, he left the den and walked into the hall. He was stunned to see a man in a wheelchair. From the expression on the man's dark face, he was equally shocked.

"Who are you?" the man asked.

"Brad Jamison. Who are you?"

The man in the wheelchair's head snapped back. "Since I live here, I think I should be asking all the questions," he shot back.

Brad stared at him. So this was the reason Michelle hadn't been involved with anyone. One thing Brad hadn't expected was a lover, and certainly not one in a wheelchair. An honorable man would make his apologies and walk away, but at the moment the claws ripping through Brad's gut made him feel anything but honorable. The smirk on the other man's face made the claws twist.

"Where is Michelle?" the stranger asked.

"Taking a call in the other room."

The man glanced toward the den and smiled. "The bedroom. I'm rather tired myself. I'll show you out."

"I think I'll wait for Michelle." This time Brad was going to let her explain.

"That wasn't an option," the man said, his voice clipped.

Brad ignored the baiting words. "I'm not leaving until I talk with Michelle."

At that moment Michelle returned and looked from one silent man to the other. "Hello, Nick. I see you've met Brad."

"We met," Nick said. "I think he was about to leave."

Brad's questioning gaze swung to Michelle, who still stood apart from both men. "Michelle, I'd like to talk with you outside," he said, his voice harsh with the strain of holding his annoyance at the other man in check.

A paperback fell from Nick's lap. Michelle moved to pick it up.

Nick looked over Michelle's bent head, and smiled his triumph.

"On second thought, it wasn't important," Brad said and turned to leave. He hadn't stooped that low.

He was halfway to his car when he heard Michelle yell his name. He kept walking.

"Brad, wait!" She ran after him. "Please wait."

He took another step toward the rental car before the pleading note in Michelle's voice stopped him. Fearing he'd either shake her or kiss her, he rammed both hands into his pants pockets before he whirled around.

Her steps faltered when she saw the chiseled hardness of his face in the dimness of the moonlight. A tongue circled her dry lips.

Brad wished for the light of one candle. He wanted to see her eyes. They were the true indicator of her feelings. He thought he'd heard longing and uncertainty in her voice when she called him, or was that just what he wanted to hear? Deciding he had to know, he took the steps to bring them together, his eyes never leaving hers.

"Do you . . ." His voice trailed off. The question turned into a muttered curse.

What difference did it make if she loved the guy or not? Except it did. Somehow he suspected that she was the type of woman who loved only one man. Until now, he hadn't wanted to admit how much he wanted to be that man.

Michelle saw the warring emotions in Brad's face, but didn't understand them. Yet, more than anything she wanted to erase that look. Lifting her hand, she tenderly placed it against the curve of his clenched jaw and moved closer until the warmth of their bodies mingled. Her thumb grazed his lips, her mouth followed.

Brad jerked her to him. His hand plowed through her hair, the lush silkiness spilling over his fingers. The kiss was hot and urgent. His mouth swept the delicate curve of her face, nibbled her earlobe. He kissed the throbbing pulse at the base of her throat. Michelle shuddered and his arms tightened.

"Come back with me."

"You know I can't."

He stared down at her, then asked the question that twisted his insides. "Is he the one you told me about?"

Michelle frowned her confusion. "I thought you met."

"I told him my name and he asked where you were. What difference does it make?" Brad asked, impatient for her answer.

Michelle framed his face in her hands. "Considering he's my brother, it makes a lot of difference."

Brad opened his mouth, then shut it. A wide grin split his face. His hands closed around her tiny waist and he twirled her around. His lips found hers before they made a complete circle. Her arms clinging around his neck, Michelle gave all he asked for and more.

After a long moment, he sat her on her feet. Her breathing harsh, she leaned against him. "I'm sorry about Nick. He's always been overprotective, but since his accident he's gotten worse."

"How long ago was that?"

After a heartbeat she said, "Nine years."

"Oh, honey." Gently, oh so gently, his lips brushed, touched, and savored hers. "I can't blame him for being possessive. I feel the same way."

"Thanks for understanding," she said, leaning away from him to stare up into his face. "He hasn't had an easy time of things."

Brad caressed her cheek. "Neither have you, and you aren't bitter."

Her fingers brushed across the sensuous curve of his lower lip. "Only because someone helped me not to be."

He nipped her finger. "I'm glad."

Her smile lit her face. "So am I."

"Are you free Saturday?"

"If not, I will be," she said without hesitation.

"That's my girl. I'll pick you up around ten that morning. Dress casual." He kissed her hard and quick. "Think of me."

She pressed her fingertips against her lips as he got into the car and drove away. "Always."

Going back inside the house Michelle found Nick in his room watching television. She switched the set off. "Why didn't you tell Brad that you were my brother?"

Leaning back in his chair, Nick casually folded his arms. "Didn't he know?"

"No, and apparently you didn't bother to tell him."

"Whose fault is that, Michelle?" he asked, his voice rising as his arms unfolded. "I know it's not likely, but if you came into the hallway and a strange woman was there and she was waiting for me, wouldn't you assume that I had told her about you?"

She stared down into his belligerent face. "Assumed, but not taken for granted. Brad was a guest in our home. It was your place to introduce yourself and make him feel welcome."

His annoyance escalated. "I don't want him here. You don't need the heartache. You don't need him!"

"That's a matter of opinion," she said. This time she wasn't backing down or soothing.

"I guess now that Jamison is around, you'll be so wrapped up in him you'll forget about the rehab center," he accused, his expression sullen.

Shock flew through her. "That remark was uncalled for. I'm doing everything possible, but nothing is going to make me shut Brad out of my life." She braced her hands on the sides of the wheelchair and leaned down to his eye level. "Is that clear?"

He looked away. "Crystal."

"Good." She clicked the TV back on. "Good night, Nick."

Gravel flew in all directions as the Mercedes fishtailed to a halt. Brad's hands gripped the balled gearshift as he remembered the frightened young girl on the beach nine years ago. Her brother had had a career-ending injury. She had no other living relatives. He'd rescued her from a man who had tried to hurt her; a man she thought had loved her.

Reason told him the similarities were coincidental, but his increased heartbeat told him he had met her at last. Resting his head on the back of the leather seat, he replayed the first time he had held her in his arms.

She had been a fleeting shadow in moonlight.

Minutes after she'd left in the taxi, he'd gone to the airport to look for her and to make sure she was all right. All he found was an uncooperative reservation clerk and a crowded airport. He could have kicked himself for not getting her name. She had touched him as nothing else had. Somehow talking with her had helped him to deal with his own problems. He had stopped blaming his parents for making him always feel like an outsider and went on to make his own way in the world.

If it was she, he owed her his thanks. If . . . No. It had to be her. He wouldn't let himself think otherwise. He had met her again and the promise of her beauty was in full bloom. Her intelligence and self-confidence were as much a part of her as her graceful walk. So was her courage.

She had beat the odds and spit in the devil's eye.

A wild hoot tore through the air. Shaking his head, he laughed. Who would have imagined Brad Jamison shouting because he had found a woman he had rescued nine years ago?

His hand raked across his face. He hadn't changed that much. Did she remember him or had she tried to forget that night? If she had, he couldn't blame her. And he wasn't about to bring it up and make her uncomfortable. She had suffered enough in her life. And he would take on anyone who tried to hurt her again. Including her brother.

Michelle was going to be his, come hell or high water.

CHAPTER ELEVEN

The next day Michelle walked into her office and froze. Her eyes widened. Her briefcase and purse dropped from her hands. Unsteady fingertips pressed against her quivering lips. Walking farther into the room, she turned in a complete circle. And everywhere she looked, there were flowers. Roses, lilacs, tulips, camellias. Blossoms, in a lavish display of pastel colors and intoxicating scents, filled the room. Brad had turned her office into a miniature greenhouse. Tears stung her eyes.

She was being wooed and courted. She smiled through her tears. For someone who wasn't clear on the rules, he had made a very romantic start. That was part of his mystique and appeal. He did everything well.

He could take you from fantasy to bone-melting realism in his arms. He knew what you craved and needed before you asked. Even worse, he appeared to control the passions that made you mindless. He was definitely a dangerous man, but that was part of his allure. Picking up the phone, Michelle called him. His secretary put her through immediately.

"They're beautiful."

"Not as beautiful as you, but they'll have to do," his deep voice said.

"Are you sure you haven't gone through this courting ritual before?" she teased.

He laughed, a warm rich sound. "Very."

Her intercom flashed. "Dana is buzzing me. My appointment is here."

"All right. I'll be out of town for the next few days." He paused. "There are some other cities I need to see before I make a final decision on relocating."

"I would have been disappointed in you if you weren't checking out other sites, but I'm betting on Dallas."

"I should expect it by now, but you never cease to amaze me. You're quite a woman."

"You're quite a man yourself." The red light flashed. "Gotta run. Have a safe trip and I'll see you Saturday."

"Good-bye. Hope you like my surprise tomorrow." The line went dead. Bemused, Michelle hung up the phone. What could top today?

A five-foot Gund teddy bear. His cottony-soft chocolate-brown fur begged Michelle to hug him. She did. She didn't care that Jacob, and the deliveryman who had been waiting in her driveway when she arrived home, had smiled and exchanged amused looks. She didn't care that Nick snorted that it was frivolous. That night she fell asleep, her hand touching the bear's fur and thinking of a like softness, Brad's hair.

The three-pound golden box of Godiva chocolates arrived after lunch the next day. They were incredibly delicious and sinfully addicting, just like the man who had sent them. Michelle savored each bite, a small smile hovering on her lips. Tomorrow was Saturday. "I wonder where we'll go for our date," she said aloud to herself.

"Come on, Michelle, just this once," Brad begged, an endearing grin on his handsome brown face.

Folding her arms across her chest, Michelle shook her head. "No, and that's final."

Strong fingers lifted her chin. "You're not afraid of a little ride, are you?"

Michelle glanced up as the Texas Giant, a seven-car roller coaster, zipped by, going sixty-two miles an hour. The cars clattered and careened around on a wooden track that was one hundred and forty-three feet above the ground. Shrieks and screams filled the air as the cars twisted and turned, swooped and climbed.

"That, I believe, is more than a little ride."

"Come on, honey. I'll be sitting beside you. You can just close your eyes and hang on."

"That's what you said when we rode the Pirate's Ship and I saw my life flash before me. You said the same thing when you talked me into parachuting two hundred feet from the Texas Shoot Out. Sitting in the front on the Log Ride was also your idea." She pulled her damp white T-shirt from her breasts.

Disregarding his soaked shirt, Brad grinned and pulled her against him. "And like a gentleman, when the log splashed into the water, I covered your body with mine."

Michelle blushed.

"Sorry about the hands. Come on, honey. Didn't you want to ride everything at Six Flags Over Texas when you were young?" he coaxed.

Pushing out of his arms, she walked over to a tree-shaded bench and sat down. "I never was able to go."

Brad sat beside her. "I did. Once. My maternal grandparents lived about twenty miles from here." His smile faded, sadness crept into his black eyes. "From the age of ten I used to spend every summer with them. My grandfather taught me how to fish and ride and hunt. I couldn't wait for school to end so I could catch a flight home."

Michelle wondered if he realized he had called his grandparents' house home. "I bet you were spoiled rotten."

He shrugged. "I guess, but I never doubted they wanted me." As if aware of what he had implied, Brad stood. "If you don't want to ride, how about a hamburger?"

Michelle rose and laced her hands with his. "They sound like wonderful people."

His hand squeezed hers. "They were. Losing them was tough. But I'm finally going to be able to keep a promise to my grandfather and buy back the land my mother sold."

Michelle frowned. "Why did she sell the property?"

"To make me beg. It didn't work."

She shivered from the coldness in his voice. Her free hand turned his face to hers. It was devoid of emotions. She wanted nothing more than to bring back the teasing Brad. "If I ride that thing, will you promise not to let me fall out?"

He kissed her palm. "I promise."

"Lead on."

To her surprise, Michelle enjoyed the scary ride. And the next one Brad dragged her to. They were two adults living a childhood fantasy and enjoying themselves immensely.

It was after eight that night when Brad pulled up in front of Michelle's house. Before he could turn off the motor, Nick came outside waving for Michelle.

Worried, she got out of the car and ran to him. "What is it? Are you all right?"

"Mr. Nash called. It seems some important

people are in town unexpectedly and he's having a cocktail party. He wanted you to come over."

"Now?"

He looked at Brad standing beside her and snorted. "I guess the rehab center doesn't matter anymore." He backed up his chair. "Sorry I bothered you."

"Nick," Brad called. "Where is the party?"

"Nash's house in Highland Park."

"Go get dressed, Michelle. I'll be back as soon as I can shower and change."

"Thank you for understanding, Brad," she said as her brother entered the house. "The rehab center means a great deal to Nick. Unless we can raise enough funds, it might not open on schedule."

"He shouldn't hold you responsible if it doesn't."

"I let him down right after his accident. I can't do it again," she said with fierce determination.

"Nine years is a long time to carry guilt." He looked over her head at the house behind them. "Seems to me you've paid him back in full and then some."

"He's my brother."

"And that's the only reason I let him talk to you the way he did. I'll be back."

Brad, in a tailor-made tuxedo, returned in thirty minutes. He took one look at Michelle as she en-

tered the den where he waited after Nick let him
inside and shot to his feet. His jaw dropped
"My goodness!"

She wore a short, strapless black silk dress
When she walked, her black stockinged leg
peeked out through a split on the side. Her hair
was artfully piled on top of her head in a profu-
sion of curls. Diamonds winked in her ears.

He swallowed. "Don't you have anything
less . . . less . . . ?"

Michelle lifted her head. "Yes, but I'm wearing this."

Brad arched a brow. "Is this a test?"

"If it is, are you going to pass?" she asked.

"Darn right. If you think I'm letting you out
dressed like that without me, you're crazy," he
said and took her arm. "But the first guy who
makes a pass is going to be in trouble."

She kissed him. "Thanks for not asking me to
change."

Brad led her out the door. Nick was nowhere
in sight. "I don't think it would have made any
difference."

"No, but it would have shown me that you
don't trust or approve of me."

"Oh, I approve of you. Soon, I'm going to
show you how much," he said, opening the door.

"Brad."

He tossed her a glance. "All right. I'll be
good."

"That's the trouble now. You're too good,"

Michelle mumbled as she slid into the passenger seat.

"Thank you, ma'am. I do try to please."

And please he did. He charmed the women, and won the respect of the men. When Michelle told everyone about the "unexpected expenses" keeping the Winslow Rehabilitation Center from opening, he donated the first ten thousand dollars. After that, the others followed. Before the night was out, she had another sixty thousand dollars and Mr. Nash was smiling again.

A little after midnight, Brad unlocked Michelle's door, then handed her the key. "I always seem to be thanking you," she said. "For the wonderful gifts, today, tonight."

He braced one hand on the doorjamb above her head. "My pleasure. I don't suppose we can go in and smooch on the couch."

"No," Michelle said, regret in her voice.

"Thought not. An audience might put a snag in things."

"I'm sorry. He—"

Warm lips stopped the words of apology. He kissed her until she was weak and pliant in his arms. "It's all right. I guess I won't be seeing you for a while since you're leaving Friday for your office retreat."

"We'll be at Alex's ranch near Austin for three days. Are you planning on being in that area?"

Michelle asked, unable to keep the wistfulness out of her voice.

"Afraid not. Now go on inside and get some rest. I'll talk with you before you leave," he said, then gently pushed her inside and closed the door.

Michelle stared at the closed door for a long time. Brad hadn't kissed her again. Could he be tiring of her already? Twin furrows raced across her brow.

They had had a wonderful time. Her lower lip tucked between her teeth, she went to her room. She was being foolish. Brad would probably call her tomorrow. Everything was going to be all right.

By the time Thursday rolled around, Michelle wasn't sure that anything would ever be all right again. Brad hadn't called, nor had he contacted her in any way. On top of that, the possibility of her raising any more funds for the rehab center looked bleak. There was only one way left to make sure that Nick had his chance. Taking a deep breath, she walked into her bank.

One hour later, Michelle left the towering granite building and got into her car. The foundation had the money. It had meant taking out a second mortgage on her home, the only real home she had known, but no one said love was cheap. The check would be ready on Tuesday, the day before Clint's deadline.

Nick and Mr. Nash were ecstatic when she called them. Neither asked where the extra funds had come from. She hadn't volunteered the information.

Pulling into the bumper-to-bumper down-town traffic, she headed for Clint's ranch. He was the main person who needed to know, but she had been unable to contact him by phone.

The padlock on the gate told its own story. He never locked it unless he went out of town. Taking the elongated key from her purse, she opened the lock and drove through. It took only a minute to push a note under the front door, then she drove back to the gate, relocked it, and left.

A strange sadness swept over her as she drove home. It was as if some cruel fate had let her glimpse the two things she wanted most in the world—a home no one could take away from her and the man she loved—then snatched them both away.

She let herself into a silent house after nine that night and went directly to her room to pack for the office retreat. Finished, she ran her bath. For once too tired to get a nightgown, she stripped and got into the tub. Closing her eyes, she leaned her head back against the rim and allowed her thoughts to drift. She didn't want to go to Alex's ranch, but if she didn't she'd have too much time on her hands to think about why Brad had walked out of her life.

"Is there room for one more?"

Her eyes sprang open as she jerked upright. Brad stepped into the room, a devastating smile on his face.

CHAPTER TWELVE

"I read in a survey that the one thing most people take into the bathtub with them is another person. I think you forgot something."

Stunned, she watched his long, tapered fingers release the last visible button on his white shirt. Without hesitation, he tugged the shirt out of his jeans and undid the remaining buttons. Muscles rippled as he pulled the shirt off. A dark matting of chest hair descended to a sharp V into his pants. Her stomach muscles tightened into a knot.

The rasp of a zipper caused her to inhale sharply. Leaning forward, Brad hooked his thumbs into his jeans.

Sanity returned with a jolt. "Brad, no," she said, her gaze finally moving up to meet his. His gaze was considerably lower than her face.

Michelle glanced down. Heat flooded her cheeks as she saw the evaporating bubbles clinging to the taut peaks of her nipples. Sliding beneath the water, she crossed her arms over her breasts. "Get out of here."

"That would take either a fool or a saint. I've never been accused of being either."

She swallowed, caught between propriety and glad to know he hadn't forgotten her. "You have no right to be in here."

"I beg to differ."

Michelle gritted her teeth and twisted in the rapidly cooling water. She'd just ignore him. Picking up the sponge, she began to wash her arm. Out of the corner of her eye, she saw him take a seat on the commode and cross one long leg over the other.

"Need any help with those hard-to-reach places?"

Hearing the laughter in his deep voice, the anger Michelle had been trying to hold on to disappeared. No matter how much she wanted to deride him for not calling her, she was happy that he was here now. "You shouldn't be in here."

"Why?"

"Why?" she parroted.

"I asked you first," he said with a wide grin.

"I think it's obvious," she said, rubbing the same spot on her arm.

"The only thing that's obvious is that you're one of the most beautiful and fascinating, not to mention spunky and intelligent, women I have ever met. You tempted me from the first time I saw you, and you're still doing it." His dark eyes narrowed. "By the way, I am fast approaching my limit," he said. "So I suggest you put that sponge down before I join you, and I promise I won't let you out until we're both shriveled like ten-year-old prunes."

The sponge stilled. "I don't know what you think you're doing, but I want you to leave. I haven't heard from you since Saturday and you appear in my bathroom and act as if nothing has happened."

"I was thinking."

"Thinking?" she shouted incredulously.

"Thinking of something extraordinary to give you next."

Her mouth tightened. "And of course you thought of yourself."

"Nope. I wanted to give you a memory," he said softly. "A memory of walking on the beach beneath the stars, of watching the fog roll in over the Golden Gate Bridge. I wanted to give you San Francisco in the springtime."

Captivated by his words, she turned her head and looked directly into his eyes. Kneeling by the tub, he was blatantly arrogant in dismissing her wish, yet so compellingly handsome Michelle was forced to admit she was glad he had.

His unsteady hand reached out to smooth a wisp of hair behind her ear, then followed its delicate curve downward over the slope of her jaw, the silky skin of her neck, and paused to feel the pounding pulse in the base of her throat. "I want to share that memory with you. Can you give it to me?"

Hunger swept through her. "Brad, I—"

The rest of her words were smothered beneath the persuasive demand of his avid mouth on hers. Vaguely, she was aware of being lifted, of her feet dangling in the air, but mostly she was aware of the naked length of her body molded intimately against his.

Her breasts brushed against his hairy chest, and a thousand delightful sensations coursed through her. Protest stumbled and died beneath the sensual onslaught of his hands and mouth. The evocative swirl of his tongue sent unleashed longing racing through her. Pressing closer, she curved her arms around his neck and laced her fingers around his head.

Slowly, seductively, Brad allowed Michelle to slide down his length until her toes, then feet, settled onto the carpeted floor. His lips never left hers.

"I take it back about not being called a fool. Only a fool would have started this," he rasped. The palms of his hands skimmed the wet, satiny skin of her back and shoulders, leaving a trail of unsatisfied flesh.

Her heart pounding, she mumbled, "Does that mean we're going to be prunes?"

Brad blinked, then threw back his head and

laughed. Michelle, who had been serious, stared at him in bewilderment.

"Not this time, sweetheart." Grabbing a giant white terry bath towel, he wrapped it around her naked body. He took particular pleasure in getting the tuck just right between her breasts. "I think I need to get temptation out of the way."

Picking her up in his arms, he left the bathroom, pausing only briefly to drag his shirt from atop the vanity.

Keeping Michelle in his arms, Brad stretched out on her chaise longue, settling her hips between his legs. His hand traveled up her arm, her shoulder, and settled in her hair. The cool breeze drifted through the open patio door, lifting the gauzy white curtains, and twirling them in a crazy dance. Crickets chirped, and began the mating ritual.

"If you leave that door open again, you're going to have a sore backside."

"If I hadn't, *you* wouldn't have been able to get inside."

"Humph. That's the only reason you're sitting so comfortably this moment." She snorted and his hand tightened. "I mean it, Michelle. This place is too isolated for you to run around with the door open. Any pervert could get in here."

"You and he would have a big surprise if I had planted cacti instead of begonias. By the way, I hope you spared some of them."

"They're safe," he told her. "Will you come with me to San Francisco?"

Sitting up, she met his piercing gaze. "When I didn't hear from you, I thought you had gotten tired of me. I don't like how I felt and I don't want to feel that way again when you leave."

"Oh, honey," he said, pulling her closer to kiss her lips. "I wish I could say that I'd be with you forever, but I can't. There are no guarantees, but I do care for you more than any other woman I have ever known. You fascinate me as much as you make me want to run with you to the near-est bed. Let that be enough, Michelle. Let that be enough."

Crushing her to him, he pressed his mouth to hers with mind-bending persuasion, but his hands were gentle, so very gentle. The dreamer in her cried for the loss of a precious memory, yet the realistic part of her wanted to accept what he offered and not think of tomorrow.

Dragging his mouth from her, he pleaded, "Come with me, Michelle." He laid his index finger over her lips when she opened her mouth to answer.

"Think about it first. Your bags are packed. In-stead of Alex's ranch, you can come with me to San Francisco. Nothing will happen unless you want it to happen."

"That's just it, Brad. I want it to happen," she confessed, her voice little more than a whisper.

"But I'm not sure I'm sophisticated enough to smile and watch you walk away later."

"Michelle." He pulled her back into his arms. She clutched him like a lifeline, her nails biting into his back. He didn't flinch.

"Brad, I'm not strong enough to fight you anymore."

His arms tightened for a fraction of a second, then he released her and stood. He watched her with a mixture of longing and regret. "I want you, Michelle, but you have to come without doubts. I don't want to kiss you into submission. I couldn't face you or myself afterward."

He walked to the sliding glass door, his shirt in his hand. "Sometimes you have to let something go before it will belong completely to you. I think we're both going to have one hell of a bad night. Have a good flight, and remember, I'll be waiting no matter how long it takes."

Michelle watched him pull the door shut and motion for her to lock it. She didn't move. Was she throwing away her only chance for happiness? Could she trust Brad with her love? There was only one way to find out. She ran to the door and jerked it open. "I want the memories."

His arms wrapped around her, crushing her to him. "Are you sure?"

"I'm sure," she whispered breathlessly, awed that she was the cause of the slight trembling in his voice. His mouth took hers with a fierce possession, and she moaned softly in sweet surrender. When he lifted his head, they were both breathing heavily.

"I'll wait in the den while you get dressed. We can tell Nick together."

Predictably Nick disapproved. Michelle stood firm. Brad wrote his home phone number on the back of his business card, and handed it to her brother. He refused to take it. Brad placed the card on a small table and ushered her outside.

A short time later they were aboard Brad's jet and waiting for clearance to take off from Addison Airport.

"Take a nap in one of the lounge chairs," Brad told her. "I'll wake you up when we land. I think the safest place for me is up front with Mack."

Michelle nodded and relaxed in the blue chair. Everything was going to be all right. Brad did care for her. Gazing out the tiny window, she buckled her seat belt and felt the small jet gathering speed to lift off. The lights of Dallas winked and blinked at her, then went out completely.

She was going to meet her destiny.

Two and a half hours later, the plane landed. Michelle barely roused as the wheels struck the asphalt, then came to a screeching halt. Something warm and soft brushed against her ear; she absently brushed it away with the back of her hand.

Brad stared down at Michelle curled up in the chair. She looked more like a little girl than a woman. He knew differently. Michelle was all woman and soon she was going to be his. "Wake up, sleepy head."

Michelle came awake slowly. "Are we there yet?"

"Almost."

She yawned. "Excuse me."

Brad smiled. "No problem. Up you go." He pulled her to her feet and headed for the door.

The chilly night breeze tinged with salt and seaweed made him breathe in deeply. He loved San Francisco. It was like no other place on earth. One of the reasons he loved it so was the magnificent coastline. He never tired of watching the ocean roll in to shore, trying with each wave to subdue the land or push it out of the way.

Once he moved to Dallas, he and Michelle would return often. His steps slowed as the thought reverberated in his head.

Michelle wasn't going to be a permanent part of his life. He enjoyed her, but when it was over, it was over. Need made a person vulnerable. He'd sworn long ago he'd never be put in that hellish position again.

Opening the door to the steel gray convertible

Mercedes, he helped Michelle inside and buckled her seat belt. When it was over it was over.

Michelle looked up at him. "Brad?"

The uncertainty in her voice brought him back to her. Something inside him reached out to calm her fears, and he knew his thoughts of a moment ago were shadows on the wind. He already cared, perhaps too much.

Leaning down, his lips brushed against hers. They were cold. The temperature was fifty-eight, a marked contrast to the nineties in Dallas.

"We'll have some heat soon."

Closing the door, he went around and got inside. The engine purred to life. Squeezing her hand, Brad left and returned shortly with her luggage.

"Thanks for the heat," she said around a yawn.

"You won't need it in the daytime unless it's windy, but the nights are chilly." He headed for the exit.

"I know. I've been here before," she said before she thought.

He glanced at her sharply. "When were you here?"

Averting her face, she toyed with the crease in her black trousers. "A long time ago." She recalled the first time as a foolish girl looking for a dream, the second time as a woman looking for her angel.

"Was the trip business or pleasure?" he asked, merging on the freeway.

"Neither." Not wanting to talk about a past that held no place in his memory, Michelle changed the subject. "Those homes on the hillside must have a fantastic view, but the insurance would put five kids through college."

"It's worth it. You can't imagine how it feels to wake up and see for miles. The beauty of the ocean both at peace or raging can't be surpassed," he said with feeling. "We'll stop and pick up the pizza I ordered from the plane and then we'll head home."

Thirty minutes later, Brad pulled into a circular driveway. "We're here."

CHAPTER THIRTEEN

Michelle saw nothing but the peak of a gable's shadow rising from behind several tall trees. Sliding out of the car, she followed Brad up winding steps. The closer she came, the louder the crash of waves against the shoreline. The house was like those Michelle had seen earlier, fighting to keep a foothold against the encroaching sea and nature's fickleness. Defiant like its owner.

"It must be very difficult to leave a place like this," she said.

He answered without looking at her. "Yeah, but that just makes coming back more enjoyable." Opening the door, he flipped on the lights. "Come inside before you get chilled."

She stepped into the room and gasped at its breathtaking beauty. Windows spanned the entire length of the immense great room and framed the ocean beyond. Glistening white walls and a white marble fireplace added to the free-flowing spaciousness of the room.

Where the condo in Dallas had accent colors of black, here Brad had chosen salmon and beige. Huge tropical plants in brass planters were everywhere.

"It's beautiful."

The pleasure her words evoked surprised him. In the past he had never given a hoot about what anyone thought except his grandparents. "I'm glad you like it."

"Who wouldn't? I don't want this pizza to get cold; where's the kitchen?"

He nodded to the left. "Through the swinging door. It steps down, so watch it. I'll put your things away."

Trying to maintain her poise, Michelle turned away. She was about to spend the night with a man, and had no idea how to act. Biological knowledge wasn't going to help her.

Opening a cabinet, she took out two plates, snatched a couple of paper towels, placed everything on top of the pizza box and returned to the living area. Stepping into the room, she saw Brad on his knees arranging logs and kindling in the fireplace. Finished, he struck a match and lit the dry twigs. Flames burst upward. *Just like when he touches me*, she thought inanely.

He spun to face her. "Do you want a pillow?"

"Pillow?"

"To sit on. I thought we'd eat in front of the fireplace."

Some of her tension eased. "The carpet is fine, but you better get something to put under this box."

"I've got just the thing." Leaving the room, he came back with a folded newspaper, a quilt, a bottle of champagne, and two long-stemmed glasses. "I always knew Grandmother's quilt would come in handy."

"Where did that come from?" she inquired, pointing toward the bottle.

"Refrigerator in the bedroom." He put the pizza box on the paper before setting the other things aside; then he spread the blanket, helped her to sit, and poured the champagne. "To us." His eyes locked with hers as he tilted the glass and drank.

Michelle tingled from Brad's heated stare as much as she did from the bubbles bursting in her mouth. Setting her glass down, she prepared their plates.

One arm draped around a bent knee, Brad accepted his plate. His food untouched, he watched Michelle eat. Flashes of her white teeth tantalized him. He groaned inwardly when her tongue flicked out to capture a wayward strand of cheese. Finally he could stand no more. Placing his plate aside, he leaned toward her.

She leaned forward to meet him. Her lips parted.

The restrained tenderness of his embrace touched her as nothing else. Michelle clung to him, her arms circling his neck, pulling him closer.

Gentle hands explored the curves of her body, the slope of her hip. Leaning her backward, he followed her down into the waiting softness, molding his muscled hardness against hers, letting her feel the depth of his arousal. Raw flames of desire licked along her nerve endings. Moving her hips in an instinctive invitation, she pressed closer to him.

Abruptly he raised his head, tangling his hand in her unbound hair. Black eyes swept her half-closed ones that were glazed with passion, then lowered to the quivering softness of her lips, the agitated movement of her breasts. He ached with wanting her. But she had to be sure. He would protect her from anyone, and that included him.

"I want you, but say the word and it stops here."

Her eyes fluttered open. Transfixed, she read the naked hunger in his eyes and her entire body surfaced with heat. She had known from the first kiss this moment was inevitable. "I want you."

Strong arms tightened around her, pulling her

closer. "It will be all right. I'll take care of you, I promise. I won't hurt you."

She laid her trembling palm against his cheek. "The only way to hurt me is to stop."

"I won't," he whispered hoarsely. "I can't." His lips covered hers. Cool skin became hot; soft skin accepted hard.

Clothes were cast aside with shameless urgency. In a lacy bra and panties, Michelle lay half-under Brad, who was only in his briefs. Giving in to temptation, she ran her hands over his wide chest, tracing the hard, ridged muscles, feeling them shift beneath her fingertips. He caught her hand, brought it to his mouth, and suckled each finger.

She moaned. The wild longing to be completely his was as untamed and as uncontrollable as the sea outside. With his tongue relearning the essence of her mouth, and his hands unerringly evoking unbearable pleasures, she forgot everything but the exquisite maleness that was uniquely his and the slow throbbing ache building inside her.

His burning lips trailed a path along her shoulders, then slanted downward to the heaving swell of her breasts. Her head thrown back, she invited him to take his pleasure and give in return.

Her bra slipped away and Brad's hands took its place. Gently kneading, his thumb circled the sensitive peaks until her breasts were taut and heavy. She twisted under him, wanting, not knowing how to ask. There was no need. He took that which craved his touch inside his mouth, nibbling, tugging. Her hands moved over his hair as sensations shot through her.

His hand slid over her stomach, then lower until he touched her dewy softness. She jerked. "Brad?"

"Shhh. It's all right," he soothed, his other hand stroking her face. "I won't hurt you or take you further than you want, but neither do I have the strength to let you go."

She relaxed. In his eyes she saw the tenderness she had dreamed of for so long, and also the vulnerability. It wasn't easy for him, yet he was doing it for her. She closed her hand over his. "I trust you."

Lifting her into his arms, he carried her to his bedroom. A bare foot kicked the door shut. Placing her on the cool sheets, he shoved his briefs from the leanness of his hips. Bending, he did the same for her.

The nervousness she expected did not materialize. Instead she felt a small thrill of pleasure that he found her desirable. There was no shame as his gaze caressed her body, nor as her eyes did the same to his. Looking ceased to be enough. The bed dipped as he lay down and drew her into his arms.

"Love me, please."

"I can do nothing else." He tore open a foil

package. He lifted his body over hers to make them one. An unexpected barrier stopped him. Surprise stiffened his body, then a wild exhilaration pulsed through his veins.

She knew the reason for his hesitation. "Please don't stop." Raining kisses on the hard line of his jaw, she lifted her hips. "Please." She called to him and he answered.

He thrust deeply. Sharp nails dug into his back. He suffered the pain gladly, knowing she felt pain as well.

"No more pain, honey." He began to move, slowly, allowing her body to adjust to his, kissing her tightly closed eyelids. Soon her hips began to move with his. He needed more. He needed to see her eyes.

"Open your eyes."

Drugged with sensations, her eyelids fluttered, then swept upward. Brad saw confusion, desire, wonder, astonishment. Regret was not there. He saw mirrored his own soul, his own reaction of wonder. Nothing was going to take this woman from him.

"Now let me show you what paradise is like."

Trembling fingers touched the warmth of his lips. "You already have."

The words snapped his control. Again and again he brought their bodies together, each time marveling at the velvet sheath of warmth enclosed around him. Whimpering moans of pleasure slipped past her lips as she chanted his name. Burying her head into the pillow, she arched her back, seeking and finding. He called out her name in answer. They were one.

Sometime later Michelle became aware of being lifted, and her eyes opened. She saw the curve of Brad's chin and smiled. Never in her life had she felt so cherished or such happiness. Her slim arms circled his neck. The dreamy smile on her face bespoke her contentment. "Thank you."

His lips brushed against her sweat-dampened neck. "Thank you. Now go back to sleep."

She yawned. "But I don't want to go back to sleep."

He smiled. She certainly didn't like being told what to do. Entering the bathroom, he sat on the marble base of the oversized tub with Michelle curled in his lap.

"Yes, you do, and I'm going to join you as soon as we take a soak." He turned on the faucet and water gushed from the spout.

"Why can't it wait until morning?"

"I promised to take care of you," he said, wondering again how someone as sensuous and giving as she had remained unclaimed. Gathering her more securely in his arms, he stepped into the water. "Just trust me."

"Ummm," she said as the water closed around her, soothing away her slight soreness.

"I take it you approve," Brad said, his chin resting on her head.

She approved, all right. The heat of his body and the touch of his muscled thighs against hers were very arousing. She wanted him again. Lifting her mouth to his, she ran her tongue along the curve of his lower lip.

"Michelle," Brad warned. "You're going to get into trouble if you keep that up."

She turned in his embrace until her breasts were pressed against his chest, her legs around his waist. Using the water as leverage, she touched her body to his.

He inhaled sharply, then let the air out of his lungs in a ragged sigh. Splaying his hands on her waist, he lifted her out of the water. His mouth caught one taut nipple and tugged. Michelle's cry of delight splintered through him, driving him on. His tongue made a searing trail down her quivering stomach until he came to the essence of her womanhood.

Shock rippled through her. "Brad, no, plea—" She gasped, her hands clutching his head to her, the pleasure pure and explosive. A cry of ecstasy tore through her. He quickly joined their bodies together. Her hands braced on his shoulders, she yielded to the burning wildness sweeping through her.

Afterward, as shocks swept through her body, he held her and cursed himself. He hadn't worn a condom. "I didn't protect you. That's never happened before. I promised to take care of you."

Her hands palmed his face. "You are. We both were caught up in the moment. I never knew it could be so beautiful."

He tenderly kissed her palm. Neither had he. "Let's get out of here." Holding her, he stepped out of the tub; then, supporting her against his body, he dragged a towel from the rack. "Your hair got wet."

"I wonder how."

"Sassy." He kneeled to dry her legs and kissed her instep. "Sit on the bench and I'll blow it dry."

Light brown eyes widened. "You don't have to do that."

"You'll find out that I never do anything I don't want to do." He came to his feet. "Now sit," he ordered, wrapping a dry towel around her.

It took Brad almost thirty minutes to blow her hair dry. His fingers combed through the long, silky black strands, sometimes stopping to massage her scalp, remembering the last time he had done this. This time Michelle was smiling at him in the mirror, not crying. Patting back a yawn, she leaned back against him.

"Time for bed." He cut off the dryer, placed it on the counter, then turned her to him. Deftly, he released the towel and let it fall to the floor. "I don't want anything between us."

"Neither do I."

Climbing into bed beside her, he curved his arm around her shoulders and drew her to him. She snuggled closer to his warmth, his strength.

"I'm glad I finally discovered the fire beneath the ice."

She tucked her head. "Oh, Brad."

A determined thumb and forefinger lifted her chin until their gazes met. "Never be ashamed of what we shared. Some people never know a hundredth of the pleasure we found. It was special for me because you're a special woman. I know it wasn't easy coming here, and your gift to me makes your coming all the more precious."

Blinking back tears of happiness, she touched the line of his jaw. "Thank you."

Drawing her fingers to his lips, he kissed them. "Go to sleep, honey, while I have the willpower to let you." Pulling her closer, he reached down and drew the sheet over them.

CHAPTER FOURTEEN

Michelle awoke the next morning lying almost on top of Brad. Her arms were around his neck, one leg thrown across his, her head under his chin. She knew her days of wanting to sleep alone were over. She never wanted to wake up again and not be in his arms.

Giving in to temptation, she raked her fingernails through the black mat of curly chest hair. The tender restraint he had shown in possessing her body only made her love him more. Then the thought came: she loved a man who might walk away from her if he tired of her. Unconsciously, her fingers clenched.

"Ouch!" Brad cried. He grabbed her forearm and pulled her up to eye level.

"I'm sorry," she quickly said, instantly regretting that she had hurt him.

His gaze narrowed. "You're going to pay for those scratches," he said playfully.

"I didn't mean to," she protested.

"I don't think you'll mind making payment," he teased. Before she had time to react he settled her in the erotic hollow of his thighs. Air hissed through her clenched teeth. His rigid hardness and the smoldering embers in his eyes told of his form of payment.

Possessive hands slid over the silken skin of her back, pausing on the curve of her hips. He squeezed the pliant flesh. "Do you?"

"Not even if I have to make a double payment." Splaying her hands on the broad expanse of his chest, she leaned down and gave his nipple a tug with her mouth. From beneath sultry lids, she searched his face. "But I wonder who will collect from whom?" she questioned, rotating her hips against his arousal.

His eyes blazed. "There's only one way to find out." Abruptly she found herself under him, his hands and lips meeting her challenge with a mastery that sent her heart rate into double time. Each kiss, each caress heightened their need for each other. Both eagerly gave in return. His hands shook as he sheathed himself, then made her his again.

Earth-shattering waves of ecstasy swept through them. She clung to him as he clung to her, the only solid things in their world. They reached satisfaction together.

• • •

Later, Brad rolled on his side, dragging her to him. "I'll always wonder how I managed to keep my hands off you as long as I did."

"I wonder the same thing about me," she said and kissed his chest.

"You're making it harder and harder to get out of bed," he told her. "If you keep looking at me like that, I'll extract double payment and we'll never get any breakfast."

Her teasing look froze. What if he expected her to cook something like quiche or, heaven forbid, a *souffle*? She swallowed. "I have a confession to make."

"Yes?" he said, half-expecting her to admit to their meeting nine years earlier.

"I can't cook," she mumbled.

The smile beginning to form on the curve of Brad's mouth ceased when he saw the desolate look on Michelle's face. He sobered. "I can't either, so I guess we'll have to tackle it together. I can fix pancakes if you're game."

Grinning, she sat up. "I can make pancakes. I thought you wanted something like quiche Lorraine."

His gaze dropped momentarily to her tempting breasts before swinging back up to her animated face. "At the moment I want something else, but unless we want to die of hunger, I suggest we head for the shower."

Color crept into her cheeks. She jerked up the sheet. Last night had been a kind of dreamlike fantasy. Showering together in broad daylight was out of the question. "I'll wait until you come out."

"That won't be necessary." Scooping her up, he headed for the bathroom. "You aren't going to hide from me. You have a beautiful, tempting body and I intend to see every delicious inch of it as often as I can. You can be prim and proper, cool and sophisticated, but never when we're alone." He set her on her feet in front of the shower door. "Is that understood?" he questioned.

Something about him telling her what to do struck a sore spot. She answered to no one. Hands on her hips, she said, "If I say otherwise?"

Cupping her mutinous face in his hands, he said softly, "Then I'll just have to be patient until you change your mind."

The fight went out of her. "How do you always know the right words to say?"

"I don't. I only know that I never want you to regret again one single moment of the time you spend with me."

Silently, she walked into the glass enclosure and held out her hand. "The last one out has to do the dishes."

The pancakes were rubbery and scorched, the coffee too strong, the eggs hard yellow-and-white pebbles. Dressed in Brad's bathrobe, the sleeves rolled up to her elbows, Michelle took another bite of her overcooked sausage and decided breakfast wasn't half-bad.

She surveyed the once-immaculate kitchen, saw the batter-splattered bowls, the two skillet handles sticking up in the sink, paper towels everywhere, and decided she was glad she was not the one doing the dishes.

"Yell when you're ready for me to dry the dishes. I'm going to change."

Brad's fork paused halfway to his mouth. "You wouldn't?"

Michelle smiled. "I should, but I won't. If you can eat my cooking, the least I can do is clean up."

Strong white teeth closed over a fork laden with syrupy pancakes. "They're better than mine. Give you a couple of weeks and they'll be floating off the griddle."

Realizing the implication of his statement, he sought her face. He hadn't meant to imply that they would be staying together, but he knew he liked waking up with her in his arms, seeing her blossom beneath his hands. But for how long? Michelle was a woman who put her career first, and he was honest and selfish enough to know he wanted to come first in any relationship. He'd sworn long ago that he'd never wait in line for anyone's affection the way he had with his parents.

Seeing the conflicting emotions play across his face, knowing he was struggling to say something that wouldn't hurt her, she tried to save them both. "I'll invite you over to breakfast and you can see for yourself." Rising, she picked up her plate and went to the sink.

His fork clattered onto his plate. She deserved more. Life had kicked her in the teeth too many times for him to let it happen again.

Michelle heard the scraping of his chair against the floor, and smelled Brad's cologne an instant before his arms slid around her waist, pulling her against him, cradling her in his arms. "Right now, I can't imagine waking up without you, but I can't make any promises. Yet, I'm selfish enough to want you to stay anyway."

Did life offer any guarantees? Happiness was often for those strong enough to take chances. Loving Brad was reckless, but as long as there was a chance of him loving her in return, she was going to take it. Setting the plate on the counter, she covered his hand with hers.

"Selfish people take with no thought of giving. You aren't selfish, Brad. It would be selfish of me to ask for more than you're willing to give. We'll just enjoy the time we have together, and when it's over, we'll just walk away. No regrets, no accusations."

Her words should have put him at ease. They didn't. The thought of any other man touching her as he had sent a wave of fury through him. Michelle was a passionate woman. She wasn't going to stop wanting to be loved because he was no longer around. "You aren't going to see anyone except me."

The note of possessiveness in his voice brought a twinkle to her eyes. He definitely reminded her of the story about the dog with two bones. "In view of what you said, don't you think it might be best if I did?"

He turned her around, a look of implacable determination stamped on his handsome face. "No, and that's final."

Michelle regaled him with a look of disappointment. "I guess so. But does that go for you too?"

"Of course it does."

"In that case, I agree to your decision. I do like a man who can make a decision and make it stick."

His accusing gaze softened. "I think you finally got one over on me. For that I'm going to buy you the biggest lobster we can find on the wharf."

By four that afternoon Brad had made good on his promise, adding strawberry crepes and a hot fudge sundae. Ghirardelli chocolates were tucked inside Michelle's oversized bag. At the moment, they were both munching on chocolate chip cookies as hand in hand they strolled through the red maze of The Cannery.

"I love it here. It's hard to believe this was

once a fruit cannery," Michelle said, craning her head over her shoulder to get a last glimpse of an African princess doll dressed in royal garb.

Brad stopped. "I take it you want to look at her?"

Licking crumbs inelegantly from her fingers, Michelle asked, "Look at whom?"

Brad smiled at Michelle. She looked like a little kid, her eyes big and shiny. "Every time I feel a slight tug of your hand and look around it's been either food or a doll. Since there are no eateries on this aisle, it must be a doll."

Glancing around, he saw her. Standing eighteen regal inches, she was resplendent in a beautiful tribal wedding gown. Pointing, he said, "Do you want to go in and see her?"

Michelle started to walk off, only to find Brad was the one balking. He wasn't moving until he had an answer. "So I'm twenty-six years old and I like dolls. Now can we go?"

"Do you have a collection? I didn't see any in your house."

"No, I don't have a collection. I just like to look at them. Now can we please just drop the subject and go?" she questioned, irritation creeping into her voice.

He pulled her resisting body into his arms, and unmindful of the people passing, kissed her thoroughly, leaving her breathless and pliant. "I wanted a train set. Every year until I was thirteen, I'd wake up expecting to see it on my birthday or Christmas morning. It never was there. I'll never forget wanting that train set. Buying it for myself after I was grown somehow didn't seem to mean as much. So I never got one."

Michelle faintly heard a child whisper about the man kissing the lady, but didn't move. How could a man be so arrogant one moment and so tender the next? "One of the foster homes I stayed in when I was seven was probably the best one. The couple gave their daughter an Egyptian doll for her birthday. She had a collection. They were so elegant and poised, and dressed so beautifully, I fell in love with them."

"Did you ever get a doll?"

"No, but I got a Tonka truck once," she said, smiling, the old hurts no longer as painful. She had made a success of her life, which was the important thing.

"A truck?"

"They had made a mistake and left me off the list. Nick gave me his gift so I wouldn't think Santa Claus had forgotten me. Growing up, he was always there for me. I owe him a lot."

"You've paid him back a lot."

"There is one final thing that I need to give him." They both knew she was referring to the rehab center. "Come on, let's catch the ferry to Sausalito. If I don't get seasick, you can take me out to dinner."

"I was hoping you would cook," he teased with a playful smile on his face.

She playfully punched him in the stomach. "For that, I'm going to push you overboard. I've always wanted to yell, 'Man overboard.' "

Brad laughed and reached for her.

"Hello, Bradford."

Michelle looked around to see a stylishly dressed, middle-aged woman in a gray raw silk suit. Several strands of pearls in varying lengths hung around her neck. Black hair, lightly streaked with gray, peeked from beneath her fedora. In one word, she was elegant. Michelle glanced around at Brad when the seconds ticked by and he said nothing, and was surprised to see anger tightening his face.

"Brad?" Michelle said, a frown knitting her brow.

His head dipped curtly toward the other woman. "Marian. We were just leaving." He grabbed Michelle's arm.

Something about the name clicked in Michelle's brain. Marian was the first name of the editor-in-chief of *Mystique* magazine. This was Brad's mother. He obviously disliked her intensely. Observing the naked pain in the older woman's face, Michelle knew she couldn't walk away. No matter what she had done, she was his mother and she was hurting. Michelle had cried herself to sleep too many times, wishing for her mother, to see Brad and his mother at odds.

Stepping out of his grasp, Michelle extended

her hand. "Hello, Mrs. Jamison. I'm Michelle Grant."

"It isn't Jamison anymore, is it, Marian? It's Foster," Brad corrected in a harsh voice.

Soft black eyes met chilly black ones. "My marriage to Carlton doesn't mean I loved you or your father any less."

A ruthless expression settled on Brad's face. "How could it when you don't know the meaning of the word 'love'? You never did and you never will."

Shock distorted Marian's smooth features. She clutched the strands of perfectly matched pearls. "You're never going to forgive me, are you?"

"You never wanted my love, why want my forgiveness?"

"Bradford, please." Marian's slim body trembled, her eyes implored.

His eyes were as cold as his voice. "I remember saying the same word to you, but you were too busy with your social life." He pulled a case from his pocket, then held out a heavily scrolled, elongated key. "You see this key? It's the key to the gate at Granddad's ranch. The ranch you sold to Clint Daniels. By this time next week it will be mine and your little scheme to make me beg will have failed."

"Oh my God!" Michelle stared at the key in Brad's hand, heard a roaring in her ears, and knew that for the first time in her life, she was going to faint.

CHAPTER FIFTEEN

"Is she all right?"

"Yes. No thanks to us, Marian."

"Bradford—"

"Haven't you done enough? Just leave."

Michelle heard the voices—one angry, one softly pleading—and struggled against the darkness engulfing her.

Something was wrong. Something . . . The key. She moaned, her hands lashing out.

"Easy, honey. Everything is all right. We're in one of the shops' office. You're all right."

Michelle concentrated on the soothing note in Brad's voice. Her lids blinked open. Brad's face, lined with worry, filled her vision. She opened her mouth to ask him about Clint's ranch. Nothing came out. Tears stung her eyes and clogged her throat. How could fate have done this to her? It wasn't fair.

Seeing her distress, Brad pulled her into his arms and held her close. "I'm taking you home."

Gathering her in his arms, he stood and brushed past the curious onlookers and his mother. But not before Marian said, "Forgive me." Tears rolled down her stricken face.

Michelle didn't know if the torturous words had been meant for her or for Brad. She only knew that Brad's forgiveness for either of them was very unlikely.

As soon as they reached the house, Brad took her into his bedroom and laid her on the bed. After undressing her with infinite care, he pulled her nightgown over her head and tucked her under the covers. Sitting on the side of the bed, he held her hand.

"Considering how close you and your brother are, I guess it's something of a shock to see Marian and me together," he said.

"Oh, Brad. Why?"

For a long moment she thought he wasn't going to answer her, then he began to speak. "I was unplanned but Marian didn't let me stand in the way of her social life or her position as editor-in-chief of *Mystique*. It was her idea that I call her Marian and my father Kyle." Brad stood and walked to the window, his back to her. "It took me a long time, but I finally accepted that she didn't want me in their lives."

No, you haven't, she thought, looking at the rigidness of his body. He wanted his mother's love, just as Michelle had wanted hers. His parents' inattentiveness was still difficult to accept or understand, but he'd walk through the fires of hell before he'd admit it. They had been wrong, but until Brad could forgive them, he'd never be able to go on with his life.

She knew forgiveness was difficult. She had hated Richard until she had seen him five years ago. To her relief, she had felt nothing except pity for wife number three, whom he was cheating on.

"What about the ranch?" she asked, trying to keep her voice steady.

Returning, he sat on the bed and covered her clasped hands with his. "Marian's last attempt to bring me to heel. Despite knowing that Granddaddy promised the ranch to me, and knowing how much the place meant to me, she sold it when I refused to play the devoted son. I've waited three long years to buy that place and now there's nothing she can do."

She felt chilled. "You think she would have tried to buy the ranch back if she had known?"

"Yes." He answered without hesitation. "The ranch was the last thing that tied us together. Once it's mine, our relationship will be severed completely. That's why all the negotiations were kept secret."

Everything Clint had said fell into place. Brad's lawyer was the one Clint had contacted. Clint hadn't told him about the bid on his ranch, therefore Brad wasn't aware that he was in competition with anyone. Since Clint was out of town, Brad didn't know that his bid had been topped and that he had lost his grandparents' ranch once again. The woman he had held in his arms last night had taken it. She closed her eyes in total misery.

"I'll understand if you want to go home."

Opening her eyes, she looked at the uncertainty in his face and knew she couldn't leave him. Not now. Not with his mother's rejection so vivid in his mind. He had been hurt as a boy and although he had learned to mask it better, he was still hurting. She opened her arms and he came into them. She wasn't betraying Nick, she was comforting the man she loved.

Lying beneath him moments later, she expected him to be rough and demanding in trying to excise the demons of his past. She was wrong. His every touch was as gentle as a baby's breath and as precious.

"I'll be here as long as you want me." This time she was his strength, his warmth.

Early the next morning, the repeated ring of the door chime finally roused Michelle from sleep. Vaguely, she remembered Brad waking her to ask if she wanted to go jogging with him. Barely able to keep her eyes open after a relentless night of making love, she had sent him off with a kiss instead.

The chime rang again. Grabbing the first

thing in sight, his beige sweater, she hurried to the door, sure that Brad must have locked himself out. Pulling the sweater over her hips, she opened the door. Embarrassment quickly followed on the heels of surprise, for on the other side of the threshold was Brad's mother.

The two women stared at each other across the strained silence. Marian, in a peach-colored cashmere sweater and trousers, looked stunning. Michelle looked exactly like what she was, a woman who had just crawled out of a man's bed.

Humiliatingly conscious of Marian's scrutiny, warmth crept beneath Michelle's cheeks. There was no way for the other woman not to know that beneath the sweater, Michelle was naked.

"Brad isn't here."

"It's you I came to see. If you're feeling better, we can talk. May I come in?" Marian asked, her voice strained.

"Me?"

"If I could come inside, I'll explain."

Confused, but unwilling to turn Brad's mother away, Michelle opened the door wider and stepped aside. "If you'll excuse me for a minute, I'll get dressed."

A jeweled hand waved in dismissal of Michelle's words. "That won't be necessary. We only have a few minutes before Brad returns and I don't want to waste them pretending this is a normal social call," she said and sat down on the sofa in the great room.

"I'm listening." Michelle took a chair across from her.

"Despite what you heard yesterday, I love my son. Yet, it's my fault he's the way he is. I turned a sensitive boy into a hard, embittered man." She held up her hand when Michelle started to interrupt. "Please."

Michelle inclined her head for her to continue.

"Bradford's father was my one great obsession. He liked nothing better than a challenge. I set out to intrigue him, and after our marriage, I felt I had to keep his interest. He was brilliant; he made things happen. Dullness and stagnation bored him. I simply had to keep up."

Marian shrugged elegant shoulders. "Bradford came along three years later, unplanned, and there was no time for him. I was in the middle of starting *Mystique* and. . . ." She looked up at Michelle, her eyes filled with regret. "I chose his father and the magazine over Bradford. I always thought there would be time for him later."

Michelle remembered again the boy growing up with only his grandparents to love him, and her heart ached. She looked at his mother again and knew she had paid for her mistake over and over and would continue paying as long as she lived. "Why are you telling me this?"

"I've always been afraid that I had made him hate and mistrust women. When I saw the two of you together yesterday, I knew that wasn't the case. Whether he has admitted it to you or not, he cares for and trusts you." She rose. "But betray that trust, and there'll be no way on God's green earth that he'll forgive you. No matter what the reason," she finished quietly.

"Brad is no longer a child."

Marian shook her head sadly. "I took Bradford's love for granted the way I did everyone else's except for Kyle's. After his father's death, I turned to him for comfort only to discover he didn't need or want me. He looked me in the eyes and said, 'You're twenty-four years too late and I have a plane to catch.' The next week his lawyers contacted me about buying the shares his father left him in Computron. Knowing he wouldn't take them any other way, I complied. The only time I see him now is accidentally, like yesterday."

Marian glanced around the room, tears glistening in her eyes. "This is the first time I've been in his house." Her eyes shut tightly. When they opened, they were haunted. "Love my son, understand him, comfort him. God knows I failed." She started toward the door. Michelle followed.

She spoke as Marian's hand closed on the knob. "May I ask you two questions?"

Marian turned and nodded.

"Why didn't you give him your parents' home?" Michelle asked, unable to keep accusation from creeping into her voice.

"An error on my part. I thought if I threatened to sell the farm, Bradford would have to come to me and ask for it back and we'd start to talk. When I saw it was useless, in a moment of anger I ordered my lawyers to sell. The second question?"

"Why didn't he ever get a train set?"

"Trains are usually played with by both father and son. I wanted all of Kyle's time once we were home." Opening the door, she stepped into the bright California sun. Neither woman felt its probing warmth.

"Good-bye, Michelle. Don't make the same mistake I did. You won't get a second chance."

Michelle watched the lonely woman get into a black Jaguar and drive away. A deep sadness crept through Michelle that two people who should have shared a deep bond were angry strangers.

Moving across the room, Michelle sat down on the floor, leaned her head against a hassock and looked out the window at the endless ocean.

Marian was right. Brad would never forgive her if she violated the trust he had placed in her. In three days, she was buying the only place he had ever felt loved and wanted.

Tears streamed down her cheeks. This time she cried for Brad, for the mother he would never believe loved him, for the love Michelle wanted to give him and was doomed not to.

The front door opened and Brad walked in. "Beautiful women should never cry."

"Brad, we need to talk."

"No. I saw Marian drive off. I'm sorry she upset you. You'll have to learn to ignore her as I do," he said. Dropping down on his knees beside her, he pulled her down on the floor just as the phone rang.

"Brad, the phone."

He tugged the sweater over her head, his lips sought hers, then moved lower to close tenderly over her pouting nipple. Michelle moaned and clasped his head to her breast.

However, by the tenth ring it was apparent the caller was not going to hang up without talking to someone. With a muttered curse Brad rolled to his feet in one smooth motion and jerked the offending object from its cradle.

"Jamison."

Michelle jumped from the whiplash in his voice. In his arms, she had forgotten how fierce his anger could be. Soon it would be directed toward her.

"Well, take care of it as we discussed this morning. I'm busy." His gaze swung to Michelle holding his sweater in front of her.

"Dammit, Patterson, I can't listen to you now. Have both men in my office in forty-five minutes and notify Lois to come in." Not giving the person a chance to answer, Brad disconnected the phone from the wall.

"Now, where were we?" He took Michelle in his arms.

"Don't you need to go to your office?" she asked.

Brad's hands trembled as he took the sweater from her. "I need to love you more."

The raw pain in his voice called out to her. He was trying and failing to block out that seeing his mother still had the power to hurt. Her arms circled his neck, pulling him down against her naked body. He went eagerly into her embrace. Flesh met flesh, giving, adjusting, yielding. For a space of time there was only the two of them locked together in passion and need and love.

CHAPTER SIXTEEN

Exactly ninety minutes after Brad had hung up the phone, he stepped out of the elevator on the executive floor of Computron's office complex with Michelle. His hand rode possessively on the small of her back. Michelle stole a glance at his stern profile and tucked her bottom lip between her teeth. She felt sorry for the person about to be on the receiving end of his ire. He opened a door at the end of the hall.

A slim woman in her late forties wearing a tailored navy blue suit looked up from behind the wire-framed glasses perched on her nose and rounded her desk. "Good morning, Mr. Jamison."

"Good morning, Lois."

"Everyone is in your office as you instructed." She opened an ornately carved door. "Do you need me to take dictation?"

"No, but I may need you to type a resignation letter or two," he informed her, his voice carrying into his office as he and Michelle entered.

Michelle's gaze darted around the spacious and elegant room that was easily twice the size of Alex's office. Three men were already there. One lounged against a wall in the back of the room; another sat in a high-backed black leather chair in front of Brad's teak desk; the third stood by the window. There wasn't a smile to be seen. Tension coiled around the room like a snake.

"I thought this was going to be a private meeting," the man by the window said, the words accusing.

Brad never paused. "This meeting is what I choose it to be, Sims, and I advise you to remember that." Seating Michelle behind his desk, Brad perched a hip on the corner, hitched up one gray pants leg, and asked, "Who screwed up?"

Two pairs of eyes scurried around the room, carefully avoiding Brad's probing black ones. "When I ask a question, I expect an answer. Since you're so anxious to talk, Sims, you start."

Sims rubbed his bald pate and shifted from one scuffed shoe to the other. He tried to swallow, took a breath and tried again. His gaze lifted to the middle of Brad's white-shirted chest. "No one knows if Verda took the microchip. Patterson is only guessing."

"Was she in your lab?" Brad asked quietly, his voice all the more menacing for its softness.

Sims gulped. "Yes, but only for a second. She didn't even want to come."

Brad stood. "You forced her to come into a restricted area?"

He swallowed. "Not exactly. I wanted her to see where I worked. I thought—"

The thud of Brad's balled fist against the desktop stopped Sims' explanation. "Dammit. Do you mean to tell me that you broke security to let a woman you've known for only a couple of days get to you so bad you put your job and the company you work for in jeopardy to impress her, when to everyone it was obvious she was conning you?"

Sims bowed his head. The bright sun glinted off his bald spot; his thin shoulders slumped in the ill-fitting tan suit. Michelle's heart went out to him. At last she understood the reason he wanted a private audience. The one thing she couldn't understand was why Brad had insisted she come along.

"If Patterson wasn't on the job, you'd be in jail keeping your lady friend company. You could have cost me over a quarter of a million dollars by acting like a teenager in the first wave of passion." If possible, Sims appeared to slump further. Brad turned away from him to the man sitting in front of the desk.

"And let's not forget about you, Richards. You let Little Miss Light-Fingers into a high-security building after hours, without a pass or clearance from me."

"I'm sorry, Mr. Jamison," he stated, raking a glance toward the cowering Sims. "He said it was okay."

"I'm sure it helped his argument that she was wearing a dress that was described as X-rated." Both Sims and Richards found something interesting to study on the gray carpet by their feet.

"When Patterson called me this morning, I planned to fire both of you, then make sure neither of you were able to get a job within a hundred miles of here." Both men gasped, defeat and horror shining in their eyes.

Brad's raised hand stopped their advances toward him. "I'm not going to do that now. For that, you both better thank the woman sitting behind my desk."

Once again three pairs of eyes swung toward Michelle, two thankful, one veiled in surprise. Waiting until he had the men's attention, Brad continued. "Next time, I advise both of you to look beyond the exposed skin to the woman beneath."

Coming around the desk, he took a stunned Michelle's elbow. "Patterson, a good job as usual. Although I sincerely hope that you won't contact me any more this weekend," Brad said, heading for the door. Patterson's dark head inclined slightly in understanding, as Sims and Richards gushed their thanks.

Opening the door, Brad looked at the smiling duo. "I don't give second chances." The door closed on their open-mouthed faces.

"Lois, we're not going to need your services after all," Brad said to his secretary, who was standing, in anticipation, outside the door. "I'd like for you to meet Michelle Grant. Michelle, Lois Hampton. The best executive secretary in the Bay Area."

Lois beamed. "Thank you, Mr. Jamison. Pleased to meet you, Ms. Grant."

Michelle's hand closed firmly around the other woman's outstretched one. "It's very nice to meet you, Ms. Hampton."

"We're off," Brad said. "Tell Patterson when he comes out that I meant what I said about not being available until after the weekend."

In the hallway, Michelle paused. "Why, Brad?"

"When I got the call from Patterson this morning and he explained the situation, all I could think about was how could any man be so gullible. Then I hung up and looked down at you. Your hair spread over my pillow, the heat of your flesh burning into mine. I realized that I was no different from Sims. The only difference was that I trust you with my life, and I know you'd never break that trust," he said solemnly, his thumb grazing her trembling mouth.

Bitter tears streamed down her cheeks and clogged her throat. She was worse than the woman who had used those two men to steal.

Michelle was stealing Brad's dream. How could she tell him now? It would hurt him too deeply. Especially after he had just showed her as a woman who could be trusted. Tears flowed faster at the hopelessness of the situation.

"Honey, don't cry. I promised myself I would never make you cry again."

"I don't deserve you," she said, her voice barely above a whisper.

Strong arms circled her shaking shoulders and pulled her to the shelter of his body. "You deserve better, but I'm getting there." After a quick squeeze, he pushed her away. Producing a handkerchief, he wiped away her tears, then kissed each eye. "No more crying. We're going to make memories, then I'm going to take you home and not let you out of bed until tomorrow."

They returned home just as the last rays of light turned the ocean into a sparkling jewel. Brad pulled Michelle down in front of the window and leisurely undressed her. By the time he unfastened her skirt, her fingers were on the last button of his shirt.

He came to her tenderly, cradling her body against his. Her eyes filled with tears. She couldn't lose him. Yet, she couldn't deny Nick his chance.

With his head bent, Brad licked the salty moisture away. "What's the matter, Michelle?"

He gave her the opening she needed, but the tenderness in his face forestalled her once again. "I'm just happy."

He frowned. "You cry when you're happy. You cry when you're sad or hurt. How am I to know the difference? It tears me up to see you cry and know I might be the cause of it."

She gently touched his cheek. "The only time I'll ever be unhappy is when I'm not in your arms. Always remember that," she pleaded, wanting to add *I love you*, yet knowing she no longer had the right.

"I never want to see you sad again." The velvet roughness of his tongue sought hers.

Once again she yielded to his mastery over her body, letting him drive away her fear and take her to their special place. She listened to his husky impassioned words mingled with those of her own, and knew that even as she was reaching for heaven, hell was her final destination.

The next morning the sun appeared to be as reluctant to begin the day's journey as the entwined couple. By noon the sun came from behind the clouds to begin burning the fog away. Brad and Michelle crawled from beneath rumpled sheets and headed for the shower. They said little afterward, each sensing that their idyllic time was over.

Buttoning her blouse, Michelle glanced up and saw Brad watching her. She tried to smile and failed.

Brad went to her. "Let's go for a walk on the beach again. I want to know if it was moonlight magic or if I really did hold the most beautiful woman in the world in my arms last night, and over the crash of the waves hear her chant my name, and feel her burn in my arms like leashed fire."

"Today is Sunday," she answered, the words stiff.

"Today is Sunday, but the weekend isn't over yet." His hands moved hers aside and began undoing the buttons. "On second thought, I have a better view of the beach from my bed."

Brad turned into Michelle's drive shortly before ten that night. Climbing out of the rental car, he retrieved her luggage from the trunk and followed her to the front door.

"You sure you won't change your mind and spend the night with me at my hotel?" he asked.

Biting her lower lip, Michelle unlocked the door and pushed it open. "I don't think that would be a good idea." Preceding him into the dimly lit hallway, she flicked on the overhead light in the den.

"It's the lies about your reputation, isn't it? I wish I knew who started those vicious rumors. They'd have to eat through a straw. I was a fool to believe that garbage for a second," he said tightly.

"It doesn't matter anymore." She turned away, knowing time was running out for her, for them, and placed her handbag on the sofa. "You can leave my things here."

Brad lifted a dark brow. "It wouldn't be any trouble to put them in the bedroom. Of course I'd like for you to show me the way again."

Her distracted hand plowed through her hair, lifted it away from her pinched face, and pushed it behind her ear. "Try to understand."

His smile faded. He tossed the flight bag over the arm of a chair and drew her into his arms. "I was just teasing, honey. You've been tense since we left San Francisco. I know we have some things to work out, and as soon as I close the deal on the Lazy R, we're going to have a long talk. For some reason the man has been stalling, but I intend to close the deal tomorrow. I don't want Marian interfering."

Michelle pushed out of his embrace. His black eyes widened, but Brad didn't try to touch her. "About the ranch—"

"We aren't going to discuss it. I know how sensitive you are about families, but there isn't any help for mine." Pulling her back into his arms, he kissed her. "Tonight is going to be a lonely one, but I expect to see you for breakfast." Turning, he left.

Michelle sagged into the nearest chair. What was she going to do? Faintly she heard the approach of Nick's wheelchair.

"Hello, Michelle. I was beginning to worry about you," Nick said, censure in his voice. "I thought you'd be home by now."

Michelle. So he was still upset. "Hi, Nick." Bone weary, she stood and picked up her flight bag and started to her room. She was too tired to argue with Nick. "I'm fine. Good night."

"You don't look fine. It's Jamis—"

"Please, Nick," she interrupted, near the breaking point. "Let it go."

His mouth flattened into a narrow line. "I can see you're tired, but with the rehab center back on schedule, you should be ecstatic, not looking like you're on your last legs. Despite what you say, I know it's because of Jamison," he said, his hands clamped on the arms of his chair.

"I'm going to bed." She started for her room again.

He followed her. "Don't you want to hear about Mr. Nash's call?"

She stopped abruptly and whirled, almost hitting her brother with her bag. "What did he want?"

Nick finally smiled. "To give me a job. You're looking at the new director of public relations for the Winslow Rehabilitation Center." The smile faded. "I guess that's why I was angry when you got home. I wanted to share it with you and you were with Jamison."

Tossing the bag aside, she hugged him. "I'm here now. I'll always be here for you, just as you've always been there for me. But that doesn't mean we have to exclude everyone else from our lives."

"I haven't asked you to do that," he flared.

Her laughter was hollow. "Yes you have, and I let you because I felt guilty because I left you when you needed me the most."

He caught her hand. "That wasn't your fault. That was Richard's."

She shook her head in denial. "It was my fault. I listened to the wrong man, believed his lies. But I'm not a kid any longer. I'm a grown woman capable of making my own decisions." She swallowed the sudden lump in her throat. "If they're wrong then I have to take responsibility. You can't shield me."

For a long time he looked at her, then away. "You're my sister. I love you."

She hunkered down in front of him. "I love you too. But you can't protect me from life."

His hand scrubbed over his face. "I'll try."

"That's all I ask." She hugged him again. "In case you didn't know it, I'm very proud of you."

He hugged her back. "I'm going to make you proud of me, Shelly."

She straightened. "I've always been proud of you."

"Well, I haven't. But things are going to change." He backed up his wheelchair. "You better get some rest."

Rest was the one thing she knew that she was not going to get that night. Her brother hadn't been that confident in years. The job offer had made him believe in himself again. If the rehab center didn't open, and she was the cause, he might never forgive her or regain his confidence. On the other hand, if Brad didn't get his grandparents' home back, and she was the cause, he'd never forgive her or stop hating his mother. As long as he carried the grudge against Marian, he'd never be completely happy.

She loved and wanted the best for both men, but there could only be one winner. And the loser would never forgive her.

CHAPTER SEVENTEEN

A frantic banging on the door, mixed with the persistent ringing of her doorbell, drew Michelle from a fitful sleep the next morning. She glanced at the clock and grimaced. Eight forty-five. She should have been up an hour ago, but after talking with Clint a little after seven that morning, she had finally been able to sleep.

The pounding worsened. Grabbing her robe, she went toward the door. She and Nick met in the hallway.

"Open this door!"

Brad! The apprehension Michelle had felt for the past two days escalated. He had found out!

"What the hell is wrong with Jamison?" Nick asked, going to the door.

Michelle stepped in front of him. "I'll take care of it." With trembling fingers, she opened the door.

Brad filled the doorway, his body vibrating with rage. His gaze flickered briefly to Nick behind her before the full force of his rage centered on Michelle. "Is it true?"

"Brad—"

"Dammit! No more lies. Is it true that you're the one trying to buy Clint's ranch from me?"

Her hand lifted toward his face. The burning fury in his midnight black eyes caused her to stop short of touching him. "Yes."

The mouth that had kissed her tears away twisted into a harsh, forbidding grimace. His arms were rigid, his balled fists tight; his body appeared to be carved in stone. Only the blazing hatred of his eyes showed any life.

An aching pain surged through her with the knowledge that whatever she said would not bring the tenderness back into his eyes. "Brad, I didn't know until you mentioned it to Marian that you were the other buyer," Michelle said, a yearning tenderness in her eyes that she made no attempt to hide. "I tried to tell you so many times, but I just couldn't find the words."

"You don't have to explain anything to him," Nick said. "He couldn't have thought that you would choose him over your brother."

A muscle jumped violently in Brad's temple. He seemed to hold his temper in check by sheer force of will.

"Nick, be quiet!" she shouted, then took a step toward Brad's rigidly held body. Tears streamed down her cheeks. She couldn't lose him. "I love you. I was wrong not to tell you. I

was afraid." She took another step. "Haven't
you ever done anything you regretted?"

"Yes," he ground out. "Trusted you."

Her eyes darkened with pain. She clutched
her stomach. "You can't mean that."

"You seem to have forgotten that Marian
made me an expert on deceit." His angry gaze
swept over her and Michelle felt chilled. "Although I must congratulate you. You even managed to get me to help you take away my
grandparents' ranch. Your little plan might have
succeeded if my lawyer hadn't become suspi-
cious when Clint wouldn't tell him why he
wanted to wait three weeks before selling."
Whirling, he started out the door.

She caught his arm, holding it despite the
coiled muscles bunched beneath her fingertips,
the blazing fury in his eyes. "I was wrong not to
tell you. Condemn me for that, but never doubt
my love for you."

"You don't know the meaning of the word
now, any more than you did nine years ago," he
said coldly. Her sharp intake of breath hissed
across the room.

Her mind whirled in confusion.

His smile chilled her to her very bones. "Oh, I
remember. You're more of a charmer than you
were then. I also remember telling you to spit in
the devil's eye. I never thought you'd become
his star pupil."

Icy fear twisted around her heart. Somehow

she had to make him understand. "I called Clint this morning and told him to sell to you." She ignored her brother's gasp of shock. "Doesn't that prove to you that I love you?"

"The only thing it proves is that you were afraid you might get caught," he said tersely.

She disregarded the slight tug of his arm. "Please, listen to me," she pleaded.

"I know, you love me," he sneered. "I'd rather have your hate. That, at least, is honest. You and Marian are a great pair. But this time I'm going to beat both of you."

Her fingers uncurled from around his arm and he walked away. Michelle didn't move, not even when the sounds of his car engine faded. She continued staring out of the door until Nick swung it shut. Her dazed eyes focused on him tugging on her hand.

"Come on, Shelly. Sit down."

Tears streaming down her cheeks, she didn't move. She felt too brittle, too raw. She couldn't take any more pain. Closing her eyes, she fought the sobs building in the back of her throat, yet knew that she battled in vain. When they came, hard and wrenching, her body sagged.

Strong arms closed around her, held her close, but they were not the arms that her body cried out for, that her soul needed for survival. "Oh, God. What am I going to do?"

No answer came. The only sound in the room

was her own cries of despair and defeat. Marian had been right. Why hadn't she listened?

She cried until her eyes were puffy and swollen, her throat raw and painful; until there were no tears left. Only then did she realize that she was sitting in her brother's lap. Since his accident, she had never sat in his lap. Her head rested on his broad shoulder, her arms circled her stomach.

"You really love him, don't you?" Nick asked gently.

"More than my life," Michelle answered.

He stroked her back. "You want to talk about it?"

Talking wouldn't help, but Nick needed to know the whole truth. "Brad saved me from a horrible experience nine years ago. I wasn't safe in a hotel as I told you later, I was alone on the beach, almost no money, and you had told me not to come home. Richard tried to attack me, and he would have succeeded if it hadn't been for Brad. He took care of me, asking nothing in return, until he could talk me into calling you."

"Shelly, oh honey." Nick's voice sounded as raw as her throat felt.

"And I thank him by trying to take away the only place where he has ever felt he belonged or felt he was loved." Slowly, she told Nick about Brad's childhood and his alienation from his mother and why. She finished by saying, "I couldn't betray him. I realized that if Brad didn't get the ranch, he'd never be able to forgive his mother and stop hating. He'd never be free. This morning I called Clint and told him I was withdrawing my support until after the sale to Brad."

"Your support?"

"Yes," she said, her voice as tired as she. "I took out a second mortgage on the house for the last hundred thousand dollars."

"This house? But you—" His eyes closed and he clutched her to him. "You make me feel like slime and ten feet tall at the same time."

Sitting up, she looked into his face. "You're not angry that I backed out?"

He shook his dark head. "How could I be when I know what the security of a home means to you? I'm angry at myself. I tried to run your life and your career. Your flamboyant image was my idea because I knew some men would come on too strong and others would be intimidated by it. Either way, you'd be turned off by them and I'd still have you with me." His brown eyes became shadowed. "You were right about me. I'm sorry.

"My greatest fear was that one day you'd leave me. Hearing the way you said Jamison's name, seeing the way your face softened, I knew even before seeing him that that day had come. I would have said or done anything to keep you two apart. But seeing the pain in his eyes, I realized that he cared about you too, and I couldn't

stand in your way and still be able to call myself
a man. Because that's what I am. I finally realized this chair didn't change that."

"Oh, Nick," Michelle cried, hugging his neck.
"I always knew one day you'd see that."

"If it hadn't been for you, I wouldn't have. I
know if it hadn't been for me, you would have
told Jamison everything." He pushed her away
and looked into her tear-stained face. "I've stood
in your way long enough. You deserve to be
happy. Go get dressed and make Jamison listen."

"Do you really think I can?" Hope shimmered
in her tear-filled eyes.

"You've never failed at anything else you
tried to do."

An hour later, Michelle entered her office building. The surreptitious glances of her co-workers
following her through the lobby caused her to
become uneasy. Obviously something was going on. Adjusting her sunglasses over her red,
swollen eyes, she headed for Alex's office. He
met her in the hallway.

"Michelle, may I see you in my office?"

"Of course," she answered to his retreating
back. Fighting the feeling of impending doom,
she followed him into his office.

Closing the door, he asked, "Now what the
hell is going on between you and Brad?"

Michelle blinked. Alex had never used profanity around her. Unsure of how to answer, she countered, "What are you talking about?"

"I'm talking about his dragging me from some very pleasant company early this morning to rage about what an unscrupulous woman you are. I tried to reason with him. It didn't do any good. I mentioned Nick and he started yelling more. What did you do to the guy? I've never seen him so angry," Alex finished.

Anguish seared her heart. "The buyer who topped the Foundation's original bid was Brad. The ranch once belonged to his maternal grandparents, but his mother sold it in a fit of anger at Brad. He's been trying to get it back ever since." Her hand gripped her purse tighter. "I found out Friday when we were in San Francisco together, but I was too much of a coward to tell him. His lawyers informed him this morning who I was and nothing I said would convince him that I hadn't tried to use him."

Alex nodded thoughtfully. "That explains why he insisted I come over here and get the key you had to Clint's gate."

Her eyes widened. "Brad was here?"

He shook his head. "No. Clint and another man picked up the key. I thought Clint acted rather edgy."

Her hand raked through her hair. "Alex, I have to talk to Brad and convince him that I love him. Now that he has the property, he might listen," she said. She'd tried calling him, but there was no answer.

"I'm sorry, Michelle. It's too late for that."

Fear twisted through her. "W-what do you mean?"

Alex pulled her against his chest. "He left for San Francisco as soon as his plane could be refueled. He also changed his mind about relocating. He mentioned something about there at least he knew who not to trust."

She sagged against him, and he gave her the final blow. "He's not coming back."

The door behind them opened, then slammed shut. Neither Alex nor Michelle acknowledged the presence of the newcomer.

"Must you have all the men?" Cassie demanded.

Michelle remained where she was, fighting tears, fighting misery. Brad was gone.

"Not now, Cassie," Alex said, annoyance in his voice.

"And why not? Half the town is buzzing because that nosy Mrs. Harden saw her and Brad at Fisherman's Wharf Friday. Michelle has most of the men in town wrapped around her finger, including you. Somehow I thought Brad had more sense," she spat.

"Cassie," Alex repeated through gritted teeth. "That's enough."

His sister spun on her heels, then slammed the door on her way out.

Michelle whimpered, and Alex's arms tightened. She stayed there a long time, then she realized that crying and feeling sorry for herself wasn't going to get Brad back. She had lost Brad by not facing her problems head-on as she had always done in the past. Not wanting to destroy her relationship with him, she had sought another way out. She should have remembered that, above all, he demanded honesty.

She pushed away from Alex. "What time do you think Brad's plane will land?"

Alex glanced at his watch. "About another hour and a half."

"That should give me enough time to speak with Clint and the Foundation." She pushed out of his arms and hurried to the door.

"Michelle," Alex called and she turned. "Don't let yourself be hurt anymore. Brad . . . Brad can be hard-nosed at times."

"I love him, Alex. I don't have much choice." The door closed behind her and she went to her office. She had three phone calls to make.

Resigning from the Foundation was easier than she had anticipated. Her one-hundred-thousand-dollar contribution went a long way toward repairing any hard feelings. To her surprise, Mr. Nash tried to talk her out of donating the money, insisting that Nick still had a job. She was adamant. Her next call was to Clint. He was equally pleased that everything had worked out. The third phone call was the hardest. Shaking hands lifted the receiver and dialed.

"Computron," answered a crisp female voice.

"Mr. Brad Jamison, please."

"One moment. Have a good day."

Two heartbeats later. "Mr. Jamison's office, Ms. Hampton speaking. May I help you?"

Michelle's grip on the receiver tightened. "Mr. Jamison, please."

"May I ask who's calling?" his executive secretary asked.

Michelle bit her lip. "Michelle Grant." A discernible pause filled the air.

"Mr. Jamison is in a meeting. Would you like to leave a message?"

If they didn't talk now Brad would continue to evade her. "Ms. Hampton, please tell him I said, Who's the coward now? I'll hold."

"Ms. Grant, I—"

"Please, just give him the message. I wouldn't ask you to disobey instructions if it wasn't important." Michelle closed her eyes and said a little prayer.

Another pause, then: "Please hold."

Michelle's head was still bowed. She said a prayer of thanks. The first hurdle was over. Now, if he would just pick up the line and listen.

"What do you want, Michelle?" Brad's tightly controlled voice snapped her upright in her seat.

For a brief moment her courage failed before she gathered her composure. "Hello, Brad."

"I'm busy. What do you want?" he rasped.

She hadn't thought he would make this easy. "I committed myself to obtaining the Lazy R months before I met you. I know I should have told you Friday, but please try to understand."

"Understand?" His control snapped. "Understand that while you lay in my arms for three nights, letting me go on about how much I trusted you, you were plotting behind my back to make a fool of me?"

"I told you that I didn't know until you told Marian."

"I suppose that you're also going to tell me that you forgot to mention that you personally donated the last hundred thousand dollars to beat me."

"I never meant to hurt you," she cried. "I love you."

"You don't love me. You used me. Richard taught you well."

Michelle held the phone until the loud, grating beep penetrated her foggy brain. Brad wasn't going to listen. Woodenly, she stood. She had survived once. She would do so again.

CHAPTER EIGHTEEN

Hours ticked into days, days into weeks. There were times when she wasn't sure if she could keep the false smile on her face another second. Going home was worse. The solace she once found in her bedroom had turned into taunting memories. Sleep was something she dreaded.

A pair of black eyes visited her in her dreams, one minute tender, the next burning in rage. Her state of mind wasn't helped by the office speculations on what had happened to make Brad decide to stay in San Francisco. Dana's sympathetic smile somehow made things worse.

Only Cassie appeared happy about their severed relationship. Michelle dreaded seeing her as much as she dreaded nightfall. But Cassie, like night, was inevitable.

"Hello, Michelle."

Michelle lifted her gaze from the papers she was going over to see Cassie, a grin on her face, strolling into her office unannounced. "Did you forget to knock?"

Cassie, in a figure-hugging white sheath, shrugged. "I don't have to. I own half-interest in this place," she said, picking up a crystal paperweight on Michelle's desk and tossing it in her hand.

"I'm busy, Cassie. Say what you came to say and leave."

The spherical-shaped object hit the desk with a thud. "Oops." Her grin widened.

Michelle resisted the urge to slap Cassie's face. Instead, she leaned back in her chair and crossed her arms. "You have two minutes."

"My, my, aren't you testy since Brad walked out on you."

Despite the constriction in her throat, Michelle smiled. "I may have lost him, but you didn't get him."

Cassie's beautiful face twisted in anger. "I will."

Michelle smiled although her insides were tied in knots. "Not if this weekend goes as planned." A lie to a selfish person like Cassie was excusable.

"I don't believe you!" She planted her hands on Michelle's desk and glared at her.

"I don't care what you believe. Your two minutes are up. There's the door." Michelle pointed in dismissal and picked up the forgotten papers.

"You can't have him! I'm sick of everything going your way. You're just a little nobody."

"Brad doesn't think so," Michelle said, turning over a sheet of paper and staring blindly at it.

"You're not going to have Brad. After I've had my say, he won't be able to stand the sight of you. You may have been able to get by the other rumors, but after I get through this time—" She stopped, but it was too late to recall the words.

Michelle's head jerked up to see Cassie's face frozen in fear. "Get out, Cassie."

"I'll deny everything!" she shouted.

Michelle surged to her feet. "Shut up! You tried to ruin my life because of your petty jealousy. We both know whom Alex will believe if I choose to tell him."

"You're not going to tell him?" Cassie was stunned.

"I won't hurt him because he has a scheming witch for a sister. Now get out of here," Michelle ordered. "If I ever hear another rumor, I'll go straight to Alex. Is that clear?"

Defeated, Cassie nodded.

Michelle watched the frightened woman leave, then grabbed her purse to follow suit. The queasiness she had felt for the past two days was becoming worse. Swallowing a wave of nausea, she vowed never to eat Mexican food again.

Two days later, Michelle was still ill. Drained from not being able to keep anything down, she lay in bed staring out at the waterfall. On the nightstand sat a carbonated drink and a half-eaten bowl of broth. They were the only things she felt up to eating. Nick was out of town doing some on-site training for his new job.

Another wave of nausea sent her racing to the bathroom. She barely made it. Once assured the sickness had passed, she splashed cold water on her face and brushed her teeth. The queasiness hit her again and her fingers tightened on the edge of the sink.

She studied her pale face in the mirror. Denial was no longer possible. She was going to have Brad's baby. A shaky hand moved to the womb nurturing their child, a myriad of emotions sweeping through her. She, of all people, knew the need for a child to have both parents. For hers, she had made that impossible. Knowing her reprieve was not going to last, she walked to the telephone and called her doctor. It was a Sunday, but her family practitioner was also a good friend.

The doorbell rang and Michelle slid her legs over the side of the sofa. The pharmacy delivery boy was cheerful and talkative. It hardly seemed fair when she felt so bad. Overpaying him for the prescription, she shoved him out the door. She went to the kitchen for a sip of water, then to bed.

Later that afternoon Michelle woke up, and for once, she didn't have to rush to the bathroom. Staring up at the ceiling, she tried to figure out what to do. One thing was certain: she was going to keep her baby. She had a good job. The hand stroking her stomach paused.

Alex was a friend, but he was also a businessman who had to think about his company. These were liberated times, but considering the rumors about her, her pregnancy might damage the reputation of Forbes Realtors. The final decision had to be made by Alex. Once again she picked up the phone and dialed.

Less than an hour later, Michelle opened her door to see Alex. The smile on his face shifted into a frown. "You don't look good. Are you all right?"

Closing the door, she turned. "I'm pregnant."

He stared at her in utter disbelief. "Oh, baby." Gentle arms drew her to him. "Have you told Brad?" She shook her head. "Don't you think he deserves to know?"

"I don't think he would want to know anything about either of us," she said, feeling her throat constrict with unshed tears.

"Brad may be hard, but he's fair. He won't turn you or the baby away," Alex told her.

"What if he does? I couldn't stand his rejection again." Michelle blinked away the moisture in her eyes. "The only thing predictable about him is his unpredictability."

"Call him."

"No, Alex. There's nothing left for Brad and me." She stepped back. "He's not why I called you. My pregnancy is going to give rise to a great deal of gossip. Do I still have a job?"

"The job is yours for as long as you want to work." He paused, then continued, "You know this is the Bible Belt, where people have strict moral codes; some of your clients are going to switch agents."

"I know." The almost-double mortgage payment on her home didn't leave room for too many clients to leave, but at least she had a job.

Alex's forefinger lifted her downcast chin. "Now that's settled, can we get back to Brad? He deserves to know."

She shook her head. Tears shimmered in her eyes. Pain lanced her heart. "Don't you think I want him with me? He doesn't love me, and telling him I'm carrying his baby is not going to change that."

Instantly she was back in Alex's arms. "It's all right, honey. Whatever you say. If I ever get my hands on Brad, he's going to regret hurting you."

She sniffed. "You'll have to get behind Nick."

"What did he say?"

"He's out of town. I haven't told him yet."

Alex's curse was explicit.

Michelle closed her eyes. "My thoughts exactly."

They were right. Nick went into a rage, yelling and calling Brad every foul name he had learned from his days as a professional football player. Only when Michelle became nauseated and left the room did Nick calm down. He followed her into the bathroom, then wet a cloth and wiped her face as she sat on the side of her bathtub.

"Don't worry, Shelly. It'll be all right."

Her gaze held his. "Nick, I want this baby."

His knuckles brushed back her sweat-dampened hair. "Would it do any good for me to call Jamison?"

"No." She'd never loved her brother more than at that moment.

"I'm sorry."

She looked at him with calm, determined eyes. "So am I, but I love my baby already, Nick. I won't regret the life growing inside me."

Nodding, he took her hand and squeezed. "How soon before I'll be an uncle?"

She almost smiled. "The end of February."

"I'll be here." His hand squeezed hers again. "Get some rest." Backing up the chair, he left.

• • •

July marched into August, hot and dry. Often Michelle felt as wilted as the parched flowers valiantly trying to survive in her front yard. Sensible pumps had long since replaced her four-inch heels. Her thickening waist would soon demand maternity clothes.

With a last look at her blue and purple petunias and violas, Michelle went inside. The cool air felt good against her perspiration-dampened skin. Calling a greeting to Nick, she started for her room. An oblong-shaped cardboard box on the sofa stopped her. Her body began to shiver when she saw the sender's address: The Doll House, San Francisco.

Sitting, before her legs gave way, she picked up the package. Her fingertips moved over the box. Brad still cared. She rushed to the kitchen for a knife.

Moments later, the African princess doll was in Michelle's trembling hands. The doll's skin was the color of dark chocolate. Her big brown eyes sparkled. Thick black braids peeked from beneath her intricately tied head wrap. Her exquisite ivory dress was accented with colorful tribal scarves. Leather sandals encased her dainty feet.

Brad remembered. He loves me!

Lifting out the wrapping paper and fillers, she searched for a card. She found none. A vague uneasiness sent her to the phone to call The Doll House.

Shortly afterward she replaced the phone.
Brad had ordered the doll the weekend they
were in San Francisco. Unmindful of the doll's
regalness, Michelle crushed her to her breast,
loving Brad more than ever. He cared once; perhaps he still cared. For all of their sakes, she had
to try one last time.

Two days later Michelle got out of the taxi in
front of Brad's house and smoothed her hand
over the peach-and-white floral silk dress she
wore. "Please wait," she said to the cabdriver
and started up the walk.

She'd come straight from the airport. It was
barely nine, but she wanted to catch Brad before
he left for work. Alex had called and checked his
schedule. Both he and Nick had wanted to
come, but she convinced them she needed to do
this alone.

She rang the chime and waited. The door
jerked open. Both she and Brad were momentarily caught in a time when words were gently
spoken and the two feet separating them would
not have been tolerated.

To Michelle, Brad looked as handsome as
ever. The weariness in his black eyes gave him a
vulnerability she found comforting.

Brad recovered first. "What are you doing
here, Michelle?"

"I need to talk with you. Five minutes is all I ask."

His hand fisted on the brass doorknob and for a second she thought he was going to close the door in her face, then he turned away leaving her to follow him into the great room. "Well?"

"I'm pregnant."

Hands stuffed into his jeans whipped out. "What?"

She swallowed. "I'm three months pregnant," she repeated, searching his face for a sign of happiness or softening and finding none.

Walking to the window, he asked, "What do you want? Money?"

I want you to look at me and hold me. I want you to tell me everything is going to be all right. I want your love. Unable to say those words, she said instead, "I thought that you should know."

"A letter or a phone call would have served the same purpose."

"I wanted to tell you in person."

Hard black eyes turned on her. "That's not all you wanted, Michelle. You wanted marriage. You'll have to take the alternative."

Shock rippled through her. Her hand automatically covered her stomach in a protective gesture. "No."

"I didn't mean that," he grated harshly. "I'm talking about adoption."

"I want to keep our baby."

A muscle leaped in his temple. "When do you plan to see this baby? You sometimes work up to fourteen hours a day. The kid will think the nanny or sitter is its mother." A bitter edge of cynicism tinged his voice.

"I won't give up our child. I spent too many days and nights wondering about my parents, thinking maybe it was something I had done for them to die and leave me."

"You're being selfish in trying to play the little mother."

"I'm not your mother," she said before she could stop the words. His nostrils flared with anger.

Michelle started to lift her hand to soothe away the pain she'd caused, but knew it would not be welcomed. Swallowing the growing lump in her throat, she tried to explain. "I shouldn't have said that. That was wrong of me. But please try to understand, I love this baby."

"You don't know what love is," he tossed back.

Sudden anger lit her eyes. She took a step closer to his rigidly held body. "I love you. Can't you see that?"

"No," he spat.

Suddenly the hopelessness of the situation overwhelmed her. "How do you want me to prove it, by walking off the nearest cliff?"

He stiffened as if she had hit him. "I don't want anything to happen to you now any more than I did nine years ago."

Joy that he remembered was tempered by the situation they were in. Her voice softened. "When did you remember?"

He smiled bitterly. "The night I met Nick. He ran your life then and he's still doing it."

Tears glistened in her eyes. This time he was pushing her out of his life instead of helping her to have one.

"Cheer up, Michelle. If I recall, your love for Richard didn't last past the hour he dumped you," he said curtly. "I'm honored you cared this long. However, I want more."

His callous words pushed her over the edge of caution. "You want! Nick wants! Clint wants! The Foundation wants! Does anyone care what I want, what I feel? I said I love you, and all you do is throw in my face what I did when I was an insecure teenager." Whirling, she ran for the door.

A steel grip on her wrist stopped her. "Michelle."

Pain-filled eyes stared up at his dark, carved features. Concern was there, but not love. "Don't worry, Brad. I have no intention of throwing myself over a cliff. I have a life growing inside me, and no matter what I want, when you love someone, what you want takes a backseat. Our baby doesn't know anything about life, but it wants to live, and I'd fight you and the devils of hell to make sure it has that chance." Her gaze touched his fingers clamped around her forearm, then flicked to his face, her eyes filled with resolve.

For a fraction of a second his curling fingers tightened. Hard black eyes searched brown defiant ones, staring at him through tear-spiked lashes. This time no tears followed. He had expected none.

She'd fight for her baby, but she wouldn't walk away from her brother for him. Marian had put his father and the magazine first, Michelle had put the baby and her brother in front of him. Brad was coming in a distant third . . . again. He stepped back.

She walked out the door toward the cab.

"Michelle?" Although Brad's voice was rough and uncertain, it accomplished what he wanted. Michelle turned. He wanted to see her face one last time. What he saw made the knife in his gut twist. He saw pain equal to his; he saw weary defeat. Her chin lifted. He checked the motion to drag her into his arms and damn the consequences. He saw acceptance.

"Yes?"

"If you need anything . . ."

Her harsh laughter ended as abruptly as it had begun. "Money won't buy what I need, and you won't give it freely. Good-bye, Brad. If you ever want to see your child you know where to find me. I hope you find whatever it is you're looking for."

Spinning on her heels, she walked to the cab

and got in. Instead of leaving, the cabdriver got out with a long rectangular box and brought it to Brad.

"The lady said to tell you that now you're even."

Brad's trembling hands closed around the box wrapped half in Christmas paper and half in birthday paper.

Sprinting back to the car, the driver got inside. It took every ounce of Brad's willpower not to run after the departing cab and beg Michelle to stay. Blindly reaching for the solidness of the door, he clutched it, then slammed it shut. Whirling, he didn't stop until he stood looking out the window at the ocean gently lapping against the shoreline.

For the first time in memory, he found no calming peace in its blue waters stretching into a cloudless horizon. This time it yawned as empty as he. He was no longer complete without Michelle. After three months, he still reached for her warmth in the night and came back with a damning fist of loneliness. Neither the ranch nor anything else meant anything to him if it cost him Michelle.

Sitting down on the hassock, he tore the paper off the box, knowing what he would find inside, yet dreading it. A train set. A lump formed in his throat. His eyes stung. Denial was no longer possible. He loved Michelle and with each ragged breath he drew, he realized that he always would. Neither time nor distance would change what he felt for her. But could he say the same for Michelle?

He was certain she felt something for him, but would it last past passion, past her need for a father for their baby? If it didn't, could he go through the pain of losing her or was it better, safer for him to let her walk out of his life now?

"When you love someone, what you want takes a backseat."

Michelle's words came back to him and his eyes closed against a wave of loneliness. Then, just as abruptly, they snapped open. She wasn't choosing the baby over him, she was choosing the baby in spite of him . . . loving unconditionally with no guarantees of being loved in return by the child she carried, or the father.

A woman capable of giving that much love didn't use people. Brad realized with a calming certainty that Michelle had spoken the truth. She loved him. The constriction in his chest eased. She and their child needed him just as much as he needed them. Standing, he moved to the phone.

All Brad got out was *Hello* before Alex tore a strip off his hide. Knowing he had it coming, Brad waited until Alex finished, then asked about Michelle's return flight plans.

"It's about time you stopped being so stubborn. American, flight 262."

"Thanks. I guess you can be my best man," Brad said, grinning.

"I am the best man," Alex countered with his usual aplomb.

Smiling, Brad hung up the phone. The train set still under his arm, he started to get his car keys. The sharp chime of the doorbell interrupted him. Chafing at the delay he went to the front door and jerked it open.

The words already formed to get rid of the caller died in his throat. Two policemen stood there.

"Brad Jamison?"

A tingle of dread clawed up his spine. "I'm Brad Jamison."

The larger and older of the two asked, "Do you know a Carolyn Michelle Grant of Dallas, Texas?"

"For God's sake, what is it?" he demanded, grabbing the man's uniform.

The policeman let Brad's hand remain where it was. The officer reached out and placed his hand on Brad's tense shoulder. "The cab she was riding in had an accident."

"No-o-o-o!" The tortured cry was caught by the endless wind and hurled to the rocky shores of the cliffs below.

CHAPTER NINETEEN

"Michelle. Michelle. Wake up, I need you."

Michelle clawed her way through the dense fog. Brad needed her. He was calling her name. He sounded hurt. Tears were in his voice. That couldn't be right. Brad would never cry.

"Michelle, sweetheart, wake up. It's me, Brad. Please, Michelle, open your eyes. I can't lose you."

Relentless fingers gripped her arm and gave her the final stimuli needed to lift her heavy lids. Blinking them to clear the last haziness, her gaze settled on Brad's face, ravaged and streaked with tears he made no attempt to wipe away.

"Who . . . who hurt you?" she whispered.

"I told you she was going to be all right," came an impatient voice from somewhere out of her field of vision.

"Who hurt you?" she repeated.

For the first time since he'd learned of her accident, the tension left Brad's body. "You did, by drifting in and out of consciousness for the past two hours."

Her brows furrowed, then she felt the throbbing ache over her left eye. Banished initially by her concern for Brad, it now pounded with the force of a thousand drums. Her eyes clamped shut.

"Dr. Foster!"

Brad's anxious cry snapped her eyes open, but instead of seeing his face a light shone in her eyes. "Follow the light, Ms. Grant. Yes, that's it. Now look at my nose. Good. How many fingers?"

"Three," Michelle answered the ebony-hued man who had a pair of glasses perched on his nose. He turned to Brad.

"Do you see and hear enough to concur with my diagnosis that it is only a slight concussion, or do you think we should take another skull series or an EEG?"

Brad came back instantly with a reply. "Only if you're sure it's not going to harm our baby."

A sharp cry from the bed caused both men to whirl. Brad almost knocked Dr. Foster over in his attempt to reach Michelle. "What's the matter, honey? Does something hurt?"

Michelle had difficulty getting the words past the knot in her throat. "The . . . the baby is all right, isn't it?"

"Your baby is fine," Dr. Foster answered. "Which is more than I can say about the father, until you woke up."

"I don't think Michelle wants to hear this." Brad shifted from one foot to the other.

"Oh, yes, I do," she said, wondering why Brad was nervous.

The doctor smiled, obviously relishing the chance to tell his story. "Brad was a basket case from the time the policemen contacted him about your accident. They had called your brother, and he told them you were in San Francisco to see Brad, so they contacted him. They tried to tell him you were going to be all right, but he wouldn't listen. They were afraid to let him drive, so they brought him to the hospital. I understand Brad became angry when they refused to use the siren. He then tried to get out of the moving police car."

The amusement slipped from Michelle's face. "Brad!"

"There's more," Dr. Foster said with a gleam in his dark eyes. "He came through the emergency room demanding to see you before your attending physician had time to complete your exam. When Brad told him that you were pregnant and the man appeared surprised, Brad assumed he was an incompetent and demanded they call the head of obstetrics and the head of neurology. If he hadn't been recognized as my stepson, he'd be in a padded cell by now."

Michelle's eyes rounded. "You're Marian's husband."

"Yes," Dr. Foster answered. "Proud of it too."

His gaze cut toward Brad. "She's a fine woman. When I was advised of the situation, I told them to contact her." He shook his graying head, grinning. "I've never seen Marian anything but poised and immaculately groomed. She was at the beauty salon under the dryer. She lost her scarf, and her hair was going in all directions. I don't think she noticed or cared. I understand from the moment she hit the door, she became more of a tiger than Brad."

"I've never seen her that way," Brad said softly, as if still unable to picture his mother as the woman who'd helped keep him sane until he could see Michelle.

"To tell you the truth, neither have I." Dr. Foster folded his arms. "Instead of trying to talk some sense into Brad, she agreed with him, then had the doctor call me on my car phone, even though I was en route here, for a consultation."

"Are you an obstetrician?" she asked, still trying to take it all in.

"No. I'm chief of staff and head of neurology. What day is today?" he asked out of nowhere.

Both men watched her closely. "Wednesday."

"What are doctors all over the country doing on Wednesday?" Dr. Foster continued.

"Playing golf," came Michelle's meek reply.

Sighing, he unfolded his arms. "For once I was winning too."

"I'm sorry, Dr. Foster, that they called you needlessly," she said, liking his kind manner.

"They didn't. I didn't want to let him know it, but for a while I was concerned about you myself," the doctor told her.

Brad's grip tightened on her fingers. Michelle glanced up into his frightened face. The accident came spiraling back. "I-I saw the other car coming toward us and I knew the cabdriver was either going over the cliff or he would hit the other car on the narrow road." She swallowed, recalling the driver's muttered curse, the sickening sound of metal grinding against metal, her own terrified screams.

"I had lost Brad. I couldn't face losing our baby too. I didn't want to wake up." She looked up at Brad, felt the moisture on her cheek; whose she didn't know or care. "Then I heard you calling me and I thought you needed me."

"I do, Michelle, more than life." His head bent, his lips taking hers in a kiss filled with tender passion.

Dr. Foster smiled. "It looks like we're going to lose a patient in the morning if you keep doing well."

"The cabdriver and the man in the other car, how are they?" Michelle asked.

"A broken wrist, bruised ribs. Both were sent home and advised to rest," he answered, slipping his hands into the pockets of his white lab coat. "I'd prescribe the same for you, but somehow I don't think that's necessary."

Brad grinned. Michelle blushed.

The doctor turned to leave, but Michelle stopped him. "Please tell Marian thanks."

"She's outside. Would you like to tell her yourself?"

Before Michelle could answer, Brad spoke, the hard edge back in his voice. "That's not necessary. I've already thanked her."

Dr. Foster's eyes narrowed.

"I haven't," Michelle said into the strained silence.

With a warning look at Brad, Dr. Foster went to the door and opened it. Almost immediately, Marian filled the doorway, her hands clutching her bag. Her husband took her arm when she made no move to enter. Marian stopped a few feet inside the door. Her uncertain gaze sought that of her son.

Michelle glanced up at Brad, saw his expressionless face, then looked back at the other woman who was turning to leave. "Thank you, Marian. From all three of us," Michelle said, one hand in Brad's, the other reaching out to his mother.

Slowly Marian crossed to the bed and took the outstretched hand. Tears glinted in her eyes. "Thank you." Both women knew she was thanking Michelle for trying to heal the discord between son and mother. "You had us worried," Marian continued.

"I heard," Michelle said. "I'm glad you were there with Brad."

Marian looked at her son, who refused to acknowledge her. "So am I," she whispered softly.

Michelle waited for Brad to thank his mother, but he remained silent, his attention once again on Michelle. He had to realize that this wasn't easy for her. She'd admittedly made a mistake, but she was doing her best to make up for it.

"Enough talking," Brad said as he continued to hover over Michelle. "You need to rest. Besides, I'm sure that with her busy schedule Marian has someplace to go."

Marian's hand trembled in Michelle's; her gaze, however, was steady. "Nothing is as important as seeing that you, Michelle, and the baby are all right."

He finally turned to her, his voice and eyes cold. "You've played the devoted mother, and I thank you for helping Michelle, but nothing has changed between us."

His mother's smile was heartbreakingly sad. "I didn't think it would. For the first time in your life since you were a baby, you needed me. That was something I needed." She looked at Michelle. "If there is anything I can do, the nurse has our number. We'll be home all evening."

"You don't have to do that," Michelle said.

"Yes, I do," Marian said firmly.

Dr. Foster draped his arm around his wife's shoulder. The smile he sent Michelle was warm; the one he sent Brad, challenging. "Call if you need us. I'll okay it for you to spend the night.

That chair opens into a bed." Nodding curtly, he turned to leave with Marian by his side.

"Brad," Michelle whispered, her eyes speaking volumes as she nodded toward the retreating backs of his mother and stepfather.

Brad looked at Michelle, loving her more with each passing second, then thought of the hell he had gone through when he thought she didn't love him. No one should be put through that. It was time he grew up. Squeezing her hand, he glanced around. "Thank you both. Marian, would you mind picking us up in the morning? I don't have my car."

His mother and stepfather stopped and looked back. Marian was wiping away tears, but she was smiling. Her husband was smiling also. "I'll be here. I'll bring Michelle some clothes too. Good night." The door closed.

Michelle squeezed his hand. "I'm proud of you."

Brad kissed her lips. "If you can forgive me, I can do the same for Marian. We all make mistakes. I'm just happy you had more courage than I did."

"You taught me." She beamed up at him.

"No, you taught me." Reaching for the white telephone on the bedside, Brad dialed Nick's number. "Nick, this is Brad." Pause. "Yes, she's fine." He stroked Michelle's cheek. "The doctor wants her to stay the night. I'll bring her home as soon as he says it's all right. Sure. Here she is."

Michelle didn't take the phone. Tears sprang to her eyes. "Don't you want me to stay with you?"

"We'll call back in a few minutes," Brad said, then hung up. Framing her face in his hands, he said softly, "I want you, I need you, I love you," punctuating each word with a kiss. "I have never told that to another living soul, and I probably won't again until our child is born. Your accident made me realize how selfish I was and how uncertain life can be. But even before the policemen arrived, I was coming to find you." He swallowed, recalling the terror he'd felt on learning she'd been hurt.

"I had no right to expect you to turn your back on everything when I wasn't willing to do the same for you. I want you any way I can have you. I want to marry you and keep you with me every possible moment. If you want a career, then we'll work it out together. The main thing is that we're together. I'm not used to sharing and I may get a little selfish at times, but don't give up on me."

Her heart and her face filled with love. "That's all right. We'll work it out. I want you and our baby. I love you, Brad. I never want to lose you."

"You won't." Reaching into his pocket, he pulled out two heavily scrolled keys and placed them in her open palm. "The ranch is yours. Grandfather was the only person who never expected the impossible of me. I loved the land, but I love you more. We'll create our own dynasty." His lips brushed across her forehead.

Tears glistened in her eyes. "I can't let you do that. The rehab center is to make dreams possible. It can't do that if the Foundation is built on the destruction of someone else's dream. Together, we'll find another site."

"Are you sure?"

"I'm sure."

He took the keys. "Your capacity for love is amazing."

She smiled up at him. "I've been saving up for the past nine years."

His lips brushed across hers. "So have I. You saved me that night as much as I saved you."

"What do you mean?" she asked with a frown.

"I'll tell you one day. Now go to sleep before they put me out of here." Still holding his hand, she did.

"How do you feel?"

Thirty-one hours later, nestled in the curve of Brad's arms, Michelle smiled. "Wonderful, and please don't flash that penlight into my eyes again," she begged. Brad had insisted on checking her pupils every hour since they had left the hospital.

Low laughter rumbled from his chest. He hugged her naked warmth. "I love you,

Michelle. I may be overprotective for a little while." He lay back down beside her.

Rising on her elbow, she stared down into his face draped in moonlight. "Other than the light, I am enjoying this attention from the man who restored my dreams, and banished the shadows from my heart. I always wanted someone to love me."

"You're my strength, Michelle. Eternity wouldn't be enough time to show you how much I love you."

Sharp teeth nipped his lip. "Then you'd better get busy."

He did, to the everlasting pleasure of them both.

Read on for a bonus short story by Francis Ray

Maybe This Time

CHAPTER ONE

"Amelia, David said he'd love me forever," Simone cried as she buried her beautiful face against her sister's shoulder, her sobs shaking both their bodies.

Closing her arms tightly around the hunched shoulders of her younger sister, Amelia wished that she could take the pain away as she had been doing since their parents' death in an automobile accident ten years ago, when Simone was twelve and Amelia was twenty.

"Simone," Amelia whispered. "I'm sorry."

Simone lifted her dark head. Tears sparkled in her big brown eyes. "You tried to warn me, but I wouldn't listen." She hiccupped. "You said men aren't to be trusted."

The almost indistinguishable sound of a snort coming from across the den drew Amelia's attention against her will. *He was still there.*

Although Shane Saunders hadn't said a word since he'd led a hysterical Simone into her house in East Dallas thirty minutes earlier, it was difficult if not impossible for Amelia to ignore him for long. Why had her sister brought her neighbor—this particular neighbor—with her?

Three inches over six feet, his commanding presence permeated the room. One broad shoulder, encased in a crisp white shirt, was braced against the oak mantel of the natural stone fireplace. The top four buttons of his shirt were unfastened, allowing a disturbing view of black whorls of hair on his wide chest. Folded arms crossed a flat stomach. The heel of his hand-tooled, eel-skin boot was snagged on the hearth. Faded denim jeans hugged and caressed long muscular legs.

But it was to his face that Amelia's eyes always returned. Square and angular, it reeked of authority. Although not handsome, it was a face that, once seen, you'd never forget. The eyes—black, vital, absorbing—wouldn't let you. Eyes that revealed nothing and saw everything.

Simone calling Amelia's name drew her attention back to her sister's tear-streaked face. Berating herself that she could be looking at a man when her sister was going through one of the most traumatic moments of her nine-month marriage, Amelia firmly turned her gaze and her thoughts away from Shane.

"What did David say?"

Drawing herself out of her sister's arms, Simone sat up on the beige leather sofa. She tunneled her fingers though her stylishly layered hair. "He said he was comforting Lois. He said his secretary had been having marital problems. She brought some papers to the house from the law firm for him to sign." She nodded toward Shane. "He saw them, too."

Shane pushed away from the mantel and strode across the room, his measured footsteps soundless on the deep white carpet. Hunkering down in front of Simone, he took her trembling hands into his large ones, his gaze fixed on her face.

"Simone, a thousand people can see the same thing and each one interprets it differently," Shane said quietly.

The deep rumble of his voice caused Amelia's hands to clench. The tone was as caressing as his thumb appeared to be as it stroked Simone's delicate wrist.

"I love him," Simone answered softly. She turned her head to her sister, her troubled gaze seeking reassurance.

Shane's followed.

Clamping her hands together tightly in her lap, Amelia fought her own battle. She was not going to let the forceful pull of Shane's enigmatic black eyes disturb her any longer. She did distrust men; because of it she hadn't dated for the past four years and wanted it no other way. Until now. Until Simone's neighbor, Shane Saunders.

And that scared Amelia as nothing else ever had.

"Amelia, do you think I should go home?"

No, she thought, but from the hopeful look on Simone's beautiful face that wasn't the answer she wanted to hear. Despite David Taylor being a spoiled only child who played at being a lawyer in his father's prestigious law firm, and spending more time with his customized Porsche than he did with Simone, she loved him.

"Simone, I can't tell you what to do, but I'll always be here for you," Amelia said, trying for a middle-of-the-road approach.

Simone bit her lower lip. "I suppose a phone call wouldn't hurt. I was so upset after I saw David with his arm around Lois on the sofa, their faces almost touching, that I dropped the shopping bags I was carrying. David stumbled over Lois's briefcase and fell as I ran out of the house crying. But he did call my name." She looked at Shane. "Thank goodness you were just getting home, that you agreed to drive me over here. I don't know how I would have managed. First you rescue Amelia, and now me."

Again Amelia felt the pull of Shane's gaze just as she felt the heat in her cheeks. Two weeks ago, Simone had brought him with her the night Amelia had locked herself out of the house. About to go to bed, she'd remembered she hadn't cut the sprinkler off in the back yard. She'd gone outside to do so, the door had swung shut—and she'd been locked out.

She'd called Simone from her car cell phone,

asking her to bring the spare key she had. In less than ten minutes, a car had pulled up in her driveway. The powerful beam of Shane's Ferrari had slashed through her cotton nightgown as if it were tissue paper. That had been the first time they had met, and she still hadn't recovered from the experience. She had seen him off and on since Simone and David had moved into the Preston Hollow neighborhood shortly after they married. For some odd reason, she could never understand why seeing him always made her restless.

"Did you take my advice and hide an extra key in the garage?" Shane now asked in the growing silence.

"Yes," Amelia said tightly. "I won't get locked out again."

Shane's heated gaze swept her body. "Pity, I'm beginning to enjoy rescuing beautiful women."

Simone managed a shaky laugh. "If the number of women I see going in and out of your house is any indication, you already have your hands fu—"

The frantic peal of the doorbell cut Simone off. Her hopeful gaze flickered to her sister. "Maybe that's David."

Amelia rose. As soon as she opened the door, Simone's husband pushed his way inside.

"I want to see Simone. I know what a man-hater you are, but I won't let you destroy my marriage," he snapped. Tall and boyishly hand-some in a gray tailored suit, he started for the den and abruptly halted when he saw Shane kneeling in front of Simone, her hands in his. "Get away from my wife, Saunders."

Shane's black eyes blazed like a stoked fur-nace for a split second, then faded to nothing. Pushing to his feet in one graceful motion, he stepped away. David and Simone rushed into each other's arms.

After a few moments Simone said, "Amelia, I'm going home with David."

"If that's what you want," Amelia replied. There wasn't a hint of happiness in her voice. She wished Simone would have stayed, but she was old enough to make her own decisions.

"It is," David said, quickly leading Simone from the room. She barely had time to say good-bye before the door shut with a resounding slam.

The moment Amelia had dreaded and feared since Shane walked through the door had ar-rived. They were alone.

"Are you?"

Amelia slowly turned to Shane. "Am I what?"

"A man-hater."

How Amelia wished that that were true; then she wouldn't be having crazy, irrational thoughts about this man who left her body hot and flushed. "No. I simply think men use women for their own gain," she said, her voice just short of contempt.

"I see." Shane walked closer until she could smell the citrus aftershave he wore. "You mean, just like women use men."

The truth of his statement somehow angered Amelia. "Thank you for helping Simone. Now, if you'll excuse me, I have work to do." Stiff-backed, she walked to the door and opened it. Shane didn't move.

"He really did a number on you, didn't he?"

Amelia's head lifted regally. "Yes, he did and so did the man after him." Shane's eyes widened. "You see, I'm a slow learner. But once I learn something I don't ever forget."

Shane started toward her, his gait slow and predatory. Inches away, he asked, "If you learned so well, why is the pulse in your throat beating like a hummingbird's wing?"

Her hand flew to her neck. He stepped closer. She retreated until her spine flattened against the wall in the entryway.

"I've dreamed of you since I saw you silhouetted in the beams of my headlights, your hair flowing around your shoulders, you body so enticing in that long white gown." A calloused thumb grazed her trembling lips. "In my dreams you open your arms to me. Guess what comes next?"

"Don't." She hated the vulnerability in her voice as much as she wanted to hate him for putting it there, for making her want a man she couldn't, wouldn't trust.

"Why?" he asked.

The deep timbre of his voice stroked her. Her tongue darted out to wet her dry lips. His thumb touched the dampness of her mouth, then he lifted his thumb to his mouth and tasted her moistness.

Desire ripped through her, tightening her nipples, making a mockery of her earlier words. She wanted him. They both knew it.

Suddenly he stepped back. "Have dinner with me tonight?"

She blinked. She hadn't expected the reprieve, nor did she want to think even for a second that perhaps he had a sense of honor. She would be a fool to go out with a man who could melt her resistance just by looking at her. "No, thank you."

"I thought you'd say no."

Surprise knitted her brows. "Then why ask unless...." She stiffened. "If you're finished playing games, please leave."

His expression hardened. "I wasn't playing games. If I were, you'd be under me right now with your—"

Her trembling fingertips pressed against his lips to stop the sensual image he was creating. His hot tongue darted across her skin. Air hissed through her teeth as she jerked her hand away. "Why are you doing this?"

"Because I want you and you want me."

Amelia shook her head as if dazed. "Men

taught me long ago that wanting wasn't enough, that it wasn't always what it seemed to be."

His sensual lips flattened into an uncompromising line. "I don't want to hear about the other men in your life."

The harsh condemnation in his voice wiped the lingering desire away. "Since we won't be seeing each other again, I can guarantee that I'll comply with your wishes." She edged past him to open the door. "Good-bye, Mr. Saunders."

He walked out the door; sunlight glinted on his black hair. "We'll play it by your rules for now, Amelia, but consider yourself forewarned. I'm not going to let your fears keep us apart. I don't plan to give you up."

"You don't have me to give up."

"Don't I?"

Amelia slammed the door in his face. Hands clenched by her side, she berated herself for letting him see how attracted she was to him. Usually she was calm and unflappable, handling men's advances with little effort. Shane had slipped through her usual defenses as if it had been child's play. Instinctively she knew that what Stephen and Clayton had done to her would be infinitesimal to the heartache Shane could put her through.

Wrapping her arms around herself she walked back into the den and sat down on the sofa. Stephen had been her college sweetheart. After her parents' death, she'd dropped out of college to take care of Simone. A month later she had made a surprise visit to see him and found herself surprised.

His frat brothers were throwing Steven a bachelor party. But the intended bride wasn't Amelia. He had been engaged for the past year to a girl from his hometown. She had cried and consoled herself that at least she wasn't marrying the cheating jerk. Five years later she met Clayton at a block party.

Clayton was older, sophisticated, with his own business and two small children. He had been good with Simone, undemanding and supportive while Amelia tried to juggle work, finish her degree part-time, and care for Simone. When he proposed six months later, she had said yes. Immediately, he wanted to look for a bigger house in a better neighborhood.

It wasn't long before it became clear to Amelia that Clayton had proposed because he needed a mother for his children. The wedding had been cancelled. She and Simone had moved into the house Amelia now lived in, and she had given up on men. Her judgment was too poor.

Being attracted to a man like Shane Saunders proved it. Restless, she pushed to her feet. A man with that kind of sex appeal had probably left a lot of women crying behind him. She wouldn't be one of them.

"Forget him," she told herself. "You have work to do."

Amelia went into her office, a converted bedroom, next to the den and sat at her neat, old-fashioned desk. She didn't need any man. She pulled down six figures with her own secretarial/accounting business which she'd run from her home for the past four years.

She went back to adding the quarterly receipts of a client. The column of numbers swirled, faded. In their place Shane's face appeared, his eyes vivid, alluring and promising the fulfillment of her every unspoken fantasy.

She snapped the ledger closed and leaned back in the chair. Forgetting Shane was going to be more difficult than she thought.

CHAPTER TWO

Wearing only a frown, Shane dove into the swimming pool in his back yard. His strokes were long and powerful. Sexual frustration drove him from one end of the pool to the other again and again.

What was there about Amelia Dennison that captivated him? Since the first time he had seen her, her black eyes huge, her lips parted in surprise, he had wanted her. The surge of desire had struck him in the solar plexus like an iron fist. The white gown had been transparent in his headlights, revealing her lush breasts, small waist, and long legs.

Desire pounded through him again, and he stroked harder. He didn't need this. Usually women ran after him, not the other way around. Yet, he knew it wasn't him they wanted. They wanted the prestige and the wealth he represented as the executive with a Fortune 500 company. Somehow, he knew if Amelia learned how wealthy he was, it wouldn't make the slightest difference. Whatever had happened in her past she didn't trust men and she certainly didn't trust him. But how could he change that if she wouldn't talk to him for more than five minutes or go out with him?

No closer to a solution, he climbed out of the pool, grabbed a towel and dried his face. Rubbing his chest, he walked back into the house and stopped as he saw the gift-wrapped packages covering the floor in the family room. The first smile in an hour lifted the corners of his mouth. Cody was coming tomorrow.

Cody was out of his private school for the summer, and he was spending the entire time with his father. After asking for weeks, Vivian had finally agreed to let Cody stay with him for the summer once Shane had assured her she'd continue to receive the same amount of money in child support. Besides, Vivian would be on vacation in Europe. Although she had gone into one of her tantrums, charging that he was wrong in thinking that the reason for her objections was monetary, Shane hadn't been fooled. Vivian went through money like water. She splurged on herself, but she also spent on Cody. Most of the clothes in the suitcase he'd unpacked after they came home from the airport were new.

Now that he had Cody, Shane reluctantly admitted that he didn't know what to do with his son for twelve weeks. While other children had cried or fidgeted during the hour flight from Austin this morning, Cody had sat quietly in his seat. The coloring books and games had been ignored.

Shane had interviewed several women for the position as housekeeper/sitter, but none of them had seemed right. A week ago he'd decided to care for Cody himself and had taken the early buy-out his company was offering.

Now what?

His smile vanished. Things between him and his only child would be different this time. They had to be. A month had passed since they'd seen each other. Surely his son would talk to him this time? He talked to everyone else, why wouldn't he talk to his father?

Because he hates you.

Shane shut his eyes, remembering the most painful words his ex-wife could have thrown at him. But he didn't believe it. Vivian had been spiteful and lying, lashing out at him because he had filed for the divorce. His son was only four years old. He couldn't hate his father. Tomorrow would be different. It had to be.

"Don't you like the toys I bought you, Cody?" Shane asked for seemingly the hundredth time. Each time he'd received the same blank look from his son that he was giving him now. Tall for his age, Cody was a miniature replica of his father, with black hair and eyes that were too solemn for a four-year-old.

Frustration caused Shane's chest to tighten. With effort he tried to keep his face calm as he glanced around the toy-strewn den. Everything that had walked, talked, squeaked or beeped on the commercials that past Saturday was now on his floor. Scared that he might not have gotten the "in" toy, he had called a few of his friends and asked what was popular with their little boys. Electronic games were the consensus. But Cody didn't want those any more than he had wanted the toy that propelled itself.

Putting the Game Boy aside, Shane pulled his small son into his arms. He waited for the child's slim arms to circle his neck, but they never did. Shane closed his eyes, fighting the stinging sensation in them and just held on.

"You don't have to play with the toys if you don't want, Cody. You're just tired from the plane trip." Even as the words formed, the image of a playful, happy child at the zoo who had laughed and giggled and called Shane "Daddy" materialized. Shane's arms tightened. That was almost a year ago, before the divorce. Cody had not spoken to him or called him Daddy since then.

Shane had filed for divorce and moved out of the house he and Vivian shared that day after he and Cody visited the zoo. He had expected to gain custody because of his wife's notorious affairs. He had been wrong. The judge didn't think Shane's high-powered job, which required a lot of time away from home and extensive traveling, would provide a stable environment for a young, impressionable child. Despite Shane assuring the judge that he'd quit his job, the judge had ruled in Vivian's favor. Shane was granted one weekend a month for visitation.

In a matter of days, Vivian had moved from Dallas to Austin, putting unnecessary distance between him and his son. Shane knew she had done it to hurt him. By the time he saw Cody again the laughter was gone from his face.

Now he was a different little boy. Everyone, including his own parents, blamed Shane. They reasoned he shouldn't have filed for divorce until his son was older. At the very least Shane should have sought help from a marriage counselor.

But Shane knew that a hundred years and twice that many marriage counselors wouldn't have changed things. The love he and Vivian had once shared was gone, if she had ever loved him at all. After they were married, she'd changed almost overnight from a sweet, caring woman to a selfish shrew. A counselor couldn't have said anything to transform her. Shane hadn't seen it while they were dating, but he'd soon learned that Vivian loved herself best. She tolerated Shane because of the big bucks he made that allowed her to quit her marketing job and stay home. If she hadn't become pregnant with Cody three months into the marriage, Shane would have left sooner.

"How about a drive? We can go see the ducks in the park or get an ice cream cone. What's your favorite?" Shane asked, holding Cody's little body away from him. No answer came, only another blank stare. This time Shane didn't need any words from his son. What caring father had to ask his four-year-old what his favorite ice cream was? Vivian always said sweets made Cody hyperactive and insisted they be kept to a minimum. Shane almost wished that were the case now.

Shane pulled Cody back to him, his hand palming his son's dark head. "It will be better, Cody. I promise."

Three hours later Shane turned into the affluent Preston Hollow neighborhood, his hands clamped around the steering wheel of his new Volvo. Cody hadn't paid any attention to the ducks or to the animals at the zoo. But Shane now knew what kind of ice cream his son liked . . . fudgesicles.

They'd been slowly making their way through the fifty-four flavors at the ice cream parlor when Shane turned to offer Cody another sample. He'd seen his son opening the freezer case. Reaching inside he had picked up a fudgesicle, grabbing one for each hand. He'd carried the prize back to his father, then tore the paper off and began to eat.

A car horn tooted behind him. He glanced into his rear-view mirror. His heart rate sped up. Behind him, Simone was driving her two-seater convertible Benz, smiling and waving. It was the person in the passenger seat who drew his gaze again and again. Amelia. She was looking out the window. Even in the mirror he could see that her body was stiff. She didn't want to see him. Tough. He needed to see her. He needed the soothing effect of her presence, even if she gave it grudgingly.

He didn't understand that need because she frustrated him and made him angry. Perhaps because she tried so hard to hide her vulnerability. She mistrusted men and had put up a defensive wall. He might have felt the same way about women after his divorce, but he had met too many good women before and after his divorce.

Pulling up in the driveway of his house, Shane unfastened his and then Cody's seat belts, and walked across the street, holding Cody's small hand in his. Walking up to the sports car on his neighbor's circular driveway, he watched Amelia get out of the car. She wore a coral button-front, sleeveless dress. A coral and hand-beaded leather tie-belt with brass finishing accented her small waist. As usual, her black hair was piled high atop her head in an intricate knot.

He looked her over. Yep, stiff as a board. But when her gaze touched Cody, her soft, red lips curved into a smile. The smile faded when her gaze came back to Shane. She hurriedly turned and went to the trunk of the car to help Simone.

"Hello, ladies," Shane said. "Looks like you helped someone meet their sales quota."

Simone, in a white mini-dress, handed Amelia two bulging shopping bags, smiled sheepishly, and picked up a third. "They're all mine. David and I are going to Palm Springs in a couple of weeks." Her attention switched to Cody. "What a cute little boy."

"Cody, meet Ms. Dennison and Mrs. Taylor," Shane said, smiling down at his son.

Cody ducked his head, touched one finger to the side of the car, and concentrated on drawing a straight line.

"Cody," Shane urged, aware that his voice was softly pleading, but there was nothing he could do about it.

"He's probably tired." Amelia bent down and smiled at Cody. "It's after two. Has he had a nap?" Something about the little boy tugged at her heart.

"Nap? I'm not sure he still takes naps." Shane frowned. "His mother didn't tell me."

Straightening, Amelia's eyes narrowed. "Pardon me for saying so, but you don't appear the babysitting type."

Shane hesitated briefly before he answered, "Cody is mine."

Amelia's gaze bounced from Shane to Cody. Shock widened her eyes, condemnation followed.

"I didn't know you were married," Simone said, accusation in her tone.

Shane kept his gaze on Amelia. "I'm not. Cody's mother and I divorced last year."

Amelia's expression didn't change. So even in this, she continued to think the worst of him.

"Let me take those for you," he said, reaching for the shopping bags. Amelia promptly moved them out of the way.

"No, thank you," she said with as much warmth as an icicle.

He turned to Simone who readily handed him her bag, then she knelt in front of Cody. "Would you like a cookie and some milk?"

Cody kept his attention focused on the car.

"I guess I should have known about the nap. We had an early flight out of Austin, then we went to the park, zoo, and had ice cream," Shane told them, the smile on his face as difficult to maintain as it was to push out the words. The only thing that bothered him more was the intense way Amelia keep looking at Cody. "He's just tired."

Her usual smile in place, Simone pushed to

her feet. "After a day of shopping I know exactly how he feels."

The front door of the Southern English manor house behind them opened and David stepped onto the imported stone porch. He took one look at Shane and bounded down the three steps and quickly crossed to them.

"Hi, honey," he greeted, kissing Simone on the cheek and pulling her into his arms, and away from Shane.

"I know you're glad to see me, but you missed everyone else. This is Shane's son, Cody," Simone teasingly chastised.

"I didn't know you had a son." David stared down at the silent child. "How old are you?"

The silence seemed to grow more pronounced when the question went unanswered.

"He's tired," Shane explained, sure he was fooling no one. "I'm going to put him to bed. Good-bye."

"What's the matter?" David asked, smiling. "Cat got your tongue?" The rage in Shane's face wiped the smile away.

"Don't be obtuse, David." Amelia thrust the shopping bags at him. "You could learn a lesson from Cody about keeping quiet and being mannerly. And Mr. Saunders, if you know your son is tired, put him to bed."

Amelia hunkered down to eye level with Cody. "From the stains on your shirt I bet your father has fed you nothing but junk food." She looked up at Shane. "Has he eaten a nutritious meal today?"

Shane shook his head. "I didn't. . . ." His voice trailed off. He hadn't thought to ask Cody after breakfast and Cody hadn't said anything about being hungry.

With an exasperated harrumph, Amelia shocked even herself by standing and taking Cody's other hand. "Let's go see what your father has in the refrigerator."

"Looks like a toy store in here."

Shane tucked his head in embarrassment. "I guess I did go a little overboard."

Amelia's brow arched. "A little? It would take ten children two lifetimes to play with all this."

"Well, Cody didn't like any of them."

"Maybe you gave him too much to choose from." Walking over to a small pull-toy dog, she picked it up. "Where's the kitchen?" She couldn't believe she was doing this, but she seemed unable to stop.

"Through here," Shane said, leading her down the long hallway into the spacious kitchen with porcelain counter tops and a hanging rack of copper pans over the island.

Amelia set the toy on the hardwood floor, pulled it in a circle around Cody, then looped the string loosely around his wrist. Leaving him by his father, she went to the refrigerator and began taking out containers. "You certainly won't starve."

Shane was still watching Cody, who hadn't moved.

Amelia took down the cutting board hanging from the rack. "How would you like it if someone kept staring at you?"

Shane glanced up, startled. "I just—"

"Let Cody alone. Where's the bread? Looks like we're having roast beef sandwiches."

Amelia and Shane ate the roast beef sandwiches. Cody ate peanut butter and jelly. Afterwards, she and Shane cleaned up the kitchen while Cody watched television on the set on the island counter. Amelia threw a glance at Cody, then motioned for Shane to step to the far end of the kitchen. "I want to talk to you."

Shane smiled lazily. "It will have to be lunch instead of dinner. I don't want to leave Cody with a sitter."

Amelia stared up at him, frowning. "That's not what I want to talk to you about!"

"Then what?" he asked impatiently, looking over his shoulder at Cody before turning back to her.

She swallowed, then forced out the words. "I realize it's none of my business, but it's about Cody."

Shane tensed. "What about him?"

Amelia took a deep breath and met his eyes squarely. "Has he always been selective in his speech or is it just lately?"

His face became shadowed. "I think you'd better leave."

"I'm not being nosey or insensitive. Simone had the same problem after—"

"That's enough," he interrupted. "You know the way out."

He wasn't ready to listen. Snatching a nearby pad and pen, she scrawled her phone number on the paper. He wasn't ready to listen. "If you ever want to get serious and talk, then call me."

She looked up at him. "I can tell you love him. And right now you have to be strong enough to help him," Amelia said, then turned and left.

CHAPTER THREE

Amelia hadn't known what to expect when she told Shane to call her, but it certainly wasn't to see him and Cody on her doorstep at eight the next morning. She might have been angry at Shane's presumptuousness, but seeing his haggard face and Cody's little bent head, her heart went out to both of them.

"Have you had breakfast?" she asked.

Shane glanced down at his son. "Cody wasn't hungry."

Amelia doubted that, but decided not to push the issue. She stepped back. "Come on into the kitchen. I'll see if I can tempt you both."

Shane's hot gaze shot up to her and she felt a frisson of heat. She didn't have a doubt in her mind that she could tempt him with very little effort. Her hand clamped around the doorknob. Her breathing became erratic.

"Thanks." Shane and Cody walked inside.

Grateful he had let the incident pass without comment, she showed them to the kitchen in the rambling one-story ranch house. Shane stood uncertainly in the middle of the sunny blue kitchen, still holding his son's hand. Amelia didn't think there were many moments in Shane's life when he hadn't known what to do.

"I was just about to fix some Mickey Mouse pancakes," she said. Out of the corner of her eye, she watched Cody's head come up just a fraction. She took a bowl from the cabinet and set it on the table. "Cody, you can be the official stirrer. Your father can help." She gave them each a whisk, then set about adding the ingredients as if it were the most natural thing in the world to have them in her kitchen.

The fact was she hadn't cooked for a man in the last four years. Buying the house had been her way of moving on with her life after the last romantic fiasco. A life that didn't include men.

"Stir like this, Cody," Shane instructed, making circular motions with the whisk.

"Maybe Cody just wants to watch this time," she offered, trying to ease the pain in Shane's dark eyes.

"Yeah, sure. Daddy will do it." Shane stirred the batter as best he could with Cody's whisk motionless in the bowl.

"The grill is ready. Shane, why don't you pick Cody up so he can see how it's done? One morning he might like to do his own with your help."

"Wouldn't that be fun, Cody?" Shane asked, his voice filled with forced brightness.

Cody remained silent.

Amelia picked up the bowl, quickly whipped the batter, and poured. She'd made enough Mickey Mouse pancakes for Simone when she was younger to be able to make them in her sleep.

Cody didn't say anything, but he did eat one of the pancakes. She was sure the only reason Shane ate the other three was that he was trying to encourage his son to eat. Afterwards she reverted to another of Simone's favorites, Saturday morning cartoons.

Cody sat in front of the TV in the den with his legs crossed under him, his hands politely in his lap. None of the zany antics of the cartoon characters that usually prompted giggles from other clients' children elicited one sound from him. Amelia and Shane moved far enough away so that Cody wouldn't hear them.

"How can I help my son?"

The words sounded torn from Shane's heart. He'd made her angry, filled her with longing, but this was the first time he had made her want to weep for him. She hugged her arms around her waist instead of hugging him. "He reminds me of Simone after our parents died in the automobile accident. She withdrew completely."

"She told me how you dropped out of school to take care of her," Shane said, his voice as gentle as it had been strained before. "But this is different. Vivian and I are alive."

"But that doesn't mean he's not as angry with you and his mother for separating, just as Simone was angry with our parents," she told him. "I didn't know what to do until her school counselor recommended professional help."

"No way," Shane said angrily.

Cody flinched and down went his head. Shane and Amelia moved at the same time. "It's all right, son. Daddy didn't mean to shout." When there was no response, Shane shut his eyes briefly, then picked up his son. "Thanks for the breakfast."

Amelia followed them to the door and opened it. "Call me if you need me."

Again there was that change in Shane's eyes that sent a jolt of heat and longing through her. "What if it's just for me?"

"Only if Cody needs me."

As silent as his son had been, Shane went to his Volvo and buckled Cody in the back seat.

"What happened to the Ferrari?" Amelia asked.

Shane straightened. "In the garage. It's safer for Cody to be in the back seat."

No one had to tell her about men and their love affair with cars. Simone's husband babied his Porsche. Amelia was pleased to realize Shane valued his son more. He was trying. He just didn't know what to do and was in too much denial to listen. She prayed it wasn't pride. "If there's a problem with dinner, call me and I'll come over."

Relief crossed Shane's darkly handsome face. "Thank you. For everything."

Nodding, Amelia went back inside and closed the door. She couldn't resist peeking through the sheer curtain in the living room to watch Shane round the car and get in. He moved with a sinuous grace that made her heart thump, her hands itch to run them over the muscled length of his body. Her eyes closed and she gave a long, slow sigh.

What on earth had possessed her to volunteer to go to Shane's house and put herself in a position to be around a man who tempted her just by breathing? *A little boy who needed her.* And whether his father admitted it or not, so did he.

Amelia tried to work on a manuscript for a client, but her mind kept wandering away from the word-processing job. Over the years as she'd worked from home so she'd be available if Simone needed her, she'd developed the ability to multi-task. She could type, talk on the phone, and fax with ease. Today she kept making mistakes. She kept looking at the phone, and hurrying the clients off when she answered.

Her mind kept straying to Shane and Cody. Were they all right? Shane had come this morning, but would he call if he needed her? Was he another of those prideful males she'd met over the years and then so easily dismissed because of their arrogance?

By six-thirty that afternoon she couldn't stand the waiting a moment longer. Grabbing her purse she headed for the garage. She'd just go check on them and make sure they were all right.

"I guess Daddy can't make them like Amelia," Shane said. "We'll go out and get a hamburger. Would you like a hamburger?"

Cody sat politely at the counter. The glass of milk by his plate remained full, the bright blue plate empty. The pancakes that should have gone on it had been charred on the outside and raw on the inside. They were now in the trash.

The doorbell rang. Shane slowly went to the intercom. He didn't want to deal with anyone. "Yes?"

"If you're having dinner, the least you could have done was invite me."

The voice was lightly teasing, but he heard the tension beneath. "Amelia, stay right there."

He scooped up Cody. "We have company," he told his son as he crossed the wide foyer to open the door.

"Hello," Amelia greeted, her gaze flickering between the two. "I thought I'd drop by."

"I'm glad you did," Shane replied, his voice filled with relief. "Come on in." Shane closed the door behind her and wondered if he could keep this beautiful woman for him and for his son. He'd like nothing better than to pull her into his arms and pretend his life wasn't falling to pieces around him.

Amelia reached up and cupped Cody's cheek. "Hi, partner."

He stared at her, thoughtful. Her smile widened.

"Hope I didn't disturb you," she told Shane.

"Come with me." Shane headed to the kitchen to show her the mess that had been lunch and dinner. "Mother said a moron could boil spaghetti. Either she was wrong or the University of Michigan gave the first moron an MBA. Just before you came I was trying to see if Cody wanted to go get a hamburger."

"Too much fat." She put her purse on the counter. "You sure he likes spaghetti?"

"His grandmother said he used to."

Her eyes narrowed and he could almost hear her wondering why his father hadn't known. "Where's the spaghetti?"

Opening the cabinet, Shane handed the package to her. He really didn't mean to slap it into her hand. Really.

Her slightly raised eyebrows said he did and that he still should know what his son liked. He had thought so too many times himself during the past few days to let it pass unanswered. "I worked sixteen hours a day as a corporate executive of one of the largest credit card companies in the country. I had to work a lot of late hours and I traveled a great deal, but I did it so Cody could have the best of everything."

"That would have been a loving father who put his son's welfare first."

He had no comeback. Absolutely none.

Amelia turned away from him. "Cody, I'm going to make you a pot of the best spaghetti and meat sauce you've ever tasted." She indicated that Shane should put the child on the floor. "Wonder where the pots are? Do you think they're under here? How about here?"

Shane watched her make a game of finding the pots. She never seemed to mind when Cody didn't answer, but only stared at her in interest.

"Found them, but which one?" She held a pan that would barely hold two cups of water and a much larger one out to Cody. "Which one do you think we should use?"

Shane watched as the seconds ticked by, watched until he felt his chest grow tight. "Amelia—"

"Relax, he's just taking his time. I wouldn't want to make the wrong decision either. But even if he did, that's all right. He and I are friends, and in the morning I'm going to come back and we're going to fix pancakes. Wonder if we could do one that looks like SpongeBob?"

Shane didn't know who the heck SpongeBob was and was about to put a stop to whatever Amelia was doing when his son's hand slowly lifted toward the big pot.

"Good choice. That was my pick too. Spaghetti needs lots of water to cook."

Shane listened to her carry on a normal conversation with his son. He turned away. He was thankful she had helped, but it hurt that his son had reached out to her and not to him. He should have been the one. Shane felt as if he had failed as a father.

"It's understandable that you feel angry. I felt the same way when the counselor called me about Simone." Cody had eaten two helpings of the spaghetti and meat sauce, then gone to sleep while he was watching *The Lion King*. She'd waited until Shane had put him to bed and had come back downstairs.

The midnight-black eyes looking at her this time were almost hard. "I love my son," Shane said.

She didn't think, just put her hand on his arm, felt the bunched muscles beneath. "Then help him to understand why his world has changed so much. Get professional help."

Shane stepped away from her. "You think I'm being stubborn."

"No, I think you're being an ass."

He whirled. "I'm just afraid that whatever's wrong with him can't be fixed." He paused. "I'm afraid of losing my son."

"Your son needs you. You're the constant in his life at the moment. You're the last face he's going to see at night, the first one he sees in the morning. He has to know that, no matter what, you'll be there this time."

Shane's mouth flattened into a thin line. "You cut deep with that tongue of yours."

"For Cody I'd cut even deeper."

Shane walked over to her. His hands settled on her waist.

Amelia forced herself not to struggle, knowing that would bring her body into contact with his. She certainly wasn't going to touch him and try to push him away. "Let me go," she said softly.

"That doesn't seem to be possible," Shane answered, his voice growing huskier. "Believe me, I've tried. I must have swum the length of the pool a thousand times since I first saw you, but nothing helps get you out of my system or makes me forget how much I want you. Maybe this will."

Amelia knew the kiss was coming. She could have twisted her head to the side. But, slow-learning fool that she was, she met him halfway. The first brush of his mouth against her was like a burst of sunshine after a lifetime of darkness.

Pure emotion, all of it wildly pleasurable, coursed through her.

Shane took his time. He'd waited weeks to taste her lips. He wasn't about to rush. She tasted as sweet and as hot as he'd imagined. He could kiss her forever and it still wouldn't be long enough.

Reluctantly Shane pulled back. Amelia deserved gentleness. If it killed him, he was going to give it to her.

"I want you, but I'll wait." He stepped back, pleased to see that she didn't appear to be any steadier on her feet than he was. "Should Cody and I pick you up in the morning?"

The tip of her tongue darted out to wet her lips, and Shane watched the motion hungrily. Her eyes widened a fraction and she took a step back.

"I–I'll drive over."

"We'll be waiting."

Amelia went to the door as if she wasn't sure what was happening. That was all right. He did.

"Drive carefully, keep your cell phone on, and call me when you get home or if there's a problem."

Amelia's eyes flashed angrily. "I'm capable of taking care of myself."

"So sue me because I care about you."

That snapped her eyes wide. His were probably just as large. He hadn't meant to say that. "Cody needs you, too," he managed to say.

"Of course." Opening the door, Amelia quickly ran across the street to where her car was parked in front of Simone's house and drove off.

Shane stepped outside and watched until the Maxima turned the corner and disappeared. Closing the door he went to his son's room. Cody was sleeping peacefully. Shane kneeled down. "Your daddy may have messed up again."

CHAPTER FOUR

The next morning, Shane opened the door, expecting to see Amelia. But it was Simone, standing there with a grocery bag in her arms at a quarter past eight. He frowned, wondering if he had scared Amelia off. "Hi, Simone. Let me take that."

"Morning, Shane." She bent to eye-level with Cody, who was holding his father's hand. "Morning, Cody. Amelia sent me over here to tell you especially that she's on her way, and to tell you that she has a surprise for lunch."

Relief swept through Shane. "She's still coming?"

Simone straightened, her beautiful face wreathed in a smile. "As fast as the traffic allows. She got held up with a client so she sent me to the grocery store for her. I love teaching, but it's great being off for the summers."

Shane's arm tightened around the bag. He wanted to ask if she had ever dealt with children like Cody, but didn't know how.

"Simone," David called from across the street. He was standing on their front steps in his tennis whites, a frown on his face. "Come on or we're going to be late for our tennis match at the club."

Simone started to turn, but Shane's hand on her arm stopped her. He might not know much about child rearing, but he knew about other men. "Men tend to appreciate more what they can't have."

The smile on her face faded. She glanced back at David who stood with his arms akimbo. "I love him. I don't want to lose him." Her voice trembled.

"Then be less agreeable and make him work for you until he meets you halfway and treats you like you deserve," Shane told her, his voice low. "My marriage might not have lasted, but I learned one partner can't give all the time. When you do, the other one just takes until there is nothing left and then you dislike them as much as you dislike yourself."

"Simone!" David's call was louder, more irritated.

Simone stared at Shane a moment longer, then she turned toward her husband. "David, I am not hard of hearing."

David blinked and his hands dropped to his side.

Shane's mouth twitched. "That should start him thinking. He's lucky to have you."

"He is, isn't he?" Simone laughed, then bent

to Cody's level again. "I teach kindergarten. I'd love to have you in my class when school starts. We have a lot of fun learning."

Shane's mouth tightened. Cody was only staying the summer. Maybe less, if he didn't start talking. As much as Shane wanted his son with him, if staying with him made him unhappy, he would take Cody back to his mother. "Thanks for the groceries. I'll bring a check over later to cover the cost."

"Don't you dare." She straightened, and pushed a lock of hair behind her ear. "Just do me a favor?"

"Sure."

"Show Amelia that some men can be trusted. You're at the top of my list for the job, you know." With a wink she started back across the street. David met her halfway, a frown still on his face. When Simone reached him, she put her arms around his neck and planted a kiss so hot on his lips that it had him looking dazed and grinning when he lifted his head.

Shane didn't blame him. If Amelia kissed him like that he wouldn't turn her loose until he had made her his.

Amelia hated being late. Hated worse that Cody might think she'd forgotten him. Being self-employed had its drawbacks at times. She'd arrived at Shane's house, ignored the little leap of her pulse when she saw him in those sinful jeans and black knit shirt that stretched across his wide chest, and had gone directly to the kitchen.

She'd put a plate of waffles and pancakes in front of Cody. He had pulled the waffles closer to him. His father had taken the pancakes. They'd both been relieved when Cody ate the waffle and half a bowl of cereal.

It had been Shane's idea to go to the park. She had piles of work waiting, but hadn't been able to say no. Shane had driven. With Cody between them they'd meandered through the park. She held off until she couldn't stand it any longer. "Have you thought about what I said about professional counseling?"

Shane was silent for a while. "I don't want to fail him."

She glanced over at Shane, noted his rigid jaw. This was difficult for him. "Then make the call."

Reaching down, Shane picked up Cody and held him close. "I'll make the call."

Relief swept through Amelia, but she had to push a little bit more. She waited until they were back at his house and Cody was watching *The Muppet Movie.* Again she pushed aside thoughts of the work waiting at home—work that would take the rest of the night to have ready for a client. She pulled Shane to the side.

"If you're going to talk to someone, you'll need to know as much as possible about when Cody first stopped talking."

His body stiffened. "I already know that. It was after the divorce and it's only with me."

"Shane, that doesn't make sense."

Unfolding his arms he turned to her, and she noticed the movement of muscle beneath skin. "Why?"

Amelia tried not to get sidetracked by the sensual pull of his body. "He hasn't said a word to me or Simone, either. If you're the only one he doesn't talk to, then why won't he talk to us?"

"I thought it was because he didn't really know you guys." He stared at Cody thoughtfully. "But now that I think about it, when I took him to see my parents in Detroit in February, he didn't say one word the entire two days we were there, either. My mother couldn't stop crying. We haven't been back since."

Deep in thought, Amelia bit her lip. "When Simone stopped talking, she also became a problem with a couple of teachers who had been her favorites. She was angry with those she loved the most. The therapist said that in Simone's mind we could have prevented what happened and we didn't. But it was the trauma of the accident that was at the heart of Simone's silence, not me."

"I'm calling his mother." Going into the kitchen Shane picked up the cordless phone and moved to stand where he could see Cody but still not be overheard.

Reaching his ex-wife took two hours of overseas calls. Vivian and her latest lover were in Paris. She wasn't pleased to hear from him. Shane came straight to the point. "Does Cody talk with other people?"

"Of course he does," she snapped. "It's just you, and I can't blame him. Even he must know that the only thing you're good for is making money." She hung up on him.

"What did she say?" Amelia asked from beside him.

"That it's just me." He got a dial tone and punched in another number.

"Who are you calling?"

"A private detective friend of mine. He did some work for my company," Shane said and waited for the ringing phone to be picked up. "I need to get in contact with Cody's teachers now and Luke will be able to locate them."

"Luke Grayson," answered a deep gravelly voice.

"I have a job for you," Shane said and gave him the details.

Less than twelve hours later, Shane had the answers to his questions. Angrier than he'd ever been in his life, he felt like kicking something. Sitting in the den, the sight of Cody watching him helped calm him down. He went to his son. "It's going to be all right. Daddy's going to do whatever it takes to make it better."

Too keyed up to sit still, he took Cody's hand. "Let's go for a walk."

He was just closing the door when Amelia pulled up behind David's Porsche. As soon as she was out of the car, she looked across the street. She took one look at Shane's face and started toward him.

He met her halfway. "You were right."

Understanding filled her eyes. "Hi, Cody," she said and then turned her attention back to Shane. "We'll talk later."

Shane took her hand, felt the leap of her pulse. "Thank you."

She nodded. Her breath trembled over lips he'd again dreamed of kissing. Keeping her hand in his, Shane started down the sidewalk.

They got a chance to talk privately while Cody squatted and watched a caterpillar inch its way across the hot concrete. "I found out that Cody has become increasingly uncommunicative in school. The school counselor spoke with Vivian several months ago and suggested professional counseling, and notifying me. Vivian adamantly refused and threatened to sue them if they brought it up again."

Amelia didn't know if Cody's mother had

been in denial or if she just hadn't cared or if she wanted to hurt his father more than she wanted to help her son.

"She's been lying to me since the divorce, just to make me feel guilty. She kept telling me it upset Cody to see me, but I visited his school anyway." Shane stuffed his hands into the pockets of his slacks. "I wanted to see him, hold him, for him to know I still loved him. I went one day and checked him out for lunch. He didn't say anything at the restaurant and he didn't show any interest in the playground equipment. When I arrived back at the school, his mother was there. Someone from the school must have called her. She was yelling that it wasn't time for my visit and he started crying. After the visit to my parents, I stayed away until a month ago because I thought it was for the best for Cody."

Amelia's hand touched his arm. "You're in his life now. That's what counts."

Shane's hand covered hers and linked, palm to palm. "I'm going to make sure it remains that way. She deliberately prevented him from getting help, so I've already instructed Luke to send everything to my lawyer. Cody is staying with me."

Three days later, Amelia sat with Cody in the outer office of a child psychologist. She stacked interlocking building blocks while Cody, sitting with his legs tucked under him, simply held his red piece.

Shane hadn't wanted Cody to be left alone when he went in to talk to the doctor first, so she had volunteered to stay with the little boy. She had really come to care about Cody. But after Simone told her of Shane's advice and Amelia had seen the change in David, she would have said yes anyway. David had stopped treating Simone as if she were a possession. He'd even switched his secretary with another lawyer's to reassure Simone further that the incident at their house was innocent. Amelia had almost fainted when she saw him drying dishes. She finally believed their marriage would work.

Dr. Fairmont had been highly recommended by noted child psychologist and author, Dr. Catherine Stewart, a close friend of Luke Grayson. The door to the psychologist's office opened. Shane and Dr. Fairmont, wearing a smart black suit, came out. She hunkered down in front of Cody and began talking softly to him. After a couple of minutes, she held out her hand. He didn't take it, but he did get up and they went into the office together.

Fists clenched by his side, Shane watched them go. Coming to her feet, Amelia took one fist, then the other, and unclenched them. "Let's sit down."

She didn't expect Shane to say anything and he didn't. When Cody came out of the room,

Shane scooped him up as if he'd never let go. "I love you, Cody."

"Next time we'll all meet together," Dr. Fairmont said. "Give me a call tomorrow and we'll talk further."

"Let's go home," Shane said, and took Amelia's hand in his.

She shouldn't have felt the sting of tears in her eyes. He didn't mean anything personal by his remark. She was just there for Cody. She hated men. She swallowed the knot in her throat and wished desperately that that were true.

Three weeks later Shane couldn't have been happier that he'd taken the buy-out from his company. He was financially able to spend the time Dr. Fairmont said he needed to let his son know he was loved, to assure Cody that the divorce didn't mean his father loved him less. Cody needed consistency in his life and, as Shane watched Cody and Amelia in the shallow end of the pool, he couldn't help thinking how much having her around had helped him and his son.

"Hot dogs ready."

Cody didn't say anything, but he looked around and started to climb out of the pool. Amelia was right behind him. Shane wondered if either of them realized they had reached for each other's hand at almost the same time. It had been a long, hectic three weeks since they'd first seen the psychologist, but Shane's gut no longer knotted when Cody didn't answer him.

Just give him love, time, and the reassurance you'll always be there.

Looking at Amelia's sleek, tempting body in the demure one-piece black swimsuit that sent his blood pressure, among other things, rising, Shane thought that advice might apply to Amelia as well. He'd held back these past weeks because he wanted to concentrate on helping Cody, but now that his son was improving, Shane was ready to help himself to Amelia.

"One or two?"

"I want one," Amelia answered. "How about you, Cody?"

One finger went up.

Shane's hand trembled as he speared the wiener and placed it inside a bun. His son was communicating with him. "Here you go. When you finish with that one, there's more."

"I'll say." Amelia folded her arms across her waist, inadvertently pushing up her breasts. "You cooked the entire package."

Shane's gaze had dropped to her tempting breasts and it took him a moment to reply. "Just in case we're hungry later on."

Amelia unfolded her arms. She'd caught him staring. "I'll have to go soon. I have work to do."

The only place he wanted her to go was to his bed where they could work on pleasing each other. He gave her a hot dog. "It's barely six. Cody and I rented a video we want you to watch with us. Isn't that right, son?"

The nod was almost imperceptible, but it was there.

"Cody, you talked me into it," she said, her voice tremulous.

The two of them took a seat on the chaise, side by side, both balancing their plates with chips and cookies on their laps. He had failed his son once with a woman who should have taken care of him and didn't. This time he was doing better.

CHAPTER FIVE

Amelia should have gone home as soon as Cody fell asleep. Instead she'd sat there like a clod and watched as Shane stretched his son out on the dark navy leather sofa on the other side of them. To rest better, Shane had said, then gave her a look hot enough to melt asphalt as he sat down beside her. The only light came from the television. They could have been the only people in the universe.

Shane picked up a curl of her hair that had slipped from the twist on top of her head and twirled it around his finger. "I've been thinking."

Amelia twisted uneasily in her seat, but the firm, hot, beckoning line of Shane's body shifted and melded with hers with every move. She swallowed. "Yes?"

"I told you about the consultant firm I'm thinking about starting once Cody begins school in the fall, didn't I?" His finger stopped playing with her hair and began to massage her scalp.

She caught back a moan of pleasure. She remembered he'd mentioned it a couple of weeks ago. She knew he'd spoken with his lawyer several times and he thought Shane had a strong case to win permanent custody of Cody. Especially since his mother hadn't sought help for the boy. Shane had, and Cody was improving almost daily. "Yes."

"I want to hire you to type up the prospectus." His fingers increased the pressure just a little and her eyes drifted shut. "You could work here in my office. We like having you here."

"Umm." Amelia rubbed her head against his hand.

"You like that?"

"It feels wonderful."

"This is going to feel even better." His mouth covered hers, taking her on a slow road to pleasure. He kissed as if he had all the time in the world to savor her.

Amelia sighed at the sweet tenderness of his kiss and gave herself up to the mastery of his touch. She had imagined how incredibly good it would feel to be held by Shane, kissed by him again. She was delighted to find out that reality was better than imagination.

"Amelia," he said against her lips. "I think we have company."

Her eyelids popped up. *Cody.* She sat up.

Cody sat there, staring at them. Amelia's

breath caught. She didn't know what to do or say. Neither apparently did Shane. They just stared at Cody until she thought her nerves could stand it no longer. She'd never do anything to hurt Cody.

A small smile touched Cody's sweet mouth. He climbed into his father's lap and closed his eyes again.

Amelia blinked back tears as Shane hugged her with one arm and his son with the other. "If you cry, I will too," he whispered.

She sniffed and put her head on his shoulder. "I promise I won't tell anyone."

"The Saunders Men Car Wash Service," Shane said, standing in Amelia's driveway.

Amelia laughed and realized she had been doing that a lot lately. Two weeks had passed since the kiss. It seemed like forever.

Shane and Cody were dressed alike in blue jeans, white T-shirts, backwards baseball caps on their heads. Cody's red pail was half the size of his father's. "I'll pay you ten dollars and not a nickel more."

Shane looked down at Cody by his side. "What do you think, son?"

He nodded.

"You have a deal." Unwrapping the water hose, Shane put a couple of inches of water in

Cody's bucket, then his own. Cody immediately went to the side of her car which was parked under a thirty-foot-tall fruitless mulberry, reached in his bucket, pulled out the sponge, and started rubbing.

Shane watched his son with a proud, happy grin on his face. "We already washed mine. Slow down, son. Got to pace yourself so maybe the beautiful customer will feed us lunch."

Cody straightened and smiled at her.

Amelia tried to get her heart to settle from Shane's compliment. "Chicken nuggets and baked French fries?"

Cody's grin widened.

Sure her emotions were under control, she faced Shane. "Coming up. Now, what do you want, Shane?"

"Everything."

Her body heated and yearned. He made a mockery of her feeble attempt not to want him.

"But I'll wait until you're ready to give it to me." Cutting off the water, he hunkered down by Cody.

Amelia went inside, but she couldn't work. Shane called to her as no man ever had. Her feelings for the other two men who'd been in her life were nothing when she compared them to what she felt for Shane. Maybe this time it would be different. But dare she take a chance?

* * *

He was wearing her down. At least he hoped so.

"Think Amelia will like her surprise, Cody?"

Cody nodded with a happy smile, then adjusted the rose beside the place setting where Amelia was to sit. His smiles came more naturally every day. After almost two months of therapy, Shane was hopeful that, by the time school started in a few weeks, he'd be talking. His lawyer had already notified Vivian that Shane planned to keep his son.

The doorbell rang. Cody took off running. Smiling, Shane went after him. He planned to do a little keeping himself tonight. Amelia was not getting away from him.

"Where is that no-good father of yours?"

Shane ran to the front door at the strident sound of Vivian's voice. Her beautiful face contorted in anger, she stood in the foyer, wearing a printed silk dress, her dyed red hair as wild as her eyes. She had her hand clamped cruelly around Cody's thin arm. His eyes were terrified.

"Let him go, Vivian."

"You're not taking him!" she yelled. "You're just trying to get out of paying child support."

Rage poured through Shane. He started for her, then stopped as she jerked Cody's little body closer to hers.

She smiled cruelly and Shane wondered how he had ever thought he loved her. "Let him go and I'll give you double. I'll write you out a check now."

"You'll pay all right. I still have permanent custody. We're leaving."

"I don't think so," Amelia said, her voice dangerously soft.

Vivian turned toward the doorway where Amelia stood. "You must be the—"

"Say it or harm Cody, and you'll regret it," Amelia said, advancing farther into the foyer.

Vivian jerked back, loosening her hold on Cody. Amelia quickly put him safely behind her. Vivian realized her mistake and grabbed for the child again. Shane was just as surprised as Vivian when Amelia deftly countered the move and with one practiced motion of her hand used Vivian's own momentum to send her flying out the door. She landed facedown on the concrete.

Vivian screamed and kept on screaming and shouting obscenities. By the time Shane reached Amelia and Cody, Cody was clinging desperately to Amelia's neck. Shane hugged them both. "It's all right, son."

"Give him back! He's mine!" Vivian screamed.

Shane held his son tighter as tears of rage filled his eyes. He had left his son with a woman who only saw him as the means for a monthly check. "I'm sorry, son."

"We've called the police," David said, hurrying up the walk with Simone. "Go inside. I'll wait here and make sure she doesn't bother you."

Shane nodded and the three of them went inside to sit on the sofa. The police were there in mere minutes. Vivian was given the choice of leaving quietly or going to jail for trespassing and disturbing the peace. She left and the police left soon afterwards. Shane thanked David and Simone, but didn't seem to have the strength to move.

A long while later, he realized Cody was asleep. "I failed him."

"You saved him."

His hold tightened. "Because of you."

"The only thing that matters is that Cody is safe and with you now," Amelia said, stroking his arm gently.

"After this incident today, my lawyer will have enough to ensure I get permanent custody, but I didn't want it to come to this. I regret that he had to see his mother like that." Shane closed his eyes.

"Having you for a father will help him heal and forget. He's already on his way."

Shane leaned his head against Amelia's. "He helped me set the table and pick out a flower for you for dinner."

"I'll take a rain check," Amelia said, snuggling closer. "Now think of something pleasant and go to sleep."

"I don't have to think. I'm holding it in my arms."

CHAPTER SIX

"Daddy, I'm hungry. Daddy, wake up."

Shane surfaced as if from a dream. It was dark outside. He must have fallen asleep. He blinked and stared into his son's face.

"I'm hungry," Cody repeated.

Shane couldn't speak. He reached out and shook Amelia, who was asleep on his shoulder.

"Emmm."

Cody crawled into her lap. "I'm hungry, Amelia."

Shane and Amelia grabbed him at the same time, rocking and laughing with happiness. "Cody says he's hungry," Shane said.

Amelia smiled at the little boy. "Name it and it's yours."

"Mickey Mouse pancakes, chicken nuggets, French fries and fudgesicles."

Laughing, the three went to the kitchen.

• • •

Cody talked nonstop. A call to the psychologist reassured Shane and Amelia. He'd finally realized he was safe and his father wasn't going away. He said his prayers with Shane and Amelia on either side of him. They sat on the side of his bed until he fell asleep, then walked into the hall, leaving the door open.

"He's going to be all right." Amelia's eyes misted.

"What did I tell you about crying?" Shane teased, but his voice was thick.

She nodded. "I'd better get home."

"I've been meaning to talk to you about that." Shane led her next door to his bedroom and partially closed the door. "I don't want to go too far in case he wakes up again."

"Of course. What did you want to talk with me about?"

"Fate."

"Fate?"

Shane curved his hands around Amelia's waist. "It was fate that brought you into my life to help me and help my son."

"I love Cody."

"But do you love his father?"

Her eyes widened.

"I planned to work my way up to it, but I don't think I can wait. I love you, Amelia. I want you in my life and in my son's life."

"Shane." Tears sparkled in her eyes.

His hands tenderly cupped her face. "Please

tell me those are tears of happiness."

"I tried not to fall in love with you. But you kept sneaking past my defenses until I decided—"

"Decided what?" Shane asked, barely able to breathe.

"I want everything, and you're the man I want it with."

"Yes!" Shane shouted, his mouth finding hers.

Amelia sensed the possessive difference in the kiss immediately. It was in the boldly erotic tongue, the crush of her breasts against his hard chest. Her emotions swirled.

"I love you, Amelia," Shane whispered, gathering her in his arms and lowering her onto the turned-down bed.

"Pretty sure of yourself," Amelia teased, tracing her finger across his lip.

"I'd hoped and dreamed." He pressed his mouth against the side of her neck. His fingers made quick work of the buttons on her blouse.

"We'll have to compare." She finished with his shirt, then sighed at the hard, muscled warmth beneath her hands. "You feel so good."

"You feel better." Off came her lacy black bra. "I've dreamed of how you'd taste." His tongue caressed the nipple.

She moaned beneath him, her hand holding his head to her. Her senses reeled. Currents of desire swept through her. "I'm not going to be able to wait."

"Same here." He quickly finished undressing them. He brought his body over hers and stared into her eyes as he brought them together. "I love you."

"I love you," Amelia repeated, her body arching toward him to meet and welcome the thrust of his body. Passion and ecstasy swamped her until she surrendered to the man she loved.

"Shane." His name was pulled from her as they found completion together.

His breathing labored, Shane pulled her to him. "How long do you think it will take you to plan a wedding? A month, right?"

Smiling, she rolled on top of him. "Keep surpassing my fantasies like you just did and I'll make it three weeks."

Shane grinned. "Since you just outdid mine, how about two weeks?"

"Convince me."

Laughing, he pulled her to him.

Francis Ray returns with
The Graysons!
Take a sneak peek at her upcoming romance

YOU AND NO OTHER
Morgan Grayson's story

Coming soon from St. Martin's Press

PROLOGUE

Ruth Grayson had made a mistake.

It was difficult for a mother to admit but, there it was, staring her in the face. Shelby Hendrix was gazing up at Morgan with what could only be described as rapt adoration as they made their way to the buffet table during the wedding reception of her oldest son, Luke, and his bride, Catherine. Shelby's reaction, pardon a mother for thinking so, was to be expected.

Morgan, her second child and son, was a handsome man. As always he was dressed impeccably, but the black, tailor-made Armani tuxedo he wore gave him a rakish, suave distinction that had woman after woman turning her head to get a second and often a third glance. And if a woman had the good fortune to catch his attention, he had a way of looking at her with those midnight-black eyes of his that assured her she had his undivided attention.

Heady for any woman, but made more potent

when it came from a man as commanding as
Morgan. The look in turn could be awe-
inspiring, intimidating or comforting, depending on his mood and the recipient. He was a
lawyer after all and, from the way his private
practice was thriving, he was an excellent one.
But then, Morgan had always excelled at everything he did. He had a single-minded determination that refused to accept defeat.

Ruth sighed and shook her head, causing the
wide brim of her sky-blue straw hat to waver.
She detested hats, but it had been necessary for
the garden wedding. She lifted her hand to remove it, then felt a prickling sensation at the
base of her neck. Even before she turned she
knew whom she'd see. Less than ten feet away
was her sister-in-law, Felicia Falcon, staring at
her with an understanding, but adamant, gaze.

The hat stayed.

Ruth withdrew her hand. Felicia's fashion
sense was impeccable. She'd come from one of
the wealthiest and most influential African-
American families in Boston. Ruth's parents had
been dirt-poor Native-American Muscogee
farmers from Oklahoma, but the two women
were extremely close, that bond strengthened by
the love of Felicia's husband and Ruth's brother,
John Henry, and their children. Ruth didn't
worry for a moment that her five children,
Catherine, her new daughter-in-law, or her
high-profile parents would disapprove of her

being hatless, but there were over five hundred people in the ballroom of the Four Seasons Hotel in Beverly Hills to consider.

Her sigh came again, this time heavy and long-suffering as she waved away a tanned young man with a tray of sparkling mineral water and champagne. Her attention returned to her second-born. You'd think with all the eligible women who had to be in a crowd this large Morgan would find one he was attracted to. *Not him.* Ruth barely refrained from gritting her teeth as she watched Morgan lead a smitten Shelby back to their table because behind the polite gaze he was bestowing upon her was utter boredom. That wasn't what Ruth had hoped for when the two of them had met earlier that evening.

Shelby was beautiful, sophisticated, and intelligent, and she had her own public relations firm in St. Louis. According to Shelby's mother, a Soror of Ruth's, Shelby enjoyed the arts, the finer things in life, and had an eclectic taste in music just as Morgan did.

But the sparks weren't there between them. Ruth might have been a widow for twenty-four years, but she could still remember the wild leap of her heart, the giddy excitement when she first met Vincent. You might fight the powerful attraction, the sensual pull, as she had done, but thank goodness her heart and Vincent's dogged determination had been stronger than her will.

They had had ten wonderful years together before the Master of Breath and God took him. But
the warm memories would remain forever.

With a sinking heart Ruth watched as Morgan, so like his father, turned his head and
stared straight at her, a small knowing smile
curving his lips. The smile grew as he tipped his
dark head in silent acknowledgment of his winning this round. Even as annoyance swept
through Ruth, she found herself smiling and
conceding defeat. She had raised intelligent,
quick-thinking children, and she couldn't help
but be proud of them.

But Morgan should remember that he'd inherited his determination from her as well. Once
she set her mind on something, she never backed
off until it was completed to her satisfaction.
She'd just have to adjust and reevaluate. She
only had to glance across the room and see how
happy Luke and Catherine were to strengthen
her resolve. Luke wasn't happy at first either
about her matchmaking. Now, he couldn't stop
smiling. He was so proud of Catherine and so
much in love with her. Catherine felt the same
about him. Their road to happiness hadn't been
an easy one, but that only served to make them
enjoy the results all the more.

All of her children deserved to be happily
married. Since Morgan, Brandon, Pierce, and
Sierra were still dragging their feet, it was her
duty as their mother to correct the matter. Felicia

had the good fortune to have her children, Daniel and Dominique, already blissfully wed. Ruth would see that hers found the same fulfillment.

Turning away from Morgan's pleased expression, Ruth began to circulate among the guests. Let him enjoy his victory tonight. His day was coming.

Morgan would be next to walk down the aisle. Not as the best man, but as the groom.

CHAPTER ONE

Morgan Grayson was in serious trouble.

Long, elegant fingers tapped out a synchronized beat on the steering wheel of his two-seater sports car to Aretha Franklin's unmistakable voice demanding respect. Morgan knew just how the lady felt.

Easing around a slow-moving Suburban, Morgan resisted the urge to press his foot down on the accelerator and take some of his growing frustrations out with a fast drive. The twisting roads beneath the San De Cristo Mountains outside of Santa Fe were unforgiving when it came to fools and speeding vehicles. Morgan wasn't a fool so he contented himself by increasing the volume of the CD and returned to pondering his problem.

His loving, stubborn, matchmaking mother.

Ruth Grayson had singled him out as the next one of her children to marry off. After she'd thrown Shelby in his path two weeks ago at

Luke's wedding, Morgan had erroneously thought she'd need a little more time to regroup. After all, she had enlisted the help of her friends and associates from around the country in looking for a wife for Luke. Knowing she was too sensitive to thrust the same women at him anytime soon, Morgan thought he was safe. But she had outwitted him.

For him she was staying local.

Last week when he'd picked up his dry cleaning, he'd even heard there was a jackpot—a little something so the lucky winner could have a blowout bachelorette party. This morning he had stopped by his mother's house for breakfast, and three of her single female colleagues from the University of St. Johns where she taught music in the graduate program were there. You'd think his mother would be subtler or that the women would have more pride. No way! They all acted as if this were some type of game. Unfortunately, he was the prize.

His mother had married off Luke, just as she predicted. As the second-born, Morgan was next. In the past he had always been pleased that he was next in line. No longer. Pierce, Brandon, and Sierra were constantly urging him to hold out. *Demanding* might be a more apt word. His younger brothers and sister didn't have to worry. He had no intention of getting married.

He was happy for Luke, and Catherine was a fantastic woman, but marriage wasn't in his

plans. His law practice was his mistress, and he
liked it that way. The woman hadn't been born
who would make him even think about getting
serious. But his mother wasn't listening to him.

His fingers flexed on the steering wheel as he
wondered how Luke had coped, but since he
and Catherine had been holed up in his moun-
tain cabin since they returned a few days ago
from their honeymoon in Bali, Morgan couldn't
ask him. Probably just as well, Morgan thought
as he came over a rise and saw the black iron
gate of the Hendersons' ranch that signaled he
was almost at his destination. Luke was an unwanted reminder that their mother had been
right in her choice for her first-born.

Slowing down, Morgan turned into the
paved driveway and saw the white stucco
ranch house at the end of the winding, mile-
long road. The red-tiled roof gleamed in the
bright morning sunlight. The aspen leaves were
thick and shimmering with life, the air scented
with the last, lingering scents of wildflowers. It
was a beautiful fall day. Too bad he couldn't enjoy it.

Stopping in the circular driveway in front of
the heavily carved, red double doors, he cut the
motor. The BMW roadster purred to a polite silence. He smiled. He'd always been a sucker for
cars. He enjoyed the finer things in life and
worked long, demanding hours in a job he loved
to afford them. With his law practice thriving,

his life was perfect in every way but one. His mother.

Thrusting his mother's matchmaking schemes from his mind, Morgan picked up the hand-stitched, leather attaché case from the seat beside him and got out. He had business to take care of. Besides, he could handle any woman she pushed in his path.

Closing the door, he started up the walkway lined with purple sage. The neigh of a horse followed by the throaty laughter of a woman caused him to pause and turn toward the sound. He was just in time to see an elegantly shaped woman take a huge roan stallion smoothly over one six-foot rail, then another. Since Morgan had a fondness for women and horses, he watched the riveting combination of grace and beauty.

The woman's long legs were encased in tan jodhpurs pressed tightly against the animal's gleaming flanks as she guided him over another obstacle. It took strength, skill, and control to handle such a big, powerful animal and to make it appear effortless. Morgan idly wondered if the woman was that controlled in bed or if she was as wild and as seductive as her laughter had been.

"Excuse me, sir. May I help you?"

The heavily accented voice effectively ended Morgan's speculations and his idle thought of finding out. Pleasure never outweighed business. Pushing the woman from his mind, he turned.

"Yes, I'm Morgan Grayson. I'm here to see Mr. Duval. He's expecting me."

The dark, austure face of the elderly servant dressed in unrelieved black became no less stern at Morgan's announcement. His closely cropped head of gray hair inclined slightly. "Yes, Mr. Grayson. Mr. Duval is expecting you. This way, please."

Morgan followed the man, his gait slow and deliberate, inside the rambling one-story ranch house. The interior was cool, the furniture sleek and ultra-modern. Morgan knew the couple who owned the house, but seldom lived there. They preferred the Mediterranean this time of year and saw the house as a tax write-off. Thanks to the investment advice of his brother, Pierce, they were able to enjoy their retirement in style.

Crossing the slate-gray carpeted floor, the servant knocked briefly on the carved mahogany door. "Mr. Duval. Mr. Grayson is here."

"Send him in," commanded a curt, male voice.

"Yes, sir." Opening the door, the servant closed it as soon as Morgan walked through. Morgan saw Andre Duval turn from looking out the window, then take a seat behind his desk. Not by word or look did he acknowledge Morgan. Thankful that his business with Duval would be brief, Morgan crossed the polished oak floor and extended his hand.

"Good afternoon, Mr. Duval. It's a pleasure to meet you." He didn't even wince at the lie.

Duval ignored the hand and stared unflinchingly back at Morgan. "You're late."

Morgan's own eyes narrowed. He'd heard that Duval, a renowned sculptor, was temperamental. Apparently he was also rude. Slowly Morgan twisted the hand he had extended and glanced at the face of the 18-karat Rolex on his wrist. "I'm seven and a half minutes early."

"Where are the papers I'm to sign?"

Not even by a flicker of his thick lashes did Morgan show his irritation. If Duval were his client, he'd walk. He wasn't. He was the client of the Lawson & Lawson law firm in Boston. Kendrick Lawson, the senior partner, had been Morgan's mentor as well as his boss when he attended Harvard. He was now a good friend. Morgan respected and liked the crafty Lawson too much to disappoint him. His firm would get a sizable commission once Duval signed the contract to have *Courage*, his best work thus far, reproduced for limited editions. Besides, a lawyer learned early to deal with unpleasant people and unavoidable situations.

"May I?" Morgan asked, lifting the briefcase over the highly polished surface of the immaculate desk.

The affirmative nod from Duval was curt.

Placing the case on the desk, Morgan opened it and handed the two contracts to Duval. A black-gloved right hand emerged from beneath the desk, took the papers and laid them carelessly aside. Cold brown eyes never left Morgan's face.

"You can leave now."

The lock snapped shut with a distinctive click. "If you have any questions I'd be happy to answer them. I understand you were expected to sign today and I could overnight them to Mr. Lawson."

"You understood wrong." Duval stood. His left hand was already in the coat pocket of his loosely constructed black jacket. He slipped his right into the other pocket. "Good-bye."

Morgan knew when he had been dismissed. He pulled a card from inside the jacket of his wheat-colored suit and placed it in the middle of the desk. "If you need to reach me. Good-bye." Lifting the briefcase off the desk, he turned to leave.

A brief knock sounded on the door before it swung open. Bubbling laughter preceded the striking young woman into the study. "Andre—" She stopped her headlong dash, her smoky gray eyes widening on seeing Morgan. For a long moment she simply stared.

Morgan was doing the same. She was even more exquisite up close. "Hello."

"Hello," she murmured a bit breathlessly, then turned to Andre. "I'm sorry. I came in the back from the stable. I didn't know you had a guest."

"No matter, my dear. Mr. Grayson was just leaving."

Morgan noted that Duval's voice had lost its

sharpness and now was almost crooning. Morgan could well understand why. If the woman's whisky voice didn't get you, the smoky gray eyes and pouting lips would. She had the kind of face that a man would go to his grave remembering, and a lush, curvaceous body created to satisfy any fantasy.

She flushed beneath her golden skin at his open appraisal. All that sex appeal and she could still blush. Innocence and carnality, an alluring and dangerous combination. Was she "La Flame," the mysterious woman reported to be the inspiration and reason for Duval's sculptured pieces to have regained their fire and vitality after a two-year absence from the art world? It would certainly explain his rush to get rid of Morgan.

Duval had an unimpeded view of the front of the house and the stable from the window in his study. It was safe to assume he had seen Morgan watching the young, vibrant woman and hadn't approved.

Morgan smiled. Living on the edge kept a man sharp. "Mr. Duval, I didn't know you had a daughter."

"I don't," Andre snapped.

A smile tugging the corners of her lush mouth, the woman came farther into the room. "I think Mr. Grayson is teasing, Andre."

"Phoenix, Morgan Grayson," Andre said grudgingly, obviously annoyed at having to do so.

"Hello, Mr. Grayson."

Morgan's large hand closed over her small delicate one and he noted the slight roughness of her palms. The unexpected contrast pleased him almost as much as the slight leap in her pulse at the base of her throat, the widening of her beautiful eyes. "Hello, Phoenix."

Moistening her lips, she withdrew her hand. He'd bet the farm that she wasn't the nervous type. Interesting. "Would you like something to drink?" she asked, her voice a fraction huskier than it had been.

Very interesting. "No—"

"Thank you, dear, but Mr. Grayson was just leaving," Andre interrupted. "Besides, you need to change after riding."

Embarrassment replaced the warmth in her face. Her hand fluttered across the front of her wrinkled white blouse, then down the side of her dusty jodhpurs. "Please excuse my appearance. I was so excited about Crimson settling in so well, I didn't think."

Morgan's own smile increased to put her at ease. Twin dimples he had always detested winked. "No apology needed. It was a pleasure watching you ride."

The corners of her very tempting mouth curved upward again. "Crimson did all the work."

"Since I ride, I know better."

"Phoenix," Andre called, his voice tight. "You really need to change out of those clothes, and don't forget to remind Hilda that we won't be dining in tonight."

Her eyes flashed, her body tensed. Morgan had seen the same thing happen when his sister, Sierra, became angry. The quiet before the storm. Morgan waited for Phoenix to tell the bossy Duval to take a flying leap. Instead, in the next breath, she seemed to retreat before his eyes, leaving only the façade and none of the brilliance of the vivacious woman who had entered the room. It was as if a shade had been placed over a bright flame. Again Morgan wondered what was the relationship between the two.

"Of course, Andre. Good-bye, Mr. Grayson."

"Good-bye, Phoenix," he said, unable to keep the disappointment out of his voice that she was leaving, and that she hadn't stood up to Duval. The door closed softly behind her.

"I'll show you out." Coming from around the desk, Andre led the way out of his study. As soon as they emerged, the same servant Morgan had seen earlier appeared. The elderly man reached the front door seconds before Duval stepped onto the terrazzo entryway. Despite the man's stiff left leg, Andre had not slowed in his haste to rid himself of Morgan.

Hands stuffed into the pockets of his jacket, Andre stood to the side as Morgan passed. "I'll mail the contracts directly back to Kenneth. There is no need to trouble yourself driving all the way back out here."

Morgan stopped in the middle of the stone walkway and turned. Duval wouldn't care if Morgan slow-roasted on a spit. They both knew it. He wondered why he even bothered to lie, and then he caught a movement . . . a flash of white behind him. Phoenix.

Inclining his head in acknowledgment, Morgan opened the car door, tossed his briefcase onto the passenger seat, then got in. Driving away, he again wondered exactly what the relationship was between Duval and Phoenix. Neither gave out signals of being lovers, but that didn't mean they hadn't been intimate.

Morgan might not like the snobbish man, but he was well respected and wielded a great deal of influence in the art world. Certain women were attracted to that type of man. But for some odd reason Morgan didn't think Phoenix was that kind of woman. In his profession he had learned to read people quickly and accurately. Users weren't guileless and they certainly didn't blush.

Flipping on the signal, Morgan pulled onto the highway and headed back toward Santa Fe. He didn't like puzzles. He liked even less the pompous way Duval had treated Phoenix. Before the roadster had gone another mile, Morgan knew he was going to find out exactly what was going on between the two.

. . .

"I thought I'd find you in here."

Phoenix turned from slipping on her smock to see Andre enter the studio. Bright sunlight streamed through the three floor-to-ceiling windows behind her. The rays weren't kind to Andre. They sought out every line in his sixty-two-year-old-face, and delineated his thin frame. Unbidden came the contrasting, and very vivid, image of Morgan Grayson.

The moment she'd seen Andre's visitor, she had been captivated by the intensity of his gaze, the raw masculinity his expensive suit couldn't hide. There had been something untamed and noble about him. Instinctively she'd known he'd make a good friend or a dangerous enemy.

"You aren't annoyed with me, are you?" Andre persisted.

She took her time buttoning the faded smock. They both knew it wouldn't matter if she were, just as they both knew he wasn't going to change. He was an artistic genius with the temperament to match. He could be rude, harsh, insensitive, but she never forgot he had saved her when no one else had cared.

She took a seat at the stool in front of the workbench. "Why were you so abrupt with him?"

"He was sizing you up."

Phoenix blinked, then laughed despite the sudden pounding of her heart. "He was doing no such thing."

"You always think the best of people," Andre sneered, looking down his nose at her. "You believed the same of Paul Jovan."

Phoenix's entire body stiffened.

"I'm sorry you made it necessary to remind you of the incident," Andre said, his black-gloved hand sweeping over her hair. "Your naïveté and beauty attracts the wrong type of men. I'm the only man you can trust. Remember that." Without another word Andre left the studio. There was no need for him to remain. He had accomplished what he had intended.

Phoenix removed the cloth from the bust, lifted a pick, and began to delicately remove the excess clay. She couldn't argue even if she wanted to. Andre was right. He was the only man . . . including her father . . . who had ever wanted her for herself. She must not ever forget that again.